I0699147

Ashes to Ascendency

The Unknown Journey Through Perseverance

Bruce Gibbons

Copyright © 2024 by Bruce Gibbons

All rights reserved.

No part of this publication may be reproduced, distributed, or transmitted in any form or by any means, including photocopying, recording, or other electronic or mechanical methods, without the prior written permission of the publisher, except as permitted by U.S. copyright law. For permission requests, contact [include publisher/author contact info].

The story, all names, characters, and incidents portrayed in this production are fictitious. No identification with actual persons (living or deceased), places, buildings, and products is intended or should be inferred.

1st edition 2024

Within the pages of this book lies a heartfelt tribute to James Gibbons, a man whose unwavering support has been my guiding light on the path towards inner peace and success. Through tumultuous times in both America and Bermuda, his wise words and comforting presence have been my pillars of strength, leading me to a place of tranquility and contentment. His influence in my life is immeasurable, and I am forever grateful for his unending guidance and inspiration. This book serves as a testament to my journey and the appreciation I am showing Mr. James Gibbons.

Contents

Prologue

"A sleeping man holds in a circle around him the sequence of the hours, the order of the years and worlds. He consults them as he wakes and reads in them in a second the point on the earth he occupies, the time that has elapsed up to his waking; but their ranks can be mixed up, broken."

Marcel Proust in 'In Search of Lost Time'

David's life began under a heavy cloud of parental strife and racial ambiguity. His father, Frank, was a tall, dark Portuguese man known for his philandering ways. He had already sired another child, a girl named Sandra, ten years before he met Wendy - a stunning, fair-skinned woman with long, wavy hair that cascaded down her back. Wendy yearned to escape her small island roots in Bermuda and the suffocating hold of her tumultuous relationship with Frank. In search of freedom and passion, she found herself entangled in an affair with William Parker, a not so handsome black American naval man stationed on the island. Despite their differences in background, they were drawn to each other like moths to a flame and eventually married.

Following their intimate nuptials, Wendy and William packed up their belongings and settled into a small village in Alameda, California, where William was stationed for his naval duties.

The community was predominantly black, but the couple, joined by their biracial son David with his fair complexion, stood out amongst the sea of diversity. Despite the hopes for acceptance and inclusivity, young David faced ostracization and cruelty from his peers. The palpable tension of racism in the 1960s America seeped into the streets of Oakland and Alameda, creating a harsh and bitter separation between races. As a result, David began showing signs of how this affected him through his disturbing behavior, possibly stemming from the psychological toll of being an outsider. One particularly terrifying incident involved David nearly setting his own home ablaze, endangering his mother and sisters.

With each passing year, David's young life seemed to spiral deeper and deeper into a maelstrom of addiction, crime, and homelessness. The weight of his past choices weighed heavily on his shoulders as he struggled to keep his head above water. A fateful incident, born out of desperation and recklessness, resulted in the accidental death of his homeless girlfriend. This tragedy landed him in state prison, where he faced harsh realities and painful truths about the consequences of his actions. After serving his sentence, David was deported back to Bermuda - the place of his origins - hoping for a fresh start and a chance at redemption. However, the island offered no sanctuary for him as he found himself constantly cycling through prison, rehabilitation programs, jobs, and failures in an endless loop of despair. With each setback, David questioned if he could ever break free from the grip of his troubled past and find true peace within himself.

After decades of living in the same place, David made a pivotal decision to start anew in England, at the ripe age of fifty-nine. His arrival in London was fraught with challenges, like crossing a tumultuous sea in a tiny boat. The bustling city was a harsh replication of the struggles that had plagued his life back in America. But David's resilience, honed through a lifetime of hardship and adversity, refused to let him succumb to defeat. Slowly, painstakingly, he carved out a path for himself, like a sculptor chipping away at marble, navigating the obstacles and emerging on the other side as a reformed man. Eventually, he settled into a well-deserved retirement in the quaint town of England, where time seemed to slow down and the cold, dark days were tolerable.

Like a phoenix rising from the ashes, David's journey was a powerful testament to the resilience and strength of the human spirit. He had endured a tumultuous childhood, marked by racial prejudice and family strife, and had been dragged down into the depths of addiction, crime, and poverty. But with unbreakable determination and unwavering perseverance, he fought his way through the gauntlet of challenges that life threw at him. And in the end, he emerged from the flames, transformed and redeemed, finding peace and contentment in the final years of his life. It was a story of triumph over adversity, an inspiring tale of how one man refused to let his past define his future.

Chapter 1

Frank

Under a scorching summer sun on the 7th of June in 1956, a boy was brought into the world. His arrival was not ordinary, for he carried with him a sense of confusion and uncertainty, seeking answers to questions he couldn't comprehend. Despite it all, he persevered. This boy was born on the island of Bermuda, a small British Overseas Territory surrounded by crystal clear waters and abundant life. Rich in history and legend, Bermuda's first encounter with humankind is said to have occurred in 1612, when an English settlement was established at St. George's - now the largest settlement on the island. Governed under Royal charter by the Somers Isles Company until 1684, Bermuda eventually becomes a crown colony. This island, lush with greenery and steeped in culture, would be the birthplace of this special boy who would serve and endure hardships for the betterment of humanity.

This boy was named David, and his mother was Wendy.

Wendy was a quintessential Bermudian beauty, with luscious curves and an alluring sensuality that radiated from her every move. At just 18 years old, she had already given birth to David, a testament to her womanhood and strength. But life in Bermuda for a young girl like Wendy was difficult. It was heavily influenced by one's family background. If you were lucky enough to come from an affluent and educated family, your future held the promise of a similar lifestyle. However, for most Bermudians living in poverty and struggling against the remnants of slavery, their destiny was defined by hard work and servitude. Sometimes, this meant serving their employers in any way necessary to make ends meet. The weight of their circumstances hung heavily in the air, creating a stark contrast against the stunning island backdrop of Bermuda.

Wendy's curvy figure (overweight) didn't stop men from wanting her. She had a beautiful face with perfect features, stunning hair, and flawless skin.

It's mesmerizing. Her complexion was a beautiful shade between saddle-brown and the color of the skin of a sweet potato. At eighteen, (living in Bermuda during the late thirties), she was more than just desirable; she was the epitome of raw, carnal desire for most men who crossed her path. The family members— like most islanders—descended from a people with roots in slavery. The colonizers brought in slaves from Africa and other Caribbean islands to help with tobacco growing and pearl diving. As time passed, the island underwent changes and individuals became more self-reliant. The blacks and Portuguese intermingled, resulting in beautiful offspring, including David. When she was sixteen, she met a man called Frank; he was a proud Portuguese farmer who had migrated to Bermuda with his parents. Frank, at the time of their meeting, was himself thirty-five. They met when Wendy was working at the bowling alley at the American Naval Base in Bermuda as a server. Frank was the gardener who took care of the land just outside the bowling alley. He wanted more than anything to talk to Wendy, but he was shy and afraid because of his lack of English, but he tried,

"Hey pretty girl, you have a boyfriend?" Frank spoke, and wiped the dripping sweat from his face with a dirty handkerchief.

Wendy caught whiff of his attempt to get her attention and so she smiles with a mouth full of perfect white teeth, "I have lots of boyfriends, can't you tell?" She smiled as she continued wiping the counter, "So why you wanna know, and besides, you are too old for me."

Frank laughed, "I'm not old. Maybe a little older than you." Looking down at his boots, Frank asked, "Wanna go for a bike ride later?"

"I see you on your red Triumph sometimes. You think you're tough, don't you?"

"Is it yes?" He gazed lovingly at her.

Frank—as were most men in Bermuda—was very proud of his motorcycle, always polishing and cleaning and even using black shoe polish on the tires to make them shine. Back home, where he lived with his mother and father, they spoke no English, only their native Portuguese tongue.

"Frank, Mr. Maderios said he saw you with a colored woman on the back of your bike. Is this true?" Asked his mother. "You should always remember not to get involved with colored girls. They're trouble, looking for a man for money to take care of them and their children. They are trouble and besides you already have a wife from the old country, and you must think of her."

"But momma, she is a nice girl, and I like her."

"Nice girl. I will tell you who is a nice girl, your wife Wilma. She will be coming to Bermuda soon to be with you and make the family whole."

As time changed and more freedoms were granted, Frank felt a discomfort with the traditional values imposed by his family, but despite his own personal beliefs Despite his parents raising him to always respect and follow their customs, Frank yearned for something different. He tried to stay within his own community, but he found something exciting about being with other people who were not Portuguese.

Ten years before he met Wendy, Frank had a secret relationship with a black woman named Shirley. Shirley didn't have the clean beautiful looks that Wendy had, but like Wendy, Shirley longed for love and a better life. Frank and Shirley met while working at the summer home of a wealthy businessman, Mr. Juan Tripp who owned Pan Am Airlines. They worked at his summer house in Bermuda. During the winter, the house was empty unless Mr. Tripp had guests. In that case, Frank did the gardening and Shirley cleaned the house. Alone there together, Shirley and Frank talked and laughed until one day they took advantage of the empty house and made love in one of the many bedrooms.

Shirley, while dressing after having made love with Frank, glanced at him from the bed, her eyes moist and brimming with emotion.

"I understand it's only temporary. I respect your life and won't pressure you."

Frank didn't stop to acknowledge what Shirley had just said, instead he just kept putting his clothes to right. He appeared anxious, rushing to dress himself before leaving the room. He never came back to that job.

Alone, Shirley fell in love with Frank. She thought about the romantic exchange of laughter between them, the way Frank looked at her and his constant suggestions of naughtiness. Frank had no intentions of marrying Shirley, but their desires clashed. He knew that his family and fellow Portuguese disapproved of mixing blood with the black. Still, that did little for his burgeoning desire for women outside his culture. His lust rendered him weak, and the dirty secret that only he knew revealed the type of man he was.

A year after their brief affair, Shirley gave birth to a baby girl. She had her mother's dark hair and her father's light complexion, but she would never get to know him. Instead, she heard only whispers and saw glimpses of him from afar on rare occasions. Each day, she yearned to meet the man her mother spoke of with mixed emotions.

Shirley accepted Frank and couldn't shake off the suspicion she felt that Frank may have strayed during her pregnancy. It was in the way he fidgeted with his hands when she tried talking to him, how he avoided the subject of love. His visits became shorter, and he was always drunk or had been drinking, and he was distant and irritable around her.

Frank's sudden disappearance from Shirley's life, much like the day he vanished when the first made love Mr. Tripp's home, left a gaping hole in her heart. The small island of Bermuda felt even smaller, and Shirley felt her heart sink as she watched Frank speed by on his motorcycle without so much as a glance in her direction. She clutched baby Sandra closer to her chest, as if to shield her from the harsh reality of her father's indifference. She couldn't understand how he could turn so cold, avoiding her and his beautiful daughter Sandra. Despite their initial happiness over the birth of their daughter, Frank's lack of love and care for their child was clear in his actions. Shirley struggled with conflicting emotions, wanting to hate him for abandoning them and longing for the man she once loved. Shirley tried to carry on, keeping up a brave face as she went about her days. She found solace in the joy that Sandra brought her, marveling at each new milestone and taking delight in her daughter's sweet smiles and coos. But each night, as Sandra slept soundly in her crib, Shirley allowed herself to cry, mourning the family she had dreamed of having with Frank. Weeks turned into months, and Frank remained an elusive figure on the fringes of their lives.

Shirley heard whispers and rumors from townsfolk, but no words directly from Frank himself. She didn't know what pained her more - his cold detachment, or the not knowing why he had done this to her.

Shirley was sitting alone in her home. It had been almost ten years since she and Frank had last spoke. The fading years, one after the other, replacing the pain that love brought, became her closest friend. She reached for an old metal tin lying beside her favorite chair; the tin was as old as she. Her gnarled fingers scraped along the edges of a photo of him and another woman (years before someone who never identified themselves mailed it to her). Her suspicions of long ago were that he had moved on with someone else and it was clear in this photo. Shirley's face stayed still as she gazed at the image, lost in thought. She rose from her chair and made her way to the fireplace, where a mirror hung above. In a trance, she held the photo to her reflection, studying the two faces together. A mixture of emotions flooded over her, causing tears to fall down her cheeks as she struggled to make sense of it all. Wendy's bright eyes, contagious smile, and styled hair - everything she was not while pregnant. She sensed the fading excitement and passion between them in the photo.

Chapter 2

Stepfather

The air was thick and wet with humidity on that breezy April day in 1956, just two months before Wendy's first child, David, was due to arrive. She had been working a long shift at the bowling alley, surrounded by the scent of sizzling meat and the tang of beer. As she wiped down the tables in the quiet early afternoon, her thoughts drifted to the life growing inside her. Suddenly, a figure caught her eye - a man dressed in the crisp white uniform of the US Navy.

William wasn't tall or short, just stocky, and his muscular build showed beneath the loose fabric of his uniform. He wore his hair short to match the balding spot on top. He wasn't a handsome man by traditional value of the word handsome, but he certainly seemed dignified in a confident yet shy sort of way. The skin on his face was dark and chocolatey, and he was clean shaven with a thin line of hair for a moustache. His nose was broad and when he smiled, he showed the most beautiful teeth.

Several weeks after they met, Wendy gave birth to an eight-ounce baby boy and named him David. There were over 12 people cramped in the small hospital room at King Edward III Memorial Hospital. And sadly, there was no father to witness the splendor, only a cacophony of noise from the crowd packed into the little hospital room. And then, through the crowd, an unfamiliar face emerged, William.

Wendy's smile became engorged with joy when she saw his face, his shiny black face in a sea of colors all lighter than his. The talk in the room sank to a hum, but you could see by the expression on everyone's face that something strange was happening.

The room suddenly filled with a tense energy as Wendy proudly introduced her friend, William Parker.

He stood proud in his Navy uniform; he stood confident, but his presence made Nell's mother Ianthe uncomfortable. In a hushed tone, she leaned towards Nell and whispered,

"What was Vendy thinking bringing this black man here on the day of her first childbirth? He's not exactly easy on the eyes." Her words laced with malice and disgust, causing Nell to shoot her mother a stern look.

"Mother! How shameful you should be ashamed of yourself for saying that It's important to remember to be kind and not say mean things. William is Wendy's friend and he's a wonderful person." But even Nell couldn't deny the unease that settled in the pit of her stomach at the tension in the room.

William had a small bouquet of mixed flowers in his hand. He lay them down on a table next to the bed and leaned over and kissed Wendy on the cheek. Everyone smiled and looked at each other. Politely everyone dropped their stinking attitudes for kinder words. In a touch of surprise, a nurse walked into the room carrying a small bundle in her arms. She walked over to Wendy and announced,

"Here's your lovely little boy, David. Isn't he just the darlingest little fella?"

Wendy left the hospital a few days later with her little baby boy in her arms. The taxi driver stopped just outside a small single house that sat on a triangular lot that exceeded the size for this house in Bailey's Bay. The small house was a pale sickly green, many places you could see the paint fading from years of sun and humidity. They lived close to the water's edge. Everywhere, grass and shrubs wildly overgrown. There was a large concrete structure just off to the right of the house. It serves as a tank for water. A dented steel galvanized bucket sat atop the tank with a rope tied to the handle, also a large steel tub. There were 3 concrete steps in front of the house, chipped and worn from years of use. A circle of dirt surrounded the house, which seemed to act as a walkway going round and round and from its edge, the grass grew. There were many items forgotten or lost in the tall grass, a child's shoe, empty tin cans, a doll, lots of empty rum bottles, and many other insignificant items. Off to the right of the house was shabby and careworn door made of old rotting wood, painted in a dark, harsh green paint that was chipping severely. Through that door exposed an old uneven floor too made of wood, and old unsophisticated cabinets with missing doors replaced with pieces of fabric. A tired sink made of cast iron, and another bucket filled with water. They could afford no plumbing then.

A frayed and faded Persian rug carpeted the living room. Old, laminated wood furniture stood as the marvel of the sitting room. Through another doorway opened into the only bedroom and in there a large iron framed bed was where Wendy, her mother Ianthe and some of the small children all slept. Everyone else found spaces on the floor, the sofa, or a chair.

As she closed the door of the taxi behind her, a moment of silence revealed the almost tormenting thought in her mind as a reminder of what she was coming back to after spending several days in the hospital. Invariably, like thunder before rain, a wall of noise hit her with full force, assaulting her senses and threatening to overwhelm her. The chaotic sound of children and adults arguing with each other with different intentions echoed throughout the cramped little house. It was late afternoon, and everyone had exhausted all their obligations for the day within an eight-hour span. Her two brothers, Michael and Richard (affectionately known as Busty) were engaged in a heated debate with her sisters Nell and Lynn while Ianthe, the conductor of this crude orchestra, tried to restore order. Woven between this band of adults were wild, unruly children, symbols of poverty that added to the chaotic atmosphere.

Wendy moved closer to the house and when she stepped inside, she noticed that welcome home was gone; it was back to business as usual. The cruel, unaffectionate welcome was just a silent unspoken reminder that she was just another piece of the income stream and now, with a new baby, this meant her cut diminished.

Despite the façade of a loving family, there were underlying tensions that threatened to tear them apart. Mother Ianthe was the glue that held everything together, but it was a brittle bond held by resentment and bitterness from a failed relationship with the girl's father. She struggled to maintain her outward show of love and faith, while inside, she simmered with anger. Christianity was her solace, a sort of disguise that socially smoothed over the discontent but even that seemed tinged with hypocrisy in the face of their strained relationships. Ianthe had succumbed to two serious relationships throughout her life. The first one resulted in the births of two boys, Michael and Richard, and a daughter named Brenda. Sadly, Ianthe gave Brenda up for adoption at birth, although back then, adoption meant being "given away."

She always said that having two sons, and a daughter changed the financial dynamics of their family, and without a man to support them, the boys would have to step up. Following that, Percy made his appearance.

1935 was the year Ianthe's life changed forever. At the raucous Cup Match between Somerset and St. George's, she caught the attention of Percival Burgess, a man who embodied everything she despised: privilege, entitlement, and arrogance. But Ianthe couldn't resist his charming smile and smooth words, and soon found herself in a passionate affair with him. However, like every other man before him, Percival eventually left her, leaving behind a trail of broken promises and shattered dreams, and in that whirlwind of dust he left behind three daughters, Wendy, Alice (Nell) and Diana (Lynn) the youngest of the three.

When the girls were in their teens, something crazy happened between Ianthe and Percival,

"Anthé, you are the love of my life, and we have been together now for almost 20 years. How do you feel about marrying me?"

There was nothing more than being married to Percy Burgess and without hesitation she accepted, "I can't believe this Percy, you wouldn't be trying to mess me around again like you have all the last hundred times?" She continued cooking his lunch. "This will not be a big formal wedding, so the registry?"

"The registry is all we need. Who wants a big formal wedding anyway, much too pretentious?"

Ianthe made all the preparations, and her kids helped. Ianthe scheduled the wedding for Friday, late afternoon after work in 1954; she didn't want to miss a day of work. Every pound and shilling mattered to her. On that day, family and friends gathered at the registry office, it was a day to be remembered as most black Bermudian women in those days rarely saw a marriage, or even a long-term relationship that stood in the terms of what a relationship was. Many mothers and fathers of children born out of wedlock remained close and in friendship, even supported in terms of finance, but somehow most first term relationships never worked in the way society proclaimed.

Only a handful of loyal friends and family remained, determined to see the wedding through to its blessed completion. They frantically prepared for the bride, Ianthe, hoping to bring her joy on the most important day of her life.

But as the minutes ticked by and the wedding registry entrance remained empty, panic set in. Where was Percy? The groom was nowhere to be found, and with each passing moment, doubt and fear crept into the hearts of those waiting. Would this special day end with heartbreak?

An icy hand of humiliation clutches at Ianthe's chest, threatening to choke her as she stands before the crowd at the registry. She can feel their curious eyes, judgmental whispers, and pitying looks burning into her skin like acid. She forces out a few fake tears, unable to let them see the crushing disappointment and rage that churns in her gut.

"That scumbag Percy, why did she want him, anyway? He's nothing but a snake!" one woman hisses to another, loud enough for everyone to hear.

"I'm sorry, Mom. It'll be okay," Wendy tries to console her mother, but they both know it won't be. Something inside Ianthe has shattered, irreparably damaged by this public betrayal. And deep down, she knows Percy is not coming because he never intended to. The bad has already happened to her, and it will haunt her for a long time.

The small crowd filters out of the registry, most people going in separate directions except for Ianthe and her children. They all stay together and catch a taxi back to Bailey's Bay. In the house there was mostly silence, only broken by a knock at the door.

The sun was setting, casting a soft orange glow over the neighborhood. Cora, a good friend of Ianthe's, stood at the door with her hands on her hips. Her short nappy hair was one big messy ball, and she wore tight-fitting Capri pants and a tee-shirt, sweating down her face into the gentle breeze coming off the ocean. Two young girls, around the same age as Ianthe's daughters, giggled at their mother's arrival.

"Where's your momma, Wendy?" Cora called out. "She's inside. Come on in. Have you heard the news?"

"That's why I'm here," Cora replied with a heavy sigh. "Poor thing. I am so sad this happened, but I have something important to tell her."

Cora walked into the house, its walls painted in warm earth tones and adorned with family photos. The only sound was the distant hum of voices coming from the living room. Ianthe sat at the end of her bed, her usually strong posture now slumped under the weight of recent events. With each movement she made, the springs of the mattress creaked and groaned beneath her. It was as if even the furniture could sense her sorrow and offered its support in any way it could.

Cora paces around Ianthe, her movements agitated. She speaks, but her words come out in a rush, as if she can't bear to say them.

"Anthé, I'm sorry. I know what I have to tell you will only bring more pain, but you deserve to know." She gazes intensely into Ianthe's eyes before placing her hands firmly on her shoulders and pulling her in for a tight hug. They were best friends, and Cora could feel the weight of this betrayal weighing heavily on both of them.

"Winnie told me something, and I didn't want to believe it, but it leads back to her. On the day you were supposed to marry Percy, he was actually going to marry Angela Raynor at St. Peter's Church." Cora's voice cracks with emotion as she finishes, leaving the heavy truth hanging between them like a dark cloud. Ianthe's heart drops and the room feels suddenly suffocating as she processes the full extent of the betrayal.

Ianthe never thought it would happen like this, but deep down, she always knew it was inevitable. After all, Percy was a notorious womanizer, and his charm made even the coldest hearts melt. She was just a lowly maid and cleaner for the wealthy, no match for the handsome and refined Percy, who was practically royalty in her eyes. She could feel the betrayal seeping into her bones, knowing that she was just another conquest for him, a disposable pawn in his game of seduction.

Three months had passed since Percy had stood her up at the church, but now he stumbled towards Ianthe's door on a late Friday afternoon, reeking of alcohol. She could see him from the kitchen window, his unsteady form approaching with each clumsy step. As he got closer, she noticed that there were three women in his car, giggling and chatting loudly. His slurred words and disheveled appearance told her all she needed to know about where he had been and what he had been doing. I Anthé couldn't help but feel a pang of sadness and anger as she watched him approach, remembering the hurt he had caused her just a few short months ago.

"Let me in, Anthé. I know I've caused you embarrassment, but please, let me explain." Percy pleaded through the locked door. Ianthe's voice dripped with anger as she cracked it. "Why should I let you in? You made me the laughingstock of the town."

Percy pushed past her into the house, his eyes blazing with frustration. "Is that all you care about, being laughed at? Well, join the club because plenty of people have laughed at me for this whole situation. It was out of my control; my mother forced me to marry Angela. But we both knew we would have been a terrible married couple. This way, we can love each other in our own way and remain friends."

"What about your crew in the car? They're not coming inside; I can tell you that." Anthé crossed her arms defiantly.

"Fuck 'em," Percy spat. "Just fix me a meal and let me rest. It's been a rough week."

On Sunday, Percy woke up early and quickly got ready. He kissed Ianthe on the cheek before leaving a few pounds on the nightstand. As he walked out to his car, the same three women still there, sleeping from Friday, woke up and off he drove.

Chapter 3

The Estuary

Holy Trinity, the small church where Wendy and William stood in front of family and friends. The soft strains of a local band filled the air as they exchanged vows. As they shared their first kiss as husband and wife, Wendy couldn't contain her excitement any longer.

"I have more news," she announced, beaming. "We're expecting a baby!" Nell let out a playful shout, "Whose baby is it?" laughing, Wendy replied,

"Your boyfriend Tony's, so you can all stop teasing me now."

The family erupted into cheers and congratulations, excited for this new addition to their already growing family.

Six months had passed since Carla's birth, and the hustle and bustle of preparing for their move to America had consumed the family. William had left earlier to take care of all the paperwork, leaving behind his wife and two young children. Even though it was an exciting time, David couldn't shake off a feeling of sadness that lingered within him.

Finally, after what seemed like endless waiting, news arrived that William had secured them an apartment in Brooklyn, New York. The thought of living in a city so different from their small hometown filled Wendy with both excitement and apprehension. But with determination, she packed up all their belongings while balancing a baby on her hip and holding onto David's small hand as he trotted alongside her.

The day of their departure came, and the family made their way to the airport. The hustle and bustle of family and friends surrounded them as they boarded a Pan Am plane bound for Kennedy International. As they settled into their seats, Wendy gazed out at the beauty of Bermuda and imagined the new life that awaited them in America.

Their time in New York was fleeting, a mere blip in the timeline of their lives. Wendy and her children, David and Carla, were anxiously awaiting their green cards, which finally arrived in 1962. With them came a fresh addition to the family, Maxine, just four years old and officially an American citizen. The past few years had transformed them into a whole new family, but as always, change was right around the corner. William's orders from the Navy commanded them to pack up again, this time out to California.

The family finally reached sunny California in the fall of 1962, thanks to William's hard work and determination. For little David, it meant starting school a year behind his peers. As he entered kindergarten, a year later than the other children, he couldn't shake off the feeling of being out of place and already falling behind. The new environment and unfamiliar faces only added to his internal conflict of trying to catch up with those who had a head start.

Despite their struggles, William had given his family a new life, one they could be proud of. Their first home together may not have been luxurious, but for an emerging young Black Military family, it was a beacon of hope.

As she stepped into their modest house, Wendy couldn't help but feel a mix of emotions - happiness at having a place to call their own in California, yet also a nagging worry about the future. This was their sanctuary, but would it be enough to withstand the challenges ahead?

As the Parker family arrived at The Estuary, a small village nestled among the industrial buildings of the Todd Shipyard, Wendy couldn't help but feel a pang of disappointment. After the lush and vibrant paradise of Bermuda, this place seemed dreary and lifeless. But she was determined to give it a chance. They settled into their cramped 2-bedroom apartment, one of many identical units in the complex. Each building followed the same monotonous style, with flat roofs and drab facades painted in muted colors. The only signs of nature were the stubborn weeds that poked through cracks in the concrete, reaching desperately for sunlight. In the center of the complex stood a desolate parking lot, littered with potholes and shards of broken glass, surrounded by a barren wasteland of gravel and asphalt. But the most imposing feature was the massive incinerator that loomed at one edge, its cold cinder block walls mocking the residents below. In this forgotten corner of town, where there was no garbage collection service available, all waste found its disposal in this place. Thick plumes of smoke billowed from its chimney, casting an eerie shadow over the already desolate landscape.

Not far from the parking lot, where one would expect to see children playing, lay a vast pit that had been dug into the earth near the apartment. The hole most suspiciously filled with waste oil from the neighboring Todd Shipyard - a looming structure that seemed to swallow up the horizon. The thick, acrid scent of chemicals and pollution hung heavily in the air, but in those days, governmental agencies or the newly formed EPA didn't heavily regulate life and society. As an uneducated black person making a living in the US Navy back then, complaints about environmental issues were unheard of; they simply weren't a part of daily life. And so, the children played fearlessly, close to the dangers of the shipyard, unaware of the potential harm it could bring.

David stood on the outskirts of the village, watching as the children ran and played with metal scraps that were once part of a ship. He felt out of place, like one of those discarded objects, neither fully belonging in the white community nor accepted by his black neighbors. Their stares were not fearful, but filled with resentment towards the biracial man who dared to exist among them. As he felt an unfamiliar fear bubble up inside him, David couldn't help but wonder if this would be his home or if he would always be an outsider

In the turbulent 1960s of America, the issue of racism was impossible to ignore. It seemed like everyone had someone to hate - white people despised Black people, and vice versa. But there was also tension within each race - those who were mixed with both faced discrimination from both sides. The country was in a constant state of conflict, and it left David feeling torn and unsure of where to fit in.

As the only child of his race, he stood out like a beacon in a sea of dark faces. Every day was a battle to fit in, but the only solace he found was in his love for spelling. At just six years old, he eagerly awaited the weekly spelling contests in class, determined to win the prize - small porcelain figurines that he could proudly present to his mother as a token of his achievement.

But even in these moments, he was isolated and alone. The other children never included him, except when it was to use him as a pawn in their cruel games. He learned this lesson the hard way when Ralph, one of the local boys, approached him with false kindness, leading him on before ultimately betraying him with a joke.

Ralph's voice pierced the summer air, sounding eager and mischievous. "David, where's your bike?" he asked with a grin. David's little red tricycle, adorned with shiny tassels on the handlebars, was his prized possession.

"In the house. You want to ride it?"

"Yeah, go get it and let's ride over to the tar pit." The tar pit was a well- known place that always piqued David's curiosity, and he couldn't resist revisiting it whenever he got the chance. He ran into the house and emerged with his beloved tricycle. As he wheeled it out onto the front porch, his mother smiled at him from the sofa without saying a word.

Ralph hopped onto the back of the tricycle, making use of the flat plate between the wheels meant for another rider to stand on. With his hands resting on David's small shoulders, Ralph pumped his foot against the ground, propelling them forward at a quick pace. They were getting closer to the pit when Ralph suddenly dismounted and gave one final push with his foot, sending David and the trike flying into the middle of the pit. Fortunately, it wasn't deep, only reaching David's ankles, but it was enough to leave him covered in black, sticky oil.

He looked up at Ralph with shock and confusion as Ralph laughed from above, clearly pleased with himself for pulling off such a prank.

"Now you look like one of us," he sneered, his voice dripping with disdain. David's sobs only seemed to amuse him more.

As Ralph strolled back towards the housing project, leaving David behind to retrieve his damaged trike and push it back to the apartment, David couldn't help but feel a burning sense of humiliation. But as he walked through the parking lot, trying to avoid eye contact with anyone, a group of girls noticed him and burst into cruel laughter. They began taunting him with a rhyme that cut deep:

"White Patty, White Patty, you don't shine cause yo momma didn't polish yo black behind."

The shame burned on David's cheeks and gnawed at his insides. He hated himself for not standing up to them, for not being confident enough to be proud of who he was. It was a constant struggle for acceptance in this community, but he longed to be like them - unafraid, bold, and unapologetically Black.

After his mother washed off the thick tar from his body, she sternly warned him to stay away from the pit or else he would end up falling in again. David nodded obediently, but inside, he felt a knot of guilt and fear forming. He couldn't bring himself to tell her about Ralph, afraid of the consequences that would follow. So instead, he lied and promised to stay away from danger.

Before heading outside, David grabbed a tin box filled with plastic army men from his room. As he walked out of the house and towards the incinerator, he couldn't shake off the feeling of unease and disgust at the mound of dirt next to it. It wasn't real dirt; it was a mixture of ash, broken glass, and charred garbage. Living in the Estuary was like living in a desolate wasteland, void of any beauty or life. The people here were hateful, especially towards half-breeds like himself who had come from countries like Bermuda. David often wondered why he had to be a part of this bleak environment, surrounded by mean individuals who showed him no kindness or mercy.

His stepfather, William, was an imposing figure - sturdy with broad shoulders and a deep voice that commanded attention, David was afraid of him.

William strode confidently towards the incinerator, a bag of garbage slung over his shoulder, and looked down at David as if he were a mere insect. In the background, the sound of girls' voices echoed in a haunting tune.

"White Patty, White Patty, you don't shine cause yo momma didn't polish yo black behind."

Without uttering a word to David, William turned towards the girls and tilted his head towards the sky in an air of superiority. It was clear who held power in this household.

"You girls shut damn noise up, ain't no white patties round here, now get." And just like that, the once lively chatter came to a halt. William then turned his intense gaze towards David, a look that could crush even the bravest of souls. David couldn't understand the intensity behind it, but he knew better than to question it. He watched as William forcefully shoved the paper bag into the crowded incinerator and then removed a box of matches from his pocket and shook them vigorously.

"Can I light the match, dad? Can I please?" David begged with trembling lips, his eyes wide with excitement and fear. He hoped desperately that his begging desire to be approved would earn him some protection from his father's wrath, but he knew deep down it would only make things worse.

William's face twisted into a mask of fury. "If I catch you playing with matches of any kind, for any reason, I will beat your ass until you can't stand," he growled, his voice dripping with menace.

David's heart dropped to his stomach as a wave of terror washed over him. But he nodded quickly, not daring to defy his father's orders. As William turned away, David felt a surge of anger towards him, something misunderstood, but recurring more often than he realized, but he pushed it down and went back to playing alone.

He crushed the tiny army men under his hands, imagining each one as a representation of himself in this never-ending battle against his father's tyranny. Each victory was hollow and meaningless, reminding him he was still just a helpless child at the mercy of a strange man.

After a few days, the Navy called William away to sea, leaving Wendy and the kids alone once again. It was during these times, when William was away at sea, Wendy packed bags and she and the kids made their way to Bermuda. But this time William would only be gone for a short time, so they had to cancel the trip to Bermuda.

Wendy and the kids drove William to the docks that morning, and stayed and watched as the ship gently rolled out to sea and was gone. It was then that David felt an immense sense of relief wash over him. He was glad that William was gone because it meant he could finally relax and go back to pretending to be who he was. David, the half-breed. The day had drifted by quickly, and Wendy wanted a little time to herself, so she put the kids to bed early. David and his two sisters slept in the same room, the two girls in one bed and David in the other. They shared bunk beds.

As David drifted off to sleep that night, a strange dream unfolded in his mind. The first thing he saw in the dream was the old incinerator out in the parking lot. He stood there frozen in front of it, unable to move as if he were waiting for something to happen. Then, suddenly, the incinerator changed form and became a giant robot. David had never seen a robot before, not even on TV, so he couldn't understand how it turned up in his mind. The robot started moving toward him and instinctively David began walking backwards, away from the robot, but no matter how fast or how far he went, the robot was always there, close behind. Eventually, he turned and ran as fast as he could until he found himself awake and standing next to his mother's bed. Eerily he stood like a zombie, not saying a word, only standing inanimately watching his mother as she slept. Then suddenly, in a flash, Wendy jolted out of her sleep to face what stood before her.

"Why are you just standing there, scaring me half to death?" David's mother hissed, her eyes wild with fear. "Tell me, boy, what's wrong with you?"

"I saw a robot, momma. It was coming for me."

"A robot? Don't be ridiculous. There's no such thing," she scoffed, trying to calm him down. "It must have been a bad dream."

"But I wasn't dreaming, I swear! It was real!" David pleaded.

His mother sighed and got up from the bed. She walked him back to his room, but her grip on his hand was tense.

"Go to sleep and don't wake up your sisters. If your father were here, I would let him deal with this mess." Her voice was strained with frustration. "Please don't tell him, momma. Please don't tell him about the robot or that I wet the bed," David begged.

"So, which is it? A robot or pee?" His mother's voice turned cold as ice. "Why would you lie to me and beg me not to tell your father? What else are you hiding from me?"

The anger in her eyes burned like fire as she left David in his room. He tried to calm himself, but his heart raced with fear and confusion. How could he make them believe the truth? But before he could figure it out, exhaustion overtook him and he fell into an uneasy sleep, haunted by the image of the relentless robot chasing after him in his own home. Your father WILL know about this when he gets back from the sea.

David shifted his weight on the cold, damp mattress beneath him, careful not to disturb his sisters, who lay in the bottom bunk. It was difficult to be quiet in the small apartment, as at any point could hear the slightest noise. When David thought his mother had drifted back to sleep, he quickly slipped out of bed and changed his pajamas, and then he changed the sheets. He climbed back into bed, where it was now dry and ready for sleep, but sleep didn't come as he may have hoped, instead he just lay there, looking at the ceiling, and then he was out. It had only been twenty minutes into his sleep when he started to twist and turn, his hands clenching violently. It was like the world was drifting, not a soul in sight, only he and the incinerator. Then he noticed that the cinder blocks were blackened and chipped, and the one metal door that everyone opened to put their garbage in was rusted and dented; he could hear it squeaking in his dream. As he stood in front of the incinerator, he looked around the neighborhood, there were no additional streets only one way in and one way out, and that small artery of a road opened into a square cul-de-sac where a dozen rectangular buildings sat in penitentiary style.

The air around the incinerator was thick with a dark cloud of smoke, burning his lungs and making it difficult to see. As he lay in bed, terror gripped his stiffened body as he watched the incinerator grow arms and legs and a head. It was like a demon coming to life, taunting him with its fiery grasp. The flames inside whipped and turned, caressing his mind with their hypnotic dance.

But then his focus shifted to the fire in the room, spreading quickly from the match he had carelessly lit. It crept up the wall behind the sofa, its orange tendrils flickering with menacing intent. In a moment of sheer panic, he ran to the kitchen and grabbed a pot, filling it with water before rushing back to toss it on the growing inferno. But the flames only seemed to grow more violent, mocking his feeble attempts to extinguish them.

He continued to fill pots with water, desperately trying to drown out the flames. But as the reality of the situation sank in, he realized that there was nothing he could do. This was no longer a nightmare; it was his horrifying reality.

As the flames crept closer and closer, he finally surrendered to defeat. Slowly, with heavy steps, he made his way to his mother's room, careful not to disturb her sleep. Standing by her bedside, he seemed like a towering figure over her delicate frame. His mind raced as he realized the gravity of the situation - a fire ignited by his own hands had trapped his family in a deadly bubble. At that moment, he regretted his foolish actions and hoped for a way out. But as he stood there, pleading silently for his mother to wake up and save him from this mess, she stirred and let out a harsh cough, signaling her awakening. The sound brought a mix of relief and dread to his heart - now she was awake and would witness the chaos he had caused.

Her heart raced as she ran into the front room of their apartment, only to be met with a horrifying sight. The flames were already engulfing everything in their path. Instinct kicked in and Wendy knew she had to act fast.

"Hurry, help me get your sisters!" she shouted at David, panic seeping into her voice. "The entire house is on fire and your father is going to be furious! Move your ass!"

With adrenaline pumping through her veins, Wendy led the way to her bedroom window and quickly guided David and his sisters out one by one. As she crawled out herself, she couldn't believe how quickly the fire had spread.

But then a sense of relief washed over her as she emerged onto the ground outside. The once quiet parking lot was now filled with people, their worried faces illuminated by flashing red and blue lights from the approaching fire trucks.

Amid all the chaos, there was one thing that stood out to David: the incinerator. It seemed to mock him as it continued to spew flames into the night sky. He couldn't believe that something so simple could cause so much destruction and almost cost them their home and their lives.

Chapter 4

Berkeley, California

In the heat of a scorching summer in 1965, the Parker family said their bittersweet goodbyes to the Estuary and embarked on a journey towards their new home in Berkeley. William had retired from the Navy and had secured a position as a custodian at the University of California at Berkeley.

In the confines of what a person knows and doesn't know, Wendy was proud of William. He may as well be taking a position as an attorney for all she knew. As they arrived at Salvo Island, another military compound, they couldn't help but be struck by the familiar architecture that mirrored their former village, only this time, the roofs were slanted and not flat.

This community held a different purpose - it was a haven for retired military personnel as they prepared for their next chapter in life. The buildings stood tall and sturdy, bearing marks of time with faded paint and weathered roofs. Each structure seemed to hold endless stories within its walls, whispering tales of past inhabitants and their journeys. The air was thick with a sense of nostalgia, as generations of families had passed through this place before moving on to fresh adventures. As the Parker family settled into their new life in this unique little village, they could only imagine the endless possibilities and memories that awaited them in this vibrant community.

David's silence about the fire spoke volumes to those who knew him. The memory of flames engulfing his childhood home and family haunted him, but he refused to give it power by speaking of it. No one dared mention the possibility of a beating from his father, as if by not acknowledging it they could erase it from existence. The Parker family's new home in the military base felt like a sanctuary compared to their previous cramped and barren barracks. Lush greenery surrounded them, a stark contrast to the charred remains of their old life. And David, with a newfound light in his eyes, was like a different person. Perhaps it was the diverse mix of children at his new school, some with skin tones that mirrored his own, others from completely different backgrounds. The new children of his life didn't care about his past, and in their acceptance of him he found solace and hope for a better future.

William had retired from the navy, but his new job as a custodian at the prestigious University of California at Berkeley didn't live up to David's expectations. At first, David was excited about the possibility of visiting the campus and enjoying its amenities, but William quickly shut down any notion of that happening. His strange warnings and paranoid thoughts made David question his decision to introduce his children to higher education through this job.

One day, David gathered courage to ask if he could visit the campus gym with his friends. But William's response sent shivers down his spine.

"I don't want you anywhere near that campus," he snarled. "You're too young and those guys will get you alone in the locker room and force their big dicks up your ass. Do you hear me?"

David didn't know how to respond. To William, everything seemed to revolve around sex - "big dicks" and "pussy". How could he introduce his children to an environment of higher learning when he knew nothing about it himself?

In stark contrast, David's mother had recently landed a job as Head Housekeeper at Shattuck Carleton Convalescent Hospital. Unlike her husband, she was always eager for her children to visit her at work. She would beam with pride as her co-workers gushed about how handsome her son was, a sharp contrast to William's obsession with sexual deviance.

David seethes with resentment as he remembers his stepfather's indifference during his childhood. He can't say for sure if the man was good or bad, but one thing is certain: he was painfully absent from their lives. Most of his time and energy were devoted to his work at the demanding University of California in Berkeley, leaving David and his sisters to fend for themselves emotionally and physically.

As a young boy, William spent most of his days with his Uncle Bob, who lived in a small town in Kentucky. Though William was born in Tuscaloosa, Alabama, he always considered Uncle Bob to be his primary caretaker and father figure. They spoke on the phone every week, and William's heart filled with joy every time he heard Uncle Bob's voice. Even though they were miles apart, they shared a special bond that couldn't be broken. When William turned eighteen, he enlisted in the navy to start his own journey and create the life he lived. But he would always cherish the memories of his childhood with Uncle Bob, who helped shape him into the person he was today.

In America during the tumultuous years of 1966-67, the ongoing Vietnam War was a significant factor. The Parker family lived in Berkeley, a crucial location during the war. The city's left-leaning government urged its residents to help protestors and soldiers, setting up designated areas for counseling and support. As if by fate, the Parkers moved to Salvo Island Village after their house in Alameda was destroyed by fire. The small village, which comprised subsidized housing within a two-block radius, became flooded with hippies, as David, one of the Parkers' children, referred to them. They set up camps on a grassy area on the Grove Street side, now known as Martin Luther King Jr. Way. David was captivated by their vibrant presence - people of all races singing, dancing, and indulging in marijuana. It was a time of free love and communal cooking in a new tin garbage bin provided by an elderly African American man named Pappa Slick. Today, there is little evidence of this once lively village.

In a quaint, tight-knit community, Carla, Maxine, and David were enrolled at Washington Elementary, a small school that was conveniently located just three blocks away from their home. The kids thrived in this environment, finding comfort and safety within mere minutes in any direction. And directly across the street from their school was Berkeley High, a bustling hub of teenage energy. After the school day, David would often linger to watch the impressive students on the track team as they trained with focused determination and grace. Their movements were like poetry, captivating and inspiring to young David's eager eyes.

A sense of giddy elation surged through David as he took in his new surroundings. It was as if the oppressive walls enforced by racism had crumbled and fallen away, freeing him from a long-held imprisonment. Berkeley in the 1960s was a kaleidoscope of colors and ideas, a bustling hub of liberal thought and demonstrations for change. The constant stream of people and diverse cultures created an atmosphere that pulsated with energy and passion. Everywhere his eyes turned, there was something new to see and experience, each individual adding their own unique hue to the vibrant spectrum of humanity. David was overwhelmed by this sense of unity and acceptance, even though he couldn't fully comprehend it. All he knew was that it felt incredible to be a part of it all.

The sun rose on a crisp Monday morning, signaling the start of another week. A full seven days had passed since the children arrived, and they were now fully settled in. As the beginning of the new school day loomed, David felt a familiar anxiety creeping in. But as soon as he stepped into the classroom, his worries dissipated at the sight of smiling faces from all walks of life. Each child brought their own unique energy and curiosity to the group, and David's own passion for learning was reignited in their presence. No longer did he feel the need to hide his enthusiasm for knowledge; instead, he revelled because there were others who shared his insatiable thirst for understanding and discovery. As he looked around at the diverse group gathered before him, he couldn't help but feel a sense of excitement and wonder at what each new day would bring.

As David walked through the halls of the school, he couldn't help but notice the dedication and passion of the staff towards their students. In his household, education was not a priority, but here at school, it was as abundant as air. On library days, David eagerly made his way to the stacks, specifically to the section on horses. He devoured every book, committing to memory each breed and its purpose - Thoroughbreds for speed in racing, Morgans preferred by police forces in New York, and Lipizzaner Stallions for their graceful Capriole movements. Each horse was unique and essential to the overall excellence of equine beauty.

As a child, David was fascinated by how people could excel in a particular interest and use it to benefit others. He often daydreamed about being near horses and helping them race to victory. One day, his family drove to Richmond for an outing, and he spotted a Thoroughbred racetrack from the car as they traveled on the freeway. Realizing it was only a short distance from their home in Albany, David's excitement grew.

The following Saturday afternoon, David deviated from his usual routine of attending a matinee and walked instead. He retraced the route his mother would drive, venturing out on his own for the first time with no destination in mind. With each step he took, the boundaries of his world expanded, revealing new and intriguing secrets. The busy streets were filled with honking cars, bustling traffic lights, and a chaotic mix of people performing various roles. As he walked, David caught whiffs of unfamiliar scents – the warm aroma of freshly baked bread from a nearby bakery, the pungent smell of gasoline from a gas station, and even the unpleasant odor of stale urine emanating from a doorway.

As he continued down University Avenue, the scene shifted to a more relaxed atmosphere. The buildings were boxy and made of metal, and there were railroad tracks running alongside the road. It was an industrialized area that carried a sense of cruelty.

But then, suddenly, the air changed. A rare scent wafted through the surroundings, stirring up a mix of excitement and unfamiliar friendliness within David. It was the rich smell of oats and hay, mingling with the earthy fragrance of alfalfa and the potent scent of horses and their urine. In that moment, David didn't know it yet, but he had stumbled upon something special.

He approached a large, wired gate and just outside of it was a small white house, big enough for one man. On tip toes, he reached up and then the face of a man with a white cowboy hat appeared.

"Mister, are there horses in there?"

"Yes, there are horses in here. Why you want to know?"

"Because I want to see them. I have never seen a horse before, and I have been reading this book on horses at school..."

"I'm sorry, son, but only allowed people are allowed," the guard told him disappointedly.

"Please! I just want to see the horses," I begged.

"Look, son, I tell you what," the man leaned closer to me, "walk in that direction," he pointed, "and turn right, there's a white pole from there you might get a look."

David did as the man instructed and walked in that direction and when he got to the white pole which was inside the fenced area, he could see rows of long buildings with no windows and set lower than most houses. He started climbing the fence and then jumped into a pile of straw that was just on the other side. After brushing himself off, he realized he was covered in horse manure and wet straw, the smell of which led him there.

Stepping inside the perimeter, David was transported into a magical world. It felt as if he had stumbled upon a place specially crafted by some powerful illusionist, filled with secrets and mysteries waiting to be unraveled. The barns that stretched before him seemed endless, each one housing a unique horse with no two alike. Every color imaginable was represented - deep blacks, rich browns, fiery bays, and dappled greys. The horses' faces were adorned with white blazes, bald patches, or socks in varying numbers. David's eyes darted from stall to stall, taking in the incredible variety before finally settling on one particular barn that seemed to call out to him. He couldn't quite explain it, but he felt an inexplicable pull towards this place - as if he belonged there. And without a doubt, he knew he did.

Life bursts with fierce, otherworldly enchantment, a deceptive facade of tangible existence; but the relentless grip of pessimism smothers any internal clarity. To David, every person experiences a fleeting moment of pure joy, a connection to something inherently essential - the one element that transforms the chaos of emptiness into a sublime symphony of fulfillment. It is the ultimate test for our souls, a commitment to something beautiful and worth living for. In childhood, these choices are simple and clear amidst a world of madness. Some embrace the beauty given upon them by life's gifts, while others reject it and seek to defy natural order out of self-loathing for their own limitations.

But as David's mind snapped back into reality, he saw with morbid fascination a man tending to the ankles of one horse. This regal creature exuded grace and strength, yet there seemed to be no rational explanation for its need for bandages.

"Why are you wrapping those bandages around the horse's ankles?" David inquired with curiosity. "Is he hurt?"

The man stopped his task and turned to face David, a kind smile on his face. "No, they're just preventative measures to protect his ankles. What's your name, son? And how did you get in here?"

"My name is David," he replied confidently.

"Well, David, it's nice to meet you. Do you know much about horses?"

David nodded eagerly. "I've read every book about them I could find. This one is a thoroughbred, right? For racing? They can run as fast as a car!"

Craig chuckled and patted the horse's sleek coat. "You really know your horses. My name is Craig, and my father is the trainer here at this barn."

As the day went on, David helped without being asked and even received $5 from Craig for his hard work.

"Unfortunately, you'll have to leave the same way you came in," Craig explained. "But if you want, you can come back and help again."

Craig had warned David that the day would start at four o'clock, but he could never have predicted just how early David would actually show up. With determination burning in his eyes, David tackled the morning, feeding like a man possessed, knowing it was the only time he had before heading off to school. But even after hours of classes and homework, his mind was consumed with thoughts of horses - studying their anatomy and care until he could recite it in his sleep. It was his escape, his sanctuary from the constant bullying he endured at school. The taunts and jeers from a group of black boys that seemed to take pleasure in tormenting him for his appearance. A fact that didn't need explaining to David, as he knew all too well that there was no other reason for their relentless attempts to break him down. But despite the pain and isolation, his love for horses remained unwavering, a hidden passion that fueled his soul and gave him strength to endure another day.

David was a fierce competitor on the sports field, his athletic abilities exuding a certain masculine energy that drew both admiration and jealousy from his peers. They often resorted to violence, trying to prove their own superiority over him. But David knew there were other reasons behind their actions - perhaps his effeminate nature made them see him as weak and easy prey. And although he was in some ways a gentle soul, he couldn't escape the confines of his societal expectations.

But when he was at the racetrack with the horses, David felt truly free. There was one horse in particular that captured his heart - Saginaw Bay, a magnificent dapple-gray gelding standing at an impressive fifteen hands tall. It was June of nineteen-sixty-seven, and the heat was relentless, but the enormous crowd surrounding the track added to the excitement hanging thick in the air.

As he watched Saginaw Bay prance and kick in anticipation of his upcoming race, David couldn't help but feel connected to the majestic animal. They were two beings intertwined by fate, bound by the same fabric of destiny. The horse's every movement showed his fiery spirit and determination, traits that set champions apart from common bloodlines. In that moment, David knew they were both ready for whatever lay ahead on the track.

David stood at the entrance of the stall; his voice was hoarse from chanting to the horse before him. Sweat dripped down his forehead as he whispered words of encouragement and praise, urging the machine of flesh and sinew to victory. With a crazed look in his eyes, he declared his love for Saginaw Bay, seducing the horse with his words until it submitted to his will.

Standing on an empty bucket, David reached up and forcefully placed the bridle on the horse's head, pulling the straps tight with ruthless determination. He could feel the power emanating from the animal's body, each hardened muscle pulsing with strength and potential. Running his hands over its body, he murmured soothing words, as if hypnotizing it into submission.

With one last caress, David released Saginaw Bay from its confines and entered the stall with trembling hands. As he stroked its powerful frame, he felt a connection between their souls, a transfer of energy that fueled them both. And in that moment, they were no longer man and beast, but one entity driven by an unbreakable bond forged through obsession and madness.

With a firm grip on the reins, Craig led Saginaw Bay to the track, their footsteps echoing against the wooden planks. David, too young to be there, watched from the sidelines with wide-eyed fascination. He could feel the energy radiating off the majestic horse, whose anxiety was almost palpable. In the starting gate, Saginaw Bay shifted restlessly from one hoof to the other, his body tense with anticipation. And then it happened - "BAM!" The gate flew open, and a flash of fury erupted as Saginaw Bay's hindquarters propelled him forward, leaving a tornado of dust and sand in his wake.

As they rounded the first corner, Saginaw Bay weaved through horses with ease, showing off his superior speed and agility. His sleek gray coat darkened under a thin sheen of sweat as he charged forward into the first stretch. With each powerful stride, he gained ground and moved up in rank. With anticipation building, David's heart pounded harder as the crowd buzzed with excitement. The rhythmic clicking of hooves on the dirt reminded him of castanets, and the earth seemed to shake beneath him as the horses thundered by. The jockeys lifted themselves slightly out of their saddles to lessen the weight on their steeds, causing them to appear as if they were levitating.

In the home stretch, Saginaw Bay ran neck and neck with another horse, both determined to win. The whip cracked in a booming roar and the crowd erupted into cheers as Saginaw Bay pulled ahead in a burst of speed and determination. With half a length between him and the second-place winner, he crossed the finish line in a triumphant blur.

David was left breathless as he basked in the thrill of victory, his heart soaring along with Saginaw Bay's. The sound of applause and chanting filled his ears as he reveled in the intoxicating joy of triumph.

'There is no greater feeling in a child than the feeling of being right without the intervention of egotism. It is the confectionary of life's reward, this sweetness of mind and soul. A child would cling to things as instruments of amusement, but of love would be guided through the closeness of human affection. Love cannot be understood when the target of its longing cannot reciprocate, love cannot grow of its own volition to occupy its state of being in the oneness of self, it must have something to bounce off, or reflect in order that it be understood, and thus the stages of life are ephemeral, as too the instruments of amusement. There is a half-life to everything that has form, and everything you cling to

will eventually be taken away, but not love, for it endures outside the boundaries of form.'

As David led Saginaw Bay back to the barn, the Senator and his wife walked behind. The purse for this race was a staggering two-hundred and fifty-thousand dollars, a testament to the horse's incredible speed and strength. Though he wasn't the owner of the magnificent animal, David had been given the honorary title of master, earning him immense respect from the Senator and his wife.

The couple showered David with praise and gratitude, as if he had just made a generous donation towards their political campaign. Besides giving him twenty-five dollars as a gift, they also asked where he lived.

"I live on Milvia street, near Berkeley High School," David replied proudly.

The senator's wife smiled warmly at him. "You know, we don't have any children," she said. "But we have a ranch in Washington State filled with all kinds of horses. Have you ever heard of it?"

David nodded eagerly. "Yes ma'am, I have."

"How would you like to come live with us?" she asked, extending the invitation with genuine sincerity.

"Yes, hell yes! I want this more than anything," David exclaimed, his eyes shining with excitement. "But first, I have to ask my mom. Can you wait that long?" My heart raced with anticipation as I sprinted towards the house, my feet pounding against the ground.

Breathless, I burst through the front door and pleaded with my mother, "Can I please go live in Washington with this Senator and his wife? They have horses and maybe I could even become a doctor someday!" My words spilled out in a frantic rush, my voice filled with urgency and hope.

My mother's face broke into a smile, but before she could answer, I cut her off with my desperate pleas, "Please, Mom! This is my chance to make something of myself. Don't ruin it for me!"

Her smile faded and she looked at me with a mixture of amusement and concern. "Are you out of your mind, boy?" But I was too consumed by my desire for a better life to listen to reason.

"You're ruining everything!" I shouted in frustration. In that moment, all that mattered to me was the promise of a new life with influential parents who could help me become someone important.

The words tore into my mother's heart, sharp and piercing like daggers. Her eyes filled with tears as she struggled to understand her son's request. David wondered if she was truly doing the right thing, his own heart heavy with conflicting emotions. He had always believed in his destiny, but now he questioned it. His mother's refusal to let him go with the senator and his wife angered him, stirring up a deep resentment towards her for interfering in his fate. Yet, this discontent was fleeting. Little did he know of the future consequences it would bring. In that moment, he stood firm in his conviction that a person's birth is not their last form, but an ongoing process of self- discovery and rebirth.

David would have abandoned the scene at the racetrack entirely, an act which supported his self-destructive nature, a scheme through which he believed was a viable road of travel, by cutting off his own hand's others would feel the phantom of its loss. David stored the disappointment close to the conscious level to be easily retrieved at a later date. It was shortly after this incident that he was late coming home from work one night. His mother was torn to pieces, thinking he had actually done the very thing she had forbidden him, going with the Senator and his wife. The police were not contacted; instead, she waited despite the depth of grief she was sinking further into. The clock was reading eight, some three hours had passed before his scheduled arrival home, and then suddenly he appeared; carrying something concealed behind his back.

"Where have you been?" She demanded with potent indignation, "I have been worried sick wondering if you had up and taken off."

And David explained, but was halted in mid-sentence, stopped before he could unleash his tiny little logic that she knew would heat and melt the icy cube of her anger, and when he knew the battle was being lost, he brought from behind his back a cake and a dish in the shape of a leaf, "Happy Birthday Mom," and thus the explanation spoken.

It couldn't be seen by an eye with clarity the underlying intent, for within the eye of the storm, a soothing balm had been applied. There is proficiency to life, a secret understanding, not so secret, of love's powers revealed to a child, lost in an adult, found again at the nearing of death.

David continued to endure his ritual daily bullying by the same gang of boys, though slowly the act was becoming less fun to them and eventually his continued submissiveness appeared more strength until the heat finally dissipated and he became an accepted equal, though held at a distance for lack of the fighting spirit.

The job at the racetrack was only seasonal from January through June, but he was always there at its opening, each year a little taller and filled with more personality.

Chapter 5

Richmond, California and Janet Wheeler

After years of living the structured and rigid life of a military family, the Parkers bought a three-bedroom house in Richmond, just ten miles from Berkeley. Their new community, Fairmede, was predominantly white and resembled something out of the tv series "Happy Days". Finally settling down, David now had his own room, signifying his growth and freedom from the constraints of their previous lifestyle.

As they settled into their new neighborhood, the surrounding faces seemed to change overnight. What was once an all-black community now transformed into an all-white one. It was a stark contrast that left the family feeling both intrigued and unsettled. Life had played a cruel trick on them, forcing them to confront issues of race and identity in a place where they least expected it.

David knew growing up meant finding acceptance among his peers. And when skin color becomes a defining factor, it can alter priorities and create a self-consuming divide. In this new environment, where race became more apparent and divisive, David questioned the direction of things.

As a child, David was taught to prioritize the assimilation of events outside of himself, but now he faces a harsh reality. False beliefs and biases have permeated his surroundings, dictating how he should perceive and interact with the world around him. The struggle for acceptance within the Black community upon first entering the United States was a grueling and endless battle. Despite small pockets of acceptance, there was a constant reminder that victory was still far from reach. The new neighborhood appeared perfect on the surface: manicured lawns, friendly neighbors of different races, and matching houses. But beneath this façade of serenity lay a toxic undercurrent of falsity and deception, ready to engulf anyone who dared to challenge it.

As the first Black family to move into Fairmede, the Parkers faced constant discrimination and racism. However, David was light-skinned and more easily accepted by his white peers. While he felt relieved to avoid being targeted himself, he also struggled with feeling guilty for not standing up for his family. In social situations, he laughed along with others at offensive jokes directed towards Black people, even though he didn't find them funny at all. It made him feel weak and ashamed of himself, torn between loyalty to his family and fitting in with his friends. With each forced laugh, he felt like a hypocrite, silently wishing for the courage to speak out against the casual racism around him.

David struggled to find his place in a world that constantly pulled him in different directions. Growing up in a community where racial tensions were high, he didn't know what it meant to stand up for his beliefs or even who he truly was. As more black families moved into his predominantly white neighborhood, the delicate balance shifted, and David found himself caught in the middle of conflicting ideologies.

With each passing day, David's inner turmoil grew as he tried to navigate a society that seemed determined to label and categorize him based on his race. Moving to Richmond only amplified these struggles, as he was forced to attend a new school and adapt to a new way of life. In this new environment, he slowly lost touch with the real person inside and instead adopted a facade that would allow him to fit in and avoid conflict.

But deep down, David longed for a more peaceful existence where race didn't dictate one's actions or identity. However, the fear of standing out and facing potential violence from both sides kept him from fully embracing this desire. He suppressed his true interests and hobbies, molding himself into someone he no longer recognized just to survive.

It was a constant battle between staying true to himself and conforming to societal expectations. And in the end, David became lost in a world where who he wanted to be was constantly at war with whom others wanted him to be.

At fifteen years old, David lived with his family in Richmond. He was a typical teenage boy, hanging out with friends and enjoying the carefree days of youth. But one fateful day, he had a sexual encounter with a friend's mother - a woman named Janet Wheeler. Both families knew each other well, but were divided by race - one white and one black.

Janet must have been in her forties or possibly older, but David never found out her true age. As he kept this secret from his friends, he lived a double life - one filled with excitement and danger, fueled by shame and fear.

The crux of his shame came from being discovered for engaging in an illicit relationship with a much older white woman - a taboo act in their society. And to make matters more complicated, Janet was not even deemed conventionally attractive. Despite all this, David couldn't deny the thrill that coursed through him every time they met in secret. It was a dangerous game they played, but one that he couldn't resist.

Janet Wheeler—the quintessential mother figure, the embodiment of the all-American homemaker, exuded a sense of nurturing warmth that drew others to her. Her hair, once a vibrant chestnut brown, now peppered with strands of gray, held hints of the wisdom and experience she carried. The slight slant in her demeanor showed the burden she carried on her shoulders, resulting from years of hardship and selflessness. Her milky white skin, adorned with visible blue veins, spoke volumes about the harsh realities she had faced. Yet, despite it all, there was an inner conflict that clung to her like a heavy cloak; remnants of emotional scars left by her previous husband's lack of love and physical abuse. Janet's family comprised Little Brucie and Perry, her two adoring sons who shared a close bond with David and lived just a short walk away in a corner dwelling at the intersection of Groom and Alta Mira.

David stood alone at the abandoned bus stop, his breath steaming in the chilly morning air. He had purposely missed the bus, determined not to attend his school that day. His eyes were fixed on Janet Wheeler's house across the street, a place shrouded in eerie darkness and an unexplainable sense of foreboding.

The plants around her house seemed to wither and die in her presence, as if they, too, were repelled by her sinister energy. The sky above was a deep, oppressive black, devoid of any light or hope.

David only knew Janet through her son Perry, but he could feel her dark gaze on him, drawing him in like a moth to a flame. She had a strange interest in him, one that he didn't fully understand. But little did he know she was plotting something far more nefarious than just simple curiosity. And as their paths crossed more and more, David found himself drawn towards her unnaturally, a dangerous attraction that threatened to consume them both.

As time trickled by, David's thoughts swirled in a chaotic mess. He stood frozen in place, unable to move as he processed the possibilities before him. Suddenly, the suffocating scent of lust seeped into his every pore and snapped him out of his trance. He scoured the eerily silent neighborhood for any signs of life, fearful that someone might catch him at this unholy hour with no valid reason for being there. Growing more anxious by the second, he carefully approached her house, moving with stealth and grace like a predator stalking its prey. A wooden trellis enveloped in overgrown vines shielded the front door from view, providing a discreet hiding spot for anyone on the porch.

He stands in front of the looming house, feeling like he's been there for hours. The darkness seems to seep from its very walls, enveloping him in a suffocating embrace. He knows she is inside. Her presence felt through the familiar shape of her VW Bug parked in the driveway. With trembling hands, he finally musters the courage to knock on the door, only to be met with a deafening hollowness that sends chills down his spine. As the door creaks open, he sees her standing there with a twisted smile stretched across her face, and he realizes too late that this house holds more than just ghosts from their past.

"Hi, Mrs. Wheeler, is Perry home?" he nervously asked.

"Perry's in juvy," [that's short for juvenile hall] she said. "Why aren't you in school?"

"I missed the bus and thought maybe Perry was at home again. I haven't seen him at school, thought maybe he was sick or something."

"Sick in the head, that's what he is. I can't seem to get through to him; ever since Mr. Wheeler—his dad—and I separated, he's been acting strange, angry at the world, I would say." She looked off nowhere. "Anyhow, I'm in the middle of my chores, so you should run along."

"I can help you." I quickly snapped out before she could turn and close the door.

"Well, come in then. I am sure I can find something for you to do," and she opened the door wider, signaling him in. She closed the door quietly, looking about outside before finally shutting it completely and while he was standing there, she pointed to a chair, and then she went into the garage and returned with a mop and bucket, "here, you can help by moping this floor." And then she turns and heads towards the rear of the house.

The task she had assigned him was simple cleaning the kitchen floor. With a fervent desire to impress her, he attacked the task with almost manic energy, scrubbing and scouring until every inch of the floor gleamed. As he finished and called out to let her know, his voice echoed throughout the hollowed-out shell of a house. But there was no answer, and he took a seat in the sparsely furnished living room, feeling almost as if he were in a waiting room or a sterile examination room, awaiting judgment from some unseen authority figure. The silence was deafening, broken only by the rhythmic ticking of a clock on the wall. David fidgeted nervously, his hands folded tightly in his lap, wondering what would come next in this strange game of submission and control.

At fifteen, David began a series of sexual encounters with Mrs. Wheeler that he can't quite explain. He remembers discovering his mother's True Romance magazines at just eleven or twelve years old and feeling both intrigued and ashamed as he secretly read them. Despite being attracted to girls his age, David found himself drawn to the idea of experimenting with an older woman. The thought of learning from someone more experienced was enticing, but also intimidating. He couldn't shake the feeling of wanting to escape the pressure of teenage relationships and expectations, yet also feeling guilty for seeking something taboo. It was this conflicting desire that led him down a path he never could have imagined at such a young age.

In the Livingroom were two cushioned chairs with carved wooden frames chipped and worn from years of use. There was a single couch with similar handiwork. On each wall, there was a papered print of still life depicting different stages of seasonal change. The room was utilitarian and industrial, a place not fit for the gathering of a loving family; the drab-colored gypsum board walls had the lingering smell of a house after it had been vacated of all life.

When Mrs. Wheeler walked into the room where David was sitting, she didn't look at him or say a word. She simply lay down carefully on the rickety couch that groaned beneath her weight, and then placed one of her arms over her eyes. The silence was only broken when David mentioned the kitchen,

"Mrs. Wheeler, I'm finished with the kitchen floor. It didn't take long. I called out to you, but you didn't answer." And she didn't say a word.

David's mind swirled with confusion as he watched the scene before him. His body tense despite that, he sat in the chair like a well-behaved child, his eyes trained on her unmoving figure. Her silver hair caught his attention, its color so strikingly different from what he had seen in other older women. It seemed to be her natural shade, not one of age or time. As his gaze traveled down her body, he couldn't help but notice the smoothness of her milky-white skin and the way her ample breasts pressed against the thin fabric of her housedress. Her legs, left exposed, appeared sleek and shapely, causing David to fidget nervously in his seat. At fifteen years old, he was unfamiliar with the subtleties of female body language, but to Janet Wheeler it may have been a calculated display of submission, a long-awaited surrender to her feminine desires and an acceptance of her role as a seductress.

David's eyes darted nervously around the room as he asked, his voice trembling. Mrs. Wheeler remained silent; her expression was unreadable. Finally, he stood up and slowly made his way over to her, hesitantly pressing his lips to hers. She didn't respond, but threw her arm down in anger and shouted at him to leave. Shocked and confused, David stood frozen for a moment before finally realizing he had made a mistake. "I only thought I was doing what you wanted," he stuttered as he backed away from her enraged form. Mrs. Wheeler continued to scream at him until he finally left, feeling utterly rejected and embarrassed.

On the walk back to his house, he couldn't help but repeat in his head how terrible a person he was. His guilt weighed heavily on him, but he had only been acting on what felt like a natural impulse. Confusion consumed him as he tried to understand why she had reacted so strongly. To him, it had simply been a compliment and an expression of a desire for a woman, especially one older than himself. Yet despite his rationalizations, a sense of filth and guilt clung to him, like a sticky sweat that refused to be washed away.

As he walked, his mind raced with unanswered questions and doubts. But deep down, he knew that challenging that moment of curiosity had brought him some relief, even if it came with its own set of consequences. He couldn't shake the feeling that maybe he had crossed a line, but at least now he could start asking himself these tough questions and perhaps find some clarity in the chaos of his thoughts.

There were whispers among the residents of the town that Mrs. Wheeler had once suffered a nervous breakdown and spent time in the Napa State Hospital. David couldn't shake off this rumor, but he didn't know if it was true or if it was just gossip. He felt a sense of guilt for even considering it, as if he was taking advantage of her vulnerability. Yet, there was a part of him that wondered if she had mentioned it to him herself, as if subconsciously inviting him into her life. It made him question his own morality and whether a fifteen-year-old could truly understand the complexities of human behavior. Was he using this information to manipulate her, or was it all just a coincidence? These thoughts plagued David's mind as he tried to make sense of his feelings towards Mrs. Wheeler.

Weeks had passed since the unsettling encounter with Mrs. Wheeler, and David had almost convinced himself that it was all just a bad dream. But on a dark and rainy night, a phone call shattered his illusion of safety. It was 10:00PM and everyone in the house was asleep, except for him.

"Hello?" David answered cautiously.

"Is this David? This is Janet Wheeler," came the familiar voice on the other end.

David's heart raced as memories flooded back. "Yes, it's me. What do you want, Mrs. Wheeler?" he whispered, trying to keep his voice steady.

"Please, just call me Janet." Still, David remained silent. "I wanted to apologize for how I treated you last time you were here," Mrs. Wheeler said, her tone filled with remorse.

David remained silent, unsure of how to respond.

"Something triggered a painful memory of my late husband, and I reacted poorly," she continued explaining, her voice cracking with emotion. "But if you'll allow me, I'd like to make it up to you by offering you a cup of cocoa."

David couldn't believe what he was hearing. A few weeks ago, this woman had been cold and unwelcoming towards him, and now she wanted to offer him this odd peace offering. It seemed too good to be true.

"Right now? You want to offer me cocoa right now?" he asked in disbelief.

"Yes, right now. Unless there's a problem," Mrs. Wheeler replied.

"No, no problem at all. I'll be there as soon as I can," and David hung up, saying nothing.

Quickly, he changed out of his pajamas, turned off the lights, and climbed quietly from his bedroom window. The rain was pounding hard, but he didn't care, didn't notice his focus was on her. 'I wonder what made her change her mind.'

As he approached her house, the weight of his emotions sank. His heart raced as he wondered what would come of this meeting, but this time, it felt like a welcome thrill instead of a burden. The rain poured down relentlessly as he hurried through the streets towards her house, the distance only taking mere minutes. By the time he arrived at her doorstep, he was completely drenched. Taking a deep breath, he steeled himself against the possibility of encountering one of her infamous neurotic episodes. Once he felt confident enough, he lightly knocked on the door and within seconds, a warm light flooded out from inside the house, enveloping him in a comforting embrace.

He could see her silhouette standing elegantly inside the doorway, backlit by the soft glow of a nearby lamp. She wore a sheer gown, which accentuated her curves and sent waves of desire coursing through him. After exchanging formalities, she motioned for him to come inside and stood guard by the doorway like a faithful sentinel. As she closed the door behind him, he couldn't help but feel grateful for being in her presence.

"Please, take a seat here," she whispered, gesturing to a nearby chair. "Let me take those wet clothes and put them in the dryer."

She moved around him gracefully, gently removing each piece of clothing until he was left standing in nothing but his damp underwear. Despite feeling vulnerable, he couldn't help but be captivated by every move.

He couldn't tear his gaze away from the animated figure wearing a flowing gown; After hanging up his coat in the musty garage, he joined her in the kitchen, where she stood by the stove, tending to a small pot of milk. The air between them was thick with unspoken words, hesitant and uneasy, like ghosts haunting a graveyard. But true to her word, she offered an offering of reconciliation as she set a steaming cup of Postum on the table before him and declared, "I'm going back to my room to finish my book." And with that, she left him alone with his thoughts and regrets. The warm, comforting aroma of the hot drink filled the room, but it paled compared to the fiery passion that still burned within him at the sight of her.

David thought it her intention to let him sit until she was reasonably sure he was discomfited. He didn't want to be the aggressor and screw things up like he had before, and so he sat until suddenly her voice broke through his thoughts.

"Why don't you come back here to the room with me?"

He followed the lingering echoes, which led to a single solitary room dimly lit by a small lamp resting atop a single nightstand; the room was intended for one. She was lying in a bed barely large enough for one person, reclining beneath unruffled blankets; propped against two large pillows in white. The room itself appeared staged in its emptiness. There was something different, composure this regal was rare. The truth had a predilection for unusual disguise, and she was the dragon at the gate. A book was open and resting atop her chest, and she seemed to look right through him, a subliminal frame within the entire cinema, a reference point of polarity within his vision, a carefully orchestrated ruse to overplay the cleverly arranged move of the evening before him.

He took a seat in the only chair which sat in a corner just opposite the bed and he sat there contemplating the novelty of the moment.

"I think you'll be more comfortable in the bed. Come on, get in." she pulled back the blanket, exposing her uplifted gown and the milky whiteness of her legs. "Now, isn't that better?"

As she shifted on her side, her body pressed against his and he delicately moved to the edge of the bed to make more room. Their words tangled together in a jumble, but suddenly her hand took hold of his and guided it to the mound of hair just beneath her navel. At that touch, his heart raced, and he moved erratically beneath the blanket. A surge of emotion welled up within him, firing off electric charges that ignited the essence of life within him. It was not lovemaking, not in any genuine sense; rather, it was a perfunctory dance of bodies, a choreography devoid of true intimacy.

For Janet Wheeler, this was love. Perhaps the absence of tenderness in her life had driven her to accept this as love, despite its lack of understanding. As for David, he saw the stark contrast between love and sex, the constant power struggle between man and woman. He saw the cruel and subversive nature of man's desire to dominate that delicate and ethereal creature known as woman.

Chapter 6

Confusion

Richmond—Fairmede, to David, was a place where the harsh reality of racial segregation took effect and show itself most prominently. Prior to this, he lived in an all-black community where racism was present but not yet fully realized. However, in this new environment where lower-class whites clung tightly to their white communities and sought to preserve the heritage of their ancestors, David found himself thrust into the middle of a different race war between blacks and whites.

It was here that drugs and alcohol first entered his life, with marijuana being the drug of choice. But more than that, it was a place where he couldn't find satisfaction in his pursuit of higher learning. He felt pressure to conform and be like everyone else, even if it went against his own desires.

This skewed perception of self, this misconception disguised as truth, was how David saw himself and how he believed others saw him as well. Because of his mixed heritage, he struggled with feelings of not belonging to either, feeling like he didn't fit in anywhere. It was a constant internal battle that only added to the turmoil of living in a racially divided community.

He saw Mrs. Wheeler occasionally, as they both still lived in the same neighborhood. But mostly he'd see her when he had been out drinking with the guys. She was a fragile secret that he wanted to keep hidden. Like most of the pleasures in his life unshared with the world, he was ashamed of his relationship with her. Most of the boys his age was dating girls young and pretty, but as he was only gradually becoming part of the black teenage culture, he found himself extremely shy around black girls; he didn't know for sure his position in the black race where relationships mattered and so he felt as if he were living otherworldly.

From an early age he found himself sexually attracted to women and girls, there was even an occasion when he was six years old and his mother's sister, his aunt, who at the time was thirteen and living with them during their time at The Estuary, invited him and his two sisters to play the game of house with her, naturally he was chosen to be the husband and his mother's sister was the wife. For some inexplicable reason, sex resonated like a gong in his head, affecting normal relationships. Mrs. Wheeler satisfied urges in him that he couldn't wait for a healthy relationship with someone else.

David's heart raced as he lay in bed, tangled in the sheets. His secret affair with Janet burned through his thoughts, a dangerous flame that threatened to consume him. He had kept it hidden from everyone, knowing the shame and embarrassment it would bring if anyone found out.

But on this morning, while his grandmother, who lived in Bermuda, was visiting, David's worst fears were realized. He could hear Janet's voice, talking to his grandmother in the living room. Panic gripped him as he listened to her reveal his secret to his unsuspecting grandmother.

Without a second thought, David leaped out of bed and charged into the living room. There she sat on the sofa, chatting casually with his grandmother. The sight of her sent a surge of anger and fear through him. How could she risk blowing their cover like this? But then he saw the look of longing on her face and heard the desperation in her words.

She was in love with him, despite the age difference and the danger it posed. And at that moment, David knew he had to do something.

"Grandma, please don't listen to a word she is saying. This woman is crazy and has been going around the neighborhood knocking on people's doors asking for me, looking for me like some maniac." And before Janet could say another word, David grabbed her by the back of her neck and lead her to the door and kicked her in the ass. "Stay away from me and my family, you sick bitch. Never come around her again." And she climbed into her VW Bug and that was the last time they spoke to each other.

David yearned to break free from the confines of his current lifestyle, and though he knew it may not be possible, he was determined to at least change his surroundings. He pleaded with his mother to help him transfer to Berkeley High, a school known for its diverse and accepting student body. Through some connections from The Estuary, a local community center, his mother reached out to the Walkers, an old family friend. With help from the Walkers, they could use the Berkeley address and falsely claim David as a resident so he could attend the school.

At Berkeley High, David found himself surrounded by like-minded individuals who valued education over superficial differences like race. Here, learning was encouraged based on personal interests and academic foundations rather than societal norms. It was a breath of fresh air for David, who finally felt at home among his peers. His art class was a haven for him, with his teacher Fred (known simply by his first name) embodying the laid-back and open- minded "Berkelium" lifestyle of healthy eating and listening to Neil Young. This atmosphere exuded the sense of peace and acceptance that David had been longing for.

David remained living in Richmond, but went to high school in Berkeley, and he still saw those same people who bullied him into being part of the group. You might think when he bullied him into the group that he was speaking about physical coercion, but it was a more subtle invitation that you couldn't refuse. Looking back, he could have refused. He could have stood up for himself, but he didn't know how to. He let people walk on him and then he became angry with himself. And not knowing how to manage the situation to be beneficial to everyone, he gave in and lived against his own feelings.

The pressures of life clawed at him relentlessly, driving him to the brink of madness. He couldn't escape the suffocating weight of responsibility that he carried on his shoulders. And in those moments, all he wanted to do was run away. But why? Why did this urge always take hold of him? Was it because he feared facing the harsh realities that awaited him? Or was it something deeper, more primal? Memories from his childhood flooded back, haunting him with images of a young boy torn away from his natural father and thrust into a new family with a stepfather who instilled fear in his heart. Though he was only two years old, the trauma still lingered, shaping his every thought and action. As hard as he tried to cope with an imperfect reality, the wounds from his past continued to fester and bleed, threatening to consume him entirely.

Like a shield, his mind protected him from the sharp edges of pain and loss, shielding him from the harsh realities of life. But in exchange, it burdened him with complex problems that seemed tailored to test his capabilities, as if his subconscious knew his true potential and constantly challenged him to rise above it. David found himself caught in the turmoil of other people's choices, forced to navigate through their conflicting needs and desires. His mother sought fulfillment for herself, while his father pursued his own selfish interests. Even his stepfather was driven by a desire for a better life, stemming from the consequences of his parents' decisions. It was as if his entire life had been shaped by the choices of others, leaving him feeling like a mere pawn in their game.

The pressures at home were suffocating, especially from his stepfather, William. With a constant need to be seen as a wonderful father figure in Wendy's eyes, William constantly pushed for perfection. But deep down, David knew that Wendy no longer cared about the life she was living under their roof. He realized he needed to escape, even if just for a short while, and find his own path in life elsewhere. The thought of leaving his family behind weighed heavily on his heart, but he couldn't continue living in this stifling environment. He yearned for the freedom to make his own choices and create a life that brought him true happiness.

Chapter 7

George Jones

Wendy had made a promise to David - she would help him get into Berkeley High School, but it wouldn't be until September when the new school year began. Until then, he had to make do with life in Richmond and the local school.

Living across the street from the Parker family were Pat and Joe, with their two children, five-year-old Tiffany and three-year-old Theron, who was autistic. David often found himself drawn to their home, where he was smitten with Pat and her cool, laid-back demeanor. On some nights, he would even earn a few extra dollars by babysitting for them. Pat, a well-known DJ at KDIA radio station in Oakland, always had the latest and greatest music playing in her house, along with some top-notch weed. Despite being only fifteen years old, she treated David as if he were her peer, making him feel accepted and valued.

The warm afternoon sun streamed through the kitchen window, casting a warm glow on Pat and David as they sat at the table playing dominoes. The loud sounds of Pharaoh Sanders' jazz music filled the room, adding to the intense atmosphere of the game. Suddenly, a sharp knock at the door interrupted their concentration.

Pat let out a frustrated sigh, trying to ignore the interruption and focus on her next move. But the persistent knocking continued, causing her to slam down her dominoes in annoyance.

"There, give me five and don't be a jive!" she shouted at David, who had been distracted by the knock. "And pass me the joint with your greedy ass before you smoke it all."

David chuckled and passed her the joint as he got up from the table to answer the door.

"No, stay there. I'll get it," Pat said, already making her way to the front door with the joint in hand.

She opened the door to find an elderly white woman standing on the porch, a concerned look on her face. Pat's eyes widened in surprise, and she just stared at the woman for a moment.

"Hello, I hate to bother you like this," the woman began, addressing Pat. "But I am looking for David. Is he here?"

Pat's voice rose in volume as she called out for David. "David, there's a white woman out here for you." Her tone was laced with sarcasm and disbelief.

David's eyebrows rose in surprise as he pushed away from the kitchen table, his chair scraping against the hardwood floor. He strode into the living room, where Pat was holding onto the open door with a look of disdain on her face. She quickly retreated back into the kitchen.

Confused and slightly annoyed, David turned to see who had interrupted their game. His heart dropped when he saw Janet Wheeler standing there, tears streaming down her face as she stared at the ground.

"What the hell are you doing here?" David whispered harshly. "How did you even find me? No, I don't care how you found me. Get your damn white-ass out of here and if you ever come looking for me again, I'll make sure you regret it. Now get the fuck out."

He slammed the door shut and watched through the window as she walked back to her car and drove away.

"Who was that crazy white woman?" Pat chuckled, breaking the tense silence.

"I don't know," David replied with a shake of his head. "Some crazy woman who can't take a hint." They both laughed nervously before returning to their domino game, trying to ignore the unsettling encounter that had just occurred.

Every day that passed, the weight of existence seemed to grow heavier on David's shoulders. The search for meaning and purpose slipped further out of reach as he was sucked into a dichotomy that suffocated him with its demands. Walking out of Pat's house, David felt like he was drowning in the quicksand of his own life.

The year was 1970. At just fourteen years old, David already felt like he was drowning in adulthood. His mind raced with questions and fears, desperate for a way to escape the chaos of his thoughts. And so, he turned to marijuana - a temporary reprieve from the overwhelming weight of growing up too fast, too soon.

With shaky hands, he dialed up Edward Porter, his best friend and go-to guy for weed. "Ed, man, I need you," David pleaded into the phone.

"What's wrong, Parker?" Ed's voice held a hint of concern, but David knew it wasn't genuine. They were all just using each other to numb the pain and confusion of adolescence - and the difference in race only added to the tension.

"I need a lid, Ed. Can you hook me up?" A lid was half a sandwich bag full of marijuana - enough to last a while, a week at least.

"I got you on this boss man it's $10, as usual. I'll bring it to your house soon. Oh, and George is with me." George was someone David hated more than anyone else. Just a few months ago, George and Edward played a dangerous prank on David.

Though David considered Edward to be his best friend, it was not known if Edward felt the same for David. When George played these nasty jokes on David, though Edward may have been there and never interceded, it was never he who profited the same as George did. The three of them walked to the local store and once there, George bought a six-pack of Old English 800 - a potent malt liquor.

"Come on, let's go behind the store and have a beer," George urged as they walked.

Edward happily agreed, but David tried to refuse. "I don't drink fellas, so knock yourself out," he said firmly.

"Fuck that. Everyone drinks. You smoke weed, so a beer won't hurt," spat George angrily. And against his better judgment, and the fear he had of George, David reluctantly followed them to the back of the store, where it was dark.

Suddenly, without provocation, George pulls out a handgun from his pocket and points it at David's face without warning.

"What the fuck, George? Get that thing out of my face!" David shouted, fear coursing through his veins.

"Grab one of those beers and drink it, or I will blow your motherfucking face off," George threatened, his grip on the gun tightening, his hands shaking amateurishly. And so, with trembling hands, David reached for a beer and took a swig without question. This was a situation he had never been in before - and because of George's manipulation and coercion, he had to do something that went against his own values. At the end of the night, George had forced David to drink four beers, which rendered him most intoxicated.

After that evening, David cursed the very ground that George walked on. The anger he felt when mad about something could be easily noticed by those closest to him, for those who were close, were not a threat. They were not the object of this proposed anger and so all they saw was the dramatic ramblings of someone who seemed like he knew how to direct his anger, but David was a coward toward black men, especially black men who carried the scars of battle on their faces. It was easier for David to align a friendship with a black person of personable nature and appearance, because he was a handsome young man and in the black community, looks were everything.

With a rush of exhilaration, David blasted Isaac Hayes' "Hot Buttered Soul" on his eight-track and furiously tidied his room. He meticulously organized his new clothes - a vibrant yellow leather jacket with sleek black trim, matching pinstripe slacks, bold two-toned knee-high boots, and a striking black and white knit shirt. Each piece carefully selected for the highly expected spring-day celebration at school. For the black students, this event was more than just a fashion show - it was a chance to stand out and be seen. He was readying himself for spring-day, a thing most high schools did every year in California. What happens is everyone or whoever wants to get dressed up for the day, it's the way the kids take time to show off. This idea of spring-day is mostly a black thing among the black kids, which in America, after years of oppression and shame, vanity is how black people show their worth and value to the public.

A loud knock on the front door startled David as he lounged on one of the makeshift beds in his bedroom. He peered out the window and saw his best friends, Edward and George, standing on the porch. Excited to see them, he ran to open the door and ushered them inside before disappearing back into his bedroom. The room was small but cozy, with two twin beds that used to be bunk beds but were now separated and turned into cushiony benches. As they settled in, Edward pulled out a baggie of weed and started rolling a joint.

"Is it cool to smoke in here?" Edward asked, glancing around the room.

"Yeah, my mom doesn't know what's going on," David replied nonchalantly.

George stayed quiet for some reason, but no one paid much attention. "Roll it up, man," David said eagerly, reaching for the joint first once it was passed around. He took a long drag and then passed it to Edward.

"Did you hear that?" George suddenly said, pressing his ear against the bedroom door.

"Hear what?" David asked, slightly annoyed at being interrupted. "I think it's your mom calling you," George informed him.

David groaned and got up to open the door. "What do you want, Mom? Can't you see I'm hanging out with my friends in my room?"

"I'm sorry, baby," his mom replied apologetically through the crack in the doorway. "I don't mean to interrupt, but could you make me a sandwich? You know yours are always the best."

David rolled his eyes but couldn't say no to his mom's request. "Fine, I'll be right back. Just save me a hit on that joint." He smiled at Edward and George before leaving the room and closing the door behind him.

"What a buzzkill," he muttered as he made his way to the kitchen to fulfill his mom's request.

David rushes into the kitchen, his heart pounding as he anxiously glances back at his bedroom door, afraid that someone might discover the smoke-filled room. With shaking hands, he carefully prepares a ham sandwich for his mother, knowing it's her favorite. He swiftly makes a cup of hot tea and brings everything to her on a tray, determined to keep her comfortable in bed.

"You're an angel, David. My million-dollar baby," his mother says with tears in her eyes.

"I know, Mom. You always tell me," David replies with a hint of impatience.

"But it's true! From the moment you could read and write at six years old, I knew you were special," his mother continues, her voice trembling with emotion.

"Mom, my friends are waiting for me. Can we talk about this later?" David interrupts, trying to hide his frustration.

"I'm sorry, dear. I'm being selfish again. But you mean everything to me," his mother says with a pleading look.

"I love you too, Mom. Now I really have to go. Bye," David says quickly before rushing out of the room, his heart heavy with conflicting emotions.

David hurries from his mother and back to his room, where both Edward and George sit quietly.

"Sorry, Parker, but we have to go. Now, where's the ten for the lid?" David hastily hands Edward the ten-dollar bill before rushing to the front door. The two friends walk out in silence, both lost in their own thoughts. Once they have left, David heads straight to the kitchen for a snack before retreating to his room. He collapses onto his bed, reaching for the half-smoked doobie Edward left in the ashtray. As he takes a drag, he looks around his room and notices something missing - his prized yellow jacket, slacks, and boots are nowhere to be found.

Frantically, David jumps off his bed and begins rifling through his closet, searching for any sign of his missing items. He moves over to the window and peers outside, hoping to glimpse his clothes somewhere outside the window, hoping maybe it all was a prank. It slowly dawns on him that George or Edward, or possibly both of them, must have snuck the clothes out while he was distracted by making his mother a sandwich.

The next day is Spring Day, a highly anticipated day for David. But now, instead of wearing the outfit he had carefully planned out weeks ago, he has to settle for a brown turtleneck and a worn brown leather coat as substitutes. Disappointed and frustrated by his friends' actions, David can't help but wonder.

Why the hell would they take my clothes? Don't they know if they or George have stolen my clothes? I would find out by seeing whoever is in them, and besides, the coat is bright yellow. How is that going to go unnoticed by George's black ass?

These thoughts were running through David's mind, but most of all, he felt humiliated. How are these people who call themselves friends acting in this nature? These are all the things David has had to deal with since the first day he arrived in California ten years ago. He tried many ways to be at peace with black people, but somehow they just didn't want to accept him. It wasn't his time, and maybe in time, as things change he would get the type of camaraderie he sought in people who were supposed to be a part of him.

That night, David found it hard to sleep because of what he feared would present itself in the morning at school. He had a feeling that Edward was not directly involved but more or less a part because he had to keep up his dignity as a black man to George. From the moment his mother took William as her husband and his stepfather, some kind of unusual fear of fighting, of standing up for oneself, took shape inside of him and that was further enhanced when they moved to Alameda and took up residence in The Estuary.

David's body trembled at the sight of George, a man who inspired terror with just one glance. His dark skin seemed to absorb the light, making him appear even darker than the average black person. His features were sharp and angular, lending an animalistic quality to his appearance. And when he looked at you with those deep, bloodshot eyes, it felt like he was peering right into your soul.

George's hair was thick and coarse, styled in a medium-length afro that added to his intimidating aura. Standing at five-foot-ten, his muscular frame spoke of strength and power. While not the most educated individual, George possessed a unique quality with using his hands in combat. And if anyone dared to insult his intellect, they would quickly find themselves on the receiving end of his aggressive nature.

In a strange twist, George often sought the company of David, drawn in by his stunning good looks and sharp intelligence. Despite this admiration, there was a simmering resentment bubbling just beneath the surface. When given the chance, George would unleash his anger in subtle ways that didn't appear violent, but asserted his dominance over David. It was a constant power struggle between the two, with George always determined to come out on top. George and David had been in a relationship with two sisters, creating an inseparable group of four. They were always together, laughing and causing mischief. But deep down, George couldn't help but feel a sense of competition with David. It was as if he had to constantly outshine him, even at the expense of their friendship.

George and David had dated two sisters, their bond strengthened by the close relationship between them and the girls. They were always seen together, like an inseparable foursome, but George couldn't resist the temptation to spoil their dynamic. At a Friday evening party at George's house, loud music blared on from the speakers as the two sisters, Ruby and Lily, arrived. As everyone mingled, it became apparent that David was not enjoying himself. His date, Ruby, lived with her brother, who was a pimp and surrounded by his prostitutes. She seemed to thrive on the dangerous and chaotic lifestyle he provided. And unknowingly, she often dragged David into situations where she expected him to handle like her brother would.

As the night wore on and alcohol and weed flowed freely, Ruby got high and started mouthing off to David. Her words were laced with insults and accusations, aimed at his lack of backbone and inability to stand up for himself. But something inside David snapped. All his pent-up frustration and resentment toward everyone, including Ruby, boiled over, and with sudden ferocity, he struck her across the face. The room fell silent as everyone watched in shock as Ruby stumbled back and landed on her ass.

In a moment of blind rage, David grabbed her by the collar of her coat and dragged her outside to the side of the house. He shoved her into a metal garbage bin before walking back into the party nonchalantly. He grabbed a drink and retreated to a corner of the dance floor, trying to calm his racing thoughts.

Minutes later, Ruby sauntered back into the party with a sly smile on her face. She walked straight up to David, rubbing her cheek with one hand.

"I knew you had it in you." She smiled while reaching out to kiss him. But he recoiled from her touch and smoothly walked out of the party without looking back. Emotions roiled inside him as he realized this was not the life for him.

David seethed with anger and confusion, unable to comprehend how someone like George could use friendships as tools for their own twisted pleasure. After a restless night, David dragged himself out of bed and reluctantly got ready for school. The moment he stepped outside, the atmosphere hit him like a brick wall - Richmond High was one big party. Everyone was trying to stand out, dressed in flashy and provocative attire that screamed for attention. It was a facade, a way to compensate for their lack of substance in a place that was nothing but a rundown dump.

As David made his way through the crowds of gangster-wannabes and self- proclaimed divas, he couldn't help but feel suffocated by the sense of conformity and superficiality. The school building itself was no better - built like a fortress, with no windows, only steel retractable doors meant for riot control.

Everything about this school and its students disgusted David. He longed to escape from the labels and stereotypes that were constantly forced upon him to exist as an individual rather than being lumped into racial categories. But here, in Richmond, he felt trapped and suffocated, drowning in a sea of meaningless existence with no purpose or direction.

Through the crowd, David could see the color yellow burst forth like the morning sun. It was the only color bright enough to be easily seen; he walked towards it. The closer he got, the more he recognized all his supposed to be friends. There was Edward, Red, Gary Moore and without a doubt George Jones in a bright yellow jacket with matching yellow pin striped slacks, and two-toned boots.

"What up fellas?" David asked, "What up George? Nice outfit looks just like the one that was stolen from my room the other day when you and Ed were round."

"This outfit, I got this a couple of weeks ago from Al's Men's Shop in Oakland. You like it?"

"Those are my clothes, George, and you know it." George gave David a really dirty look, the sort of look that David knew all too well. Suddenly he felt helpless, especially because all the other guys were laughing, not at him or anyone in particular just laughing at the whole scene which could probably give George the impression they were laughing at him even if they weren't, and of course David would get the blame, so he decided to just let it go.

"You know what if those clothes mean that much to you than you truly deserve them? Maybe one day you'll be able to afford to buy yourself something nice using real money."

"You want to fight me for 'em, you punk ass motherfucker?"

"No, George, I don't want to fight you for some pieces of cloth. You keep them and keep your fight too, and fuck all y'all."

And David walked out of the school.

Chapter 8

Charles Kirk and the Air Force

After leaving school that morning, David trudged wearily towards his home. But as he passed by an Army Recruiting office on the way, something inside him stirred. Maybe it was the allure of adventure and escape from his mundane life, or perhaps the promise of a fresh start away from his family and toxic group of friends. Whatever it was, David couldn't resist the pull towards the military life.

School was supposed to stand for something, a place of solace, but how could that ever be when everyone resists the better half of life for something not worth living for? David loved English class, where he excelled. But now, with peer pressure weighing down on him like a marble quarry, he could barely keep up with his studies. He felt suffocated by the constant need to conform and fit in, the ever playing out of a role that wasn't his. Drugs were becoming a regular part of his routine, starting with harmless marijuana and the more dangerous substances like alcohol. In this haze of peer pressure and self-destruction, David no longer recognized himself. He had lost touch with his true values and identity, and it scared him more than anything else.

David idolized Charles Kirk, a manipulative older friend who seemed to have it all. But he couldn't help but feel that something must be wrong with Charles' perfect life - the constant string of affairs, his tumultuous relationship with girlfriend, Pinky, and his lack of actual success despite all his grand ideas. At age unknown, Charles still lived at home with his mother and two sisters, Barbette and Beverly - both of whom David had also been involved with at one point.

Despite being unfamiliar with this lifestyle, David found himself infatuated with Charles. He longed to be in his shoes, even though he knew it would come at a heavy price. To gain equal footing with Charles, David offered his high school sweetheart Lilly as a gift to him. But it was all for naught, as Charles only used her for sex and then discarded her, leaving her to return to David.

Desperate to prove himself, David attempted to join the army like Charles had. But he was met with rejection and left behind while Charles went off without him. In the end, David was left empty-handed - rejected by the army and used by Charles, all in his desperate pursuit of admiration and affection from someone like him. Charles' departure for the army left David feeling alone, with his best friend gone and stuck in this childish life of disbelief.

Berkeley High School was David's dream destination. When he attended Richmond High, he spent more time ditching classes and riding around with friends visiting other high schools just to chat up girls and smoke weed. Deep inside lived another person yearning to be set free, but this other person who lived inside of him was the antithesis of his fake self.

It had only been a few weeks since Charles left for the Army, and David was already feeling the weight of his absence.

Wendy was surprised when Fanny Walker, an old friend from The Estuary, who was now living with her family in Berkeley, called her out of the blue.

"Wendy, honey, how have you been? I've been trying my best to get everything set up for David at Berkeley High School. He can transfer easily from Richmond now. You just need to get the paperwork done with the school." Wendy was beyond grateful and thanked Fanny profusely. She knew how much this meant to David, and she couldn't wait to tell him the good news. They made plans to catch up soon, and Wendy hung up feeling a sense of relief and happiness.

As usual, Wendy sent her husband William to handle the paperwork for David's transfer. She never enjoyed getting involved in anything related to the kids' school. This often-caused tension between her and David, who silently resented not having his mother's support or involvement in his education. He would act out and purposely get suspended from school just to get her attention, but it always backfired, ending with William doing the dirty work of a parent.

But now that he was at Berkeley High, things were going to be different. The atmosphere was full of determination and hope for a better future through education. David finally felt like he fitted in among his peers. His favorite class was art, though English was his true love. He discovered another side of people, a side where he could express himself freely under the guidance of his laid-back art teacher, Fred. The classroom always smelled of incense, and David would often eat lunch there with other students who shared his passion for art.

Despite enjoying school, David still had a strong desire to leave home and join the military. With only six months until graduation, he made the impulsive decision to drop out and enlist. This marked the beginning of a pattern of self- destructive behavior that would plague him for years to come, although he didn't realize it. He would often feel guilty about his actions, but couldn't quite understand why. It wasn't until much later that he would finally make the positive changes in his life.

By the skin of his teeth, he scraped by on a GED examination, a flimsy high school equivalency certificate that barely satisfied the government's requirements. The Army was not his first choice, but desperate and directionless. He instead enlisted in the US Air Force.

Years before enlisting in the Air Force, while still attending school in Richmond, just before his transfer to Berkeley, David had skipped class for a week to attend a track meet at Berkeley High. His absence caught the attention of the guidance counselor, who called his parents to inquire about his whereabouts for the week. It was William, his stepfather, who confronted him with bristling anger about his truancy. Wendy, ever keen on avoiding any responsibility or confrontation, let William do her dirty work as she always did. She was quick to shirk accountability and place blame on her children - whether it was bouncing checks or overdue bills. Wendy's neglectful parenting paved the way for many of her sons' future mistakes.

As he trudged back home on that Friday afternoon, David knew he was in for a rough encounter. His mother and stepfather (dad) were waiting for him as soon as he walked through the door. William's expression was stern and cold, while Wendy watched from the couch with a similar air of disapproval.

"Where have you been?" William's first words were accusatory.

"I was at school," David replied, meeting his mother's steely gaze. She always seemed to read his thoughts, but it wasn't some supernatural ability - she just knew her son well.

"Well, guess what? The school called here, your counselor, a woman, I believe. She said you haven't been to school all week. So, do I need to ask you again where you've been?" William's tone was tinged with anger.

"Come on, dad, I already told you. I was at school. I don't know why the counselor would say otherwise. Is it so easy for you to believe her over me?" Wendy abruptly got up and left the room.

"I can't understand why the counselor would lie about you not being in school. Does that make sense to you?" David didn't answer. "Well then, you might as well go to your room because you're going to get an ass whipping." William stood up and pointed towards David's bedroom, but something snapped inside of David at that moment. He had endured enough.

"You're not whipping me anymore! And besides, you're not even my real father!" David spat out defiantly.

William continued advancing towards him, nudging him towards the bedroom, and in a fit of unvarnished rage, David balled his fist and punched William as hard as he could in the stomach. But the blow did little to affect his stepfather—who was a stout, compact man with a tough hide—instead William gasped briefly before quickly regaining composure. Realizing he had no chance against William's strength, David turned and made a desperate sprint towards the patio and out into the backyard. Fear propelled him away from a man he once trusted but now saw as capable of destroying him.

The backyard stretched out behind the house, ending abruptly at a long drop onto the property belonging to the East Bay Mud. There was no fence to protect anyone from falling into the deep gorge below, a constant reminder of the disrepair that plagued their home. William, a man who rarely did handy chores around the house, always turned to David for help.

As David fled towards the edge of the backyard, his heart racing with fear and determination, he knew he had to use this steep drop as his means of escape. He didn't care if it meant risking severe injury; anything was better than facing William's wrath. But just as he reached the edge and lifted off the ground with the wind under his wings, he felt a powerful tug at the back of his shirt and suddenly found himself flat on his back. William had caught him.

Struggling against William's two-hundred-pound frame pinning down his ninety-pound body, David could feel panic and desperation rising within him. With one elbow in the crease of his throat and a large wooden plank in hand, William snarled,

"I will fuck you up, boy. Do you understand me?" The whites of his eyes were now a fierce shade of violet.

In that moment, David's only instinct was to call out for his mother. "Momma, Momma, help me please!" he screamed, hoping she would come to his rescue. And in mere seconds, she appeared, her calm presence bringing relief and a sense of redemption to David. But instead of coming to his aid, she raised her hand and struck him hard across the face.

"Shut up, boy, before the neighbors hear you," she scolded.

That day marked the breaking point for David. It was the final straw that drove him to leave home and everything he had known behind. With joining the Air Force as his escape plan, he believed he could finally find the freedom and happiness he longed for. Little did he know, this journey would lead to much more than just physical distance from his past. It would open his eyes to the harsh realities of life and the true meaning of becoming a man.

Wendy reluctantly signed the papers, allowing David to join the Air Force before graduating high school. She couldn't shake off the feeling of unease. The induction center in Oakland was cold and dark, a stark contrast to their hometown of sunny California. After completing all the testing, they put David and ninety-nine other men onto a plane headed for Lackland Air Force Base in San Antonio, Texas. It almost seemed secretive, like some kind of covert operation.

Boot camp was a grueling eight weeks for David, but he surprised himself by making it through. Instead of combat training, there were mostly psychological tactics taught. Living with a large group of guys from different parts of the US and different ages was an eye-opening experience for him. After boot camp, he was sent to Rantoul, Illinois, to train as a jet engine mechanic.

But David had always dreamed of working in administration, not as a mechanic. He blamed his discontent on the recruiter who had promised him the career field of his choice. Yet despite his reservations, he found himself in sub-zero temperatures in Illinois, constantly threatened with being relegated to bathroom cleaning duty if he didn't shape up. So, night after night, fueled by mescaline, he studied and memorized everything about jet engines until he successfully completed the ten-week program.

Despite all his achievements, David couldn't shake off the bitterness towards those who seemed to think they knew what was best for him. The Air Force may have had good intentions, but it didn't change the fact that he resented their control over his life.

After completing tech school, he was stationed at George Air Force Base in Victorville, California. His close friend Roberto had received a different assignment, and they switched, resulting in David's first duty station being in this desert town filled with bikers and migrant workers from Mexico.

David's mind was constantly at war with the negative energy that surrounded him on the base. From the moment he was assigned there after completing his training as a jet mechanic, he struggled to find peace among the chaos. After completing tech school, he was granted a brief leave before being deployed for full duty.

Eagerly he made the journey back to his hometown of Richmond. As he walked through the familiar streets, a mix of excitement and bittersweet emotions flooded his mind, bringing back memories of family gatherings and childhood adventures. Standing outside his childhood home, David felt a pang of nostalgia but ultimately decided against going in. Instead, he turned and decided to go to the base early and with his duffel bag slung over his shoulders he caught the local bus to Oakland, where he got a ticket on a Greyhound to Victorville, California.

The bus station was on busy San Pablo Avenue, known for its seedy reputation and filled with prostitutes, hustlers, panhandlers, and drug addicts. Despite knowing the dangers, David couldn't help but feel drawn to the chaotic street life. Back in high school he remembered often boasting to his friends that he was going to be a pimp someday. The environment he found himself in was corrupting his thoughts and pulling him towards a dangerous path. But deep down, he knew this wasn't who he truly was. That uncertainty and inner turmoil eventually led him to join the Air Force as a possible salvation.

Taking a seat in one chair at the bus station, David watched the built-in black-and-white TV for twenty minutes for just a quarter. He couldn't help but wonder if this fleeting distraction from reality was worth it in the end.

The bus station was pulsing with a chaotic energy, a sea of humanity swirling in a constant ebb and flow. People from all walks of life congregated, carrying their burdens in bags, suitcases, and boxes held together by masking tape. A sickly stench hung heavy in the air, a putrid reminder of the overcrowding and desperation that permeated the station.

The thought of spending another minute in this suffocating atmosphere made him anxious. He despised being surrounded by those who seemed to have given up on life. It was a tragic waste to be stuck in this never-ending search for something better. But David knew all too well the harsh reality of having a terrible life that drove one to seek something more.

Finally, a bus pulled into one bay and David could just about make out the destination posted at the top of the front of the bus, Los Angeles.

Victorville was further south, and Los Angeles was a major bus stop where other destinations branched off from there. As he boarded the bus and took a seat towards the back, he couldn't help but feel relieved to be away from the throngs of people. At nineteen years old, he was entering a new phase of life that would require him to take care of himself and his responsibilities. It was daunting, considering he had never learned how to carry his own weight. For as long as he could remember, he had lived with his parents.

The bus began its journey with only a handful of passengers scattered throughout the vehicle. David, a young man with sociable tendencies but a guarded nature, had chosen a solitary spot at the back of the bus. He kept himself wary of strangers because of his sheltered upbringing.

As the bus rolled towards Los Angeles, David couldn't shake off an uneasy feeling that settled in the pit of his stomach. Despite the sun still glowing in the sky, the thought of spending eight long hours cooped up in a moving coffin caused him great discomfort.

After several monotonous hours of passing through mostly arid land, the scenery suddenly shifted as they arrived at a small city: Modesto. The Greyhound bus made frequent stops along the way, and Modesto was one of the major towns on their route. With the driver announcing an hour-long layover, David stretched his legs by heading into the lounge for a much- needed snack.

When it was time to board again, David returned to his same spot near the rear of the bus. But just as he thought they were leaving; the driver opened the doors to let two rough-looking men on board. One man had distinct Indian features - deep, unblemished skin, high cheekbones, and long black hair pulled back into a ponytail. His leather vest was adorned with bohemian- style braided beads and his hip was adorned with a large buck knife. His companion was equally intimidating, dressed like a biker fresh out of prison with long dirty-blonde hair, a Levi vest adorned with patches symbolizing their lifestyle, and a chain hanging from his back pocket.

The two men took seats directly across from David and were loud in their conversations. David sat silently, not daring to make eye contact until they reached Turlock - only 12 miles away from Modesto. This time, the bus didn't have a long layover and quickly picked up four new passengers. David noticed they were all young men, dressed in Letterman jackets. Three of them were white, and the fourth was a large black man who David suspected must have been a linebacker for the football team.

At the front of the bus, a group of young men in school jackets were boisterously laughing and chatting. Their loudness was grating on the nerves of two individuals sitting across from David. The more the four boys laughed, the more they drank from a bottle of whiskey that seemed to make its rounds among them.

Suddenly, one man turned towards David with a sly grin and held out the bottle. "Hey kid, take a swig of this bottle and put some hair on your chest," he slurred.

Not wanting to seem uncool, David nervously took the bottle and took a sip, feeling his insides churn. "Where you headed, kid? And what's your name anyway?" asked the biker as he snatched the bottle back for another drink.

"Victorville, heading to my duty station at the Air Force base there," replied David, trying to sound confident despite his shaking hands.

"A soldier boy, huh? I served in the Army myself, in Vietnam. Lot of shit went down over there," boasted the biker. "But let me tell you, it was cool getting high every day. And fucking around with those coka girls…that's what we called them back then."

The two men continued to chat among themselves, occasionally bringing David into their conversation. As an hour passed by from Turlock, the four guys at the front finally settled down. However, the two men next to David began discussing their plans for when they reached Bakersfield.

"We're gonna fuck those guys up before we get to our stop. That means we have 2 more hours," declared the biker, still not bothering to introduce himself or his companion. "What about you, kid? What's your name?"

"David," whispering timidly.

"Well, David, consider yourself lucky today. You're about to get in on some ground floor shit. Gonna make a man out of you, boy," chuckled the biker, his eyes glinting with mischief. "You see those fucking assholes up there? Think they are better than everyone. Well, we are gonna take them out, so listen up. We are only a short way from Bakersfield," then Indian took his big knife out and wiped the blade across his dirty jeans, "pass him the knife, now we are going to take out three of the guys, easy doing, and you are going to take out the nigger."

David didn't know what to say. He took the knife and looked at it curiously.

'Why do they want me to take out the black guy, the nigger, shit he is the biggest of them all and Christ I can't beat that fellow and besides I don't want to take anybody out, this fucking crazy but what am I gonna do? If I don't do as they say, they are going to fuck me up, so I am fucked either way.'

The two men sitting across from David were just sitting there finishing the rest of their whiskey, sort of forgetting what they had just planned out. Moments turned to minutes turned to hours and then out of nowhere, after cruising the long dusty I-5 the Greyhound bus pulled into the Bakersfield station where everyone got off the bus. Indian man grabbed his knife out of David's hand.

"You little pussy, we could have had those guys." As if it were David's fault, the plan had failed, but the look of relief that covered David's face was priceless.

After an hour's layover, the bus reloaded with continuing passengers and new, only this time the two ruffians were not there. It was smooth sailing for the rest of the trip to L.A.

Chapter 9

First Air Force Base Duty

As the Greyhound bus resumed its journey, there was a sigh of relief not seeing the two bikers, (Indian and his friend), who had disembarked in Bakersfield. He wasn't sure how he would've reacted if their plan had played out as they'd initially discussed. The incident made him realize that life on the road held more dangers than he had ever imagined.

Miles passed by, and as the sun set, the bus pulled into Union Station in Los Angeles. David alighted, with his duffel bag slung over his shoulder, looking around in awe at the hustle and bustle of the station. The smell of exhaust fumes mingled with the scents of food wafting from nearby stalls, creating a pungent cocktail that was uniquely L.A.

The entire station was glassed off in sections, a sort of protective barrier from the unwanted people who filled the station each day looking for easy prey. David walked briskly through the crowded station, keeping his head down and avoiding eye contact with the clusters of people loitering around. He felt their gaze follow him as he passed, but he didn't dare meet it. The transparent shields that sectioned off parts of the station provided some relief, allowing him to see his destination up ahead without having to actually engage with the crush of bodies that filled the corridors.

As he approached the next shielded section, the doors slid open automatically, closing swiftly behind him once he was through. The din of the crowd faded to a dull murmur, and he let out a breath. There is still a way to go before his bus arrives, but at least here he could blend into the flow of commuters and feel relatively at ease. The shields may have been installed to discourage the desperate and destitute, but they also created a sense of sanctuary, a respite from the unpredictability that seemed to permeate the rest of the station.

After what felt like an endless two-and-a-half-hour journey, the bus finally came to a halt in a desolate part of town. There was no grand station or bustling crowd, just a simple stop-sign and bare surroundings. The town, though small, seemed to blend seamlessly into the vast expanse of the Mojave Desert, making it appear an appendage of the bigger desert. A panoramic view spread out before them, but the lack of greenery gave it a barren feeling. The harsh desert sun beat down on the few buildings that dotted the landscape, their exteriors cracked and faded from years of exposure. It was as if they belonged in a post-apocalyptic world, abandoned and forgotten. Only patches of dirt and brown vegetation could be seen, devoid of any vibrancy or life. This place seemed to have been stripped of all colors, leaving behind a dull and muted existence, except for the tiny shack with the neon sign blinking in the window. This was where the bus had left him.

David secured his duffel bag over his shoulder. It was 1975, a time zone which David didn't understand. This was what he wanted, a chance to break free of the life he thought was too much for him. He felt the world was conspiring against him, something that most young people felt on their way to adulthood. But how could you know where you were going if you didn't know from where you came?

Entering different environments and mingling with different cultures could sometimes be a dangerous expedition. In America alone, there was a savagery bred from the poverty life shared with many groups of people and from the looks of this new town he had just arrived; life has not spared the people much.

David started walking down a lonely dusty stretch of road toward George Air Force Base. The sun was beating down on the cracked and broken road as he walked. Sometimes it felt as if the soles of his boots were sticking to the tarmac underfoot. The duffel bag felt heavy as it caused his shoulders to sag wearily, in it filled with all his military possessions. It looked as if he didn't have a plan, only a desperate desire to get away and the Air Force was it. Looking at him, you would think he was just another vagabond roaming the roads of California, but he was on his way to his new life.

As he walked, doubts crept into his mind. Was this the right thing to do? His mother, who he had cut out of his life after the incident in the backyard with William, often came to his mind. He thought of sisters Carla and Maxine, who looked up to him, and felt a pang of guilt, but quickly suppressed it. This was his life, and he needed to control it if not understand it.

From behind, an old pickup truck approached, kicking up plumes of dust. David stuck out his thumb. The truck slowed, and he opened the passenger door. "Where you headed?" the driver asked in a gruff voice.

"George Air Force Base, are you going in that direction?" David replied. The man nodded and David got in.

Directly in front of the base gate, the old truck driver let David out, and to his surprise, he felt like he had just entered a dream. What David saw from outside of the base looked like an oasis. There were palm trees everywhere, lush green grass and just off to the left of the gate the noise of people loudly playing in a pool. After showing his ID, David was instructed to go to guest housing where he should wait until someone came and got him.

David walked along the palm tree-lined path towards the guest housing, the sound of laughter and splashing fading behind him. Despite the oasis- like surroundings, he felt uneasy. The guest housing was a simple concrete building, cool and dim inside. David placed his bag on the bed and sat down, listening to the whirring of the air conditioner. He didn't know how long he would stay here or what was in store for him, so David just waited to see if anyone would come get him no matter how long it took.

The idea of not acting on his own behalf was a conscious decision he made so he could use his inactivity as a form of uninformed knowledge. He used it to hide behind stupidity. Two weeks had passed and still no one showed up for him and though he was using the services of the base like the chow hall for food and the base stores for other personal items, he shut himself away in that room unknown by anyone until finally someone showed up.

The knock at the door startled David from his brooding. He hadn't spoken to another soul in weeks, subsisting on base meals and supplies. Who could have found him in this forgotten wing of the base? He opened the door and standing outside was someone of higher rank.

"Airmen Parker?" the Sergeant barked. David nodded mutely. "You've been AWOL for 17 days. Explain yourself!"

David took a deep breath. This was the confrontation he had both dreaded and hoped for. "Sir, I was told to come to the base guest house and that someone would come and get me, and I have been here for two weeks now." "After you noticed no one had come for you, why didn't you alert someone instead of just sitting on your ass? This is not a good start, Airmen. Get your stuff and I'll take you over to the dorm and then the commander." The Sergeant was angry, and it showed in the creases that stretched across his forehead.

David was not punished too severely; however, he was given a strict order,

"Airmen Parker, you have displayed no regard for your position as an Airman. You have, by staying anonymous in the guest housing, gone AWOL and could be court-martialed for such and offense, but since this is your first, let's call it a mistake, mistake I am letting you go in hopes you have learned something important today, do you understand, son?" Daid took the Colonels words to heart.

He was taken to his room on the second floor of the dormitory. It was quiet this time of the morning as everyone who stayed here would not be at work. After getting settled into the room, he wandered around the dorm and on the floor below he ran into a black man coming out of the bathroom with just a pair of bikini underwear on. He thought this strange because it was an all-male dorm of military men. Certainly, everyone wore the Air Force issued boxers.

"Hey, you must be new. Don't get too used to this place because these motherfuckers are crazy. I'm Silvio, Silvio Mojica. Who are you?" A dark- skinned man with thick cracked lips and blood-shot eyes filled with tears that didn't fall. His words followed a nervousness, and it could be seen in trembling lips as he spoke.

"Bruce, my name is Bruce and yes I am new here, well sort of new. I was hanging out in the guest housing for the last two weeks. That didn't go too well with the commander." A silence closed the gap between the two men. "Why are you here in the dorm alone? Why aren't you out working like the other guys?"

"I am waiting to be discharged. I'm gay or a faggot as everyone calls me. It's against the law in the military to be a homosexual, so I have been court- martialed and given a bad conduct discharge, I am just waiting my time."

David and Silvio became friends, from time to time he would go to Silvio's room for a Tequila Sunrise, and every time David would visit Silvio would try to engage him in sex, but David just ignored his advances as the way of the queer.

Despite excelling in his role as a jet engine mechanic in the Air Force, David struggled socially with his work colleagues. During lunch breaks, when all his white colleagues gathered together, he would isolate himself and think to himself. He couldn't relate to their sexist discussions about sexual conquests over the weekend, and found it hard to connect with them on any level. While this may have been attributed to cultural differences or differing masculine ideals, it shouldn't have been enough to drive him into complete seclusion. But his immediate supervisor saw things differently. He found David's behavior odd and concerning enough to warrant him seeing the Base Psychologist and he did every Friday for a one-hour session. The focus of these sessions always seemed to revolve around David's relationship with his own father, not his stepfather William, but his real father, Frank. And as the weeks went by, the psychologist framed the best diagnosis he could with the knowledge of that time and so he labeled David as an "Antisociopathicmanic," a label that only furthered David's sense of isolation and confusion about his place in the world.

"What the fuck is that?" David demanded.

"It simply means," The psychologist stated calmly, "that like the Italians who prefer animals over humans; you don't like people."

"That's not true. I am not like that. I do like people. You just don't know what you are talking about like everyone else around here who thinks they know more of the next man's problems; you are totally out of order." Bruce said.

But through it all, he wanted an explanation; he wanted someone to tell him what was going on in his life. Why did he feel the way he did and why did he have such a low opinion of himself?

And the doctor looked at the loafers he was wearing, and Bruce could sense something was out of order. This was all he got after eight weeks of sharing his soul.

Being surrounded by white people in a more intimate setting, as the Air Force was a constant source of unease for David. Despite living in a community of whites back in Richmond, he had never truly integrated with them. In their small neighborhood, it was easy to avoid interacting with neighbors, but in the Air Force, where unity and teamwork were essential, race became a silenced subject. And for David, who felt uncomfortable socializing with anyone outside his own race, this posed a unique challenge. David grew up in a black family and carried with him some negative preconceptions about white people, influenced by his stepfather's biased views. However, as he interacted with his fellow airmen on the base, he realized that these were just false images. The white race wasn't against him, and he was accepted as part of the group based on his character, not his race.

But deep down, David struggled with his mixed-race identity. He felt like an outsider among both black and white communities, and this internal turmoil led him to self-sabotage. He would subconsciously create situations where he would fail, unable to see past the color of his skin and how it affected his perception of himself and others. In hindsight, it becomes clear how this issue with his racial identity played a significant role in the trajectory of his life.

His stepfather William, a product of the rural South and a former Navy serviceman who experienced firsthand the effects of segregation and racism, drilled into David's head the idea that white people were superior. Growing up under such toxic beliefs left him feeling defenseless against the realities of the world outside.

It was in the Estuary where he first encountered the harsh truth about being black. He was forced to identify as part of the black race, not by choice but because of his immediate family. But then, to be rejected and isolated by those who treated him as an outsider and simultaneously indoctrinated by his stepfather in the supposed virtues of being white left him confused and without a clear sense of identity.

As time went on, he found more people on the base he could relate to. It didn't matter about the color of your skin because on this base people had a collective identity called drug addiction

In real life, when people got home from a hard day's work, they grabbed a cold beer. This was the American way. Now try to imagine the same circumstances. Only these American Airmen managed it differently; they grabbed a cold needle. Everyone he encountered was addicted to heroin, a group of functioning heroin addicts. He found it sickening at the time and also feeling like the odd one, but he'd rather feel odd and left out and keep his sanctity, then to fall on that side of immorality through drug addiction. David did do a little grass and had a few drinks, but never anything harder than that.

Chapter 10

Janette Hardy

David fell in love for the first time in his pre-adult life. All the other loves he had were mere factors of a simulated preparedness compared to what he had found in Jeanette Hardy.

Born in the small town of Tunica, Mississippi in 1948, Jeanette Hardy was a woman who could light up a room with her presence. In 1972, she joined the Air Force as a Motor Pool Mechanic, a year before David did. Her smooth almond-colored skin radiated warmth and beauty, complementing her medium build and five-foot-four-inch stature. With her infectious smile and perfect white teeth, she exuded confidence and charm. Her soft Afro, a crown of semi- coarse reddish-brown curls, was always adorned with a spritz of Afro-sheen that gave off a faintly sweet fragrance. Unlike most Black women with curvaceous backsides, Jeanette's haunches were small. Whenever they walked together, David couldn't help but smile at the comical sight of her tiny steps next to his own larger ones.

In our conversations, she often wistfully reminisced about her former life in Mississippi. She painted a picture of a mundane existence, filled with backbreaking labor and rural hardships. The harsh elements of extreme poverty were constantly present, making every day a struggle to survive. But it wasn't just the physical challenges that plagued her; there was also the shadow of moral degradation that lingered over her past. Growing up in a community where incestuous acts were not uncommon, she had been a victim herself, forced into sexual servitude by uncles and cousins who saw her as nothing more than an object. The toxic effects of this abuse had seeped into every aspect of her life, leaving an imbalance that was impossible to ignore. Even the pungent smell of unfiltered sewage, a constant reminder of their impoverished state, served as a cruel reminder of the indignity she and her family endured. Despite her resilience, it was becoming increasingly clear that these conditions were taking their toll on her spirit and willpower.

A woman of sharp wit and undeniable beauty, she wasted no time in enlisting in the Air Force as soon as she was able. With her head held high and determination shining in her eyes, she boarded that plane with hopes of never looking back

The vast expanse of the Mojave Desert stretched out before her, a barren landscape that radiated an intense, dehydrating heat. The scent of dry earth and scorching air filled her nostrils, overpowering any lingering memories of the decaying swamps of Tunica. But in this arid desert, she felt alive again. Resuscitated by the rejuvenating energy of the land, she could once again feel the delicate nuances of femininity coursing through her veins. Yet deep within her, there lay a darkness, a side that all humans possess, waiting to be unleashed under the brutal sun and merciless sky.

Life moves at an alarming pace, often hitting you with a shock that leaves you gasping for air. The allure of the city, with its neon lights and seductive temptations, can be overwhelming for a small-town girl like Jeanette. She fell into the fast-paced lifestyle of California, swept up in the whirlwind of parties and vices. But as the weekend flings away from the safety of home on the Base and into the clutches of L.A., she began to realize the toll it was taking on her. Cocaine, alcohol, promiscuity, and heroin became her escape from reality, until one day she woke up and saw the ugliness of it all. In a moment of clarity, she cut ties with that toxic world and was left with nothing but emptiness. Her time in this Garden of Eden showed her that indulging in pleasure can also reveal the raw, primal nature of humanity. There is a limit to how high one can climb before pleasure turns into pain. And at the root of it all is our constant pursuit for pleasure - whether it's through sex, food, possessions or vanity. But there is one form of pleasure that transcends all others - love. It may bring us pleasure, but it also eludes the crude hedonism that plagues our souls.

In her search for the ultimate escape, she was fortunate enough to see the illusion and the associated insanity of the artifice of pleasure. Like a drug that has worn off and is no longer providing the feeling intended of its use; you crash. In that mangling of body and soul you either repair to some semblance of originality or succumb to the inability to endure pain long enough to see its end.

The brutal ugliness of Mississippi was all an illusion given form when she failed to realize that it was to be her wake up call. The step of moving forward and out of that cinema killed the illusion, L.A. and a different ugliness revived that which she was trying to escape. After coming to terms with this reckless lifestyle, she realized it was a little too flamboyant and risky for her capacity and so she withdrew, trying as she could to harvest the last remaining goodness within her.

Crawling back into functionality, she shifted her life into one of simplicity, strung by sensible terms; however there remained a new element that she had overlooked her addiction to heroin?

From outside of the motor pool Jeanette looked up at the bright blue sky from underneath the hood of one of the service cars. Though she had joined the Air Force to get away from the life in Mississippi, some days felt harder than others. She often had to work twice as hard to prove herself as a Black woman in the motor pool, but she persevered with grace. Jeanette knew her skills would speak for themself if given the chance. She got back to tuning the engine she was working on, humming a gospel tune her mama used to sing. The soothing melody lifted her spirits, reminding her of why she was here - to open doors for those who would come after. Jeanette poured her hope for a brighter future into each turn of the wrench. This was her place, and she would show she belonged.

David had been on his way to Test Cell this one morning, Test Cell was a division within in the Base's framework of engine repair that dealt with the testing of jet engines after they're repaired or serviced; this segment dealt with the engine 'After Burners.'

Passing by the motor pool, he noticed a woman leaning over the open hood of a car, inspecting some aspect of its engine. He stopped long enough to get a good look, to truly realize that a woman was working on a car engine and pretty one too, woman that is.

"Hey there, how you doing?" He waved as he called out and received a toothy smile.

She grabbed a rag and began wiping her hands, and then she walked over to the fence where he was standing just on the other side.

"You work here?" He asked, lost in small talk. He was uncomfortable introducing himself to a woman, but this woman was different in an ultra- pleasant way, her beauty and southern charm overpowered him.

"Yes, yes I do work here." She replied, "what about you, where are you working, I haven't seen you here before?"

"I work over there as a matter of fact," he pointed to the building just off to the right, "jet engine mechanic, greasy work like yours, but too greasy you know, car engines are more greasy jet engines don't really have grease or oil all over the place." He staggered on in his conversation.

When David was ten or eleven, his mother began seeing a man named James Logan. It was an affair that tore at the seams of her already troubled marriage to William. But despite the betrayal, it seemed as though James had something to offer that William never could - charm, romance, and a sense of being wanted.

James was a small, impeccably dressed man who drove a flashy car and knew just how to make a woman feel special. And David's mother fell for it hook, line, and sinker. She brought David along on one of their secret rendezvous, hoping to gauge his reaction and determine whether this relationship was worth pursuing.

To her surprise, David and James hit it off immediately.

As he grew older, David couldn't help but admire certain aspects of James - his smooth talk, his confident demeanor - without fully understanding the implications behind them. And when the relationship between Wendy and James came to an end, David found himself inadvertently emulating James in his own relationships with women, this man had become the father figure David had longed for.

Looking back, he realized that James had become a sort of mentor to him without even realizing it. And now, as an adult navigating through life and love, David couldn't shake the feeling of conflict between the admiration he once had for James and the realization that he had unknowingly adopted some of his manipulative ways.

Jeanette and David began dating.

They spent a lot of their Friday evenings at the Airmen's club. They even sometimes dressed in matching outfits.

One Friday—only a few weeks into the relationship—she called David. "Would you like to come to my place for dinner?" she sounded drowsy. "I would like that more than anything, how do we do this being that you

live in the women's dorm?" David was excited about this as it would be their first time together alone without people around. And then he thought about the sound of her voice, how different it sounded.

"Have you been drinking?" He asked.

"Noooo, whyyy..." she answered in a playful tone. "Just asked, you sound different."

"Are you coming, or not?" She slurred.

"I'll be there baby," he said, "I love you." And as he tried hanging up, he caught the last thing she said.

"No, I love you," and the phone went silent.

He hung up the phone thinking about what had just happened and then dismissed it as another bad habit of his, overthinking. When he arrived, she answered the door barely dressed. Not that it should have surprised him, but when he noticed she was not wearing a bra, he found it strange because they were such a new couple, and he hadn't been used to having a formal girlfriend, not one who was this experienced.

It was him who was moving a little too slow, this dating thing was new to him and though most people just naturally feel comfortable with dating David found it terrifying.

Jeanette's room was small, hollow and dark lit by several votive candles and scented by the fresh perfume of incense. On the stereo were the mellow sounds of the Isley Brothers, and looking at her, the picture of *Billie Holiday* came to mind. Her smile was wide and bright and after kissing he took her hand and kissed it too. She led him to her bed, which was the only major piece of furniture in the room.

"Ly back and relax, don't move, let me do everything, I'm going to feed you myself with these items I picked up from the deli." she fluffed a set of pillows, and he did as she asked. David was thinking all sorts of weird thoughts, *is she going to make love to me? Is she going to take my clothes off, I hope not. Fuck-it, just go with the flow David, what can it hurt, you might like it.*

On this day, she emanated a sense of duality. In one moment, she was a timid and gentle creature, while in the next, she transformed into an alluring and mysterious being. David couldn't help but find this contrast intriguing.

As he removed his shoes and sank into the pillows she had carefully arranged, he felt himself becoming enveloped in the atmosphere she had created. She draped a soft cloth napkin over his chest before unveiling an array of small white boxes filled with cold deli foods. Just as she had promised, she began to feed him in a maternal manner, offering bites of shrimp salad, pickled mushrooms, and coleslaw. There was something undeniably alluring about her submissive actions, drawing him in closer and igniting feelings of seduction within him for the first time. He found himself unable to resist her charms.

He paid rapt attention to every detail of this experiment, his mind fully engaged in the analysis of a quintessential directive between two opposing sexes. In this moment, he realized that the pursuit of pleasure was far more costly than the simple contentment of happiness. As she reached for the last bite, he motioned for her to put it in her mouth instead. She complied and he watched as she patted the corners of his mouth with a delicate napkin, leaving behind a lingering touch that ended in a soft kiss. The flavors danced on their tongues, each bite bursting with a symphony of tastes and textures. And in that moment, they both knew that this was what true fulfillment felt like - not just momentary pleasure, but lasting joy and satisfaction.

"Don't move," she said as she reached atop the chest of drawers and retrieved a small jar.

"What's that?" He asked.

"Something for your lips, my special blend, well not truly my special blend but something like a lot and feels good on your lips so be still." She said and with a small dab on her fingertip she applied the cream to his lips.

"Oooo, that feels sooo good," He cooed and closed his eyes, savoring this unusual sensation, and there was a scent mixed in with the cream that was delightful.

For the rest of the evening, they made love and then fell into a deep peaceful sleep. But in the morning things changed, her personality was no longer that of the loving woman, she was now in torment, a pain that he hadn't seen before in a person. Though the feeling of love still permeated the room, Jeanette had somehow awakened to a torrent of unexplained illness; the likes of which transformed her mood monstrously.

Jeanette writhed in agony; her face contorted in pain. David rushed to her side, panic rising in his chest. "What's wrong? What's happening?" he cried. Jeanette could only moan in response, her body wracked by tremors. David's mind raced - could this have something to do with the food from last night? What was causing Jeanette such torment?

David cradled Jeanette in his arms, murmuring words of comfort as her moans subsided. After what seemed like an eternity, her body went limp as she lost consciousness.

"Honey, tell me what I can do to make you feel better," David pleaded, his hands massaging her tense neck and back. But she snapped at him, her voice dripping with anger and frustration.

"I don't need your help! Just leave me alone," she retorted, turning her head to face the empty wall. David felt a wall between them, a barrier he couldn't break through no matter how hard he tried. He may have been naive about many things in life, but he knew when someone was pushing him away with all their might.

"Do you want me to leave?" David asked softly, though he already knew the answer. Despite her condition being reason enough for isolation, she wanted to be honest with him.

"There's something I need to confess," she said, avoiding his gaze as guilt consumed her. But before she could explain, David interrupted and told her he had an inkling of what was going on.

Her eyes dropped even lower, filled with shame and regret. She had been so scared to tell him, afraid of his judgement and rejection. And now that it was out in the open, she couldn't bear to face him.

"How did you know?" she whispered, still unable to meet his eyes. "I'm so ashamed..."

"It's okay," David reassured her gently. "These things are never easy to deal with, especially when you feel like you have no one to turn to."

"I hate what my life has become," she admitted tearfully. "Sometimes I can't even believe this is happening to me."

As she slowly raised her eyes to meet him, David could see the raw emotions pouring out of her. And at that moment, he reached out and hugged her tight.

"I promise we'll get through this together," he whispered into her ear. "No matter what happens."

He was so innocent and inexperienced when it came to the topic of drug addiction. It was a foreign language to him, something he had only heard about from people at school or seen in movies. The concept of intervention was foreign to him, but he believed that kindness and support could overcome anything short of a life-threatening situation.

As the weekend passed, so did the sickness that had gripped her. Fortunately, she was only in the early stages of her addiction and her body hadn't yet been completely consumed by it. By Monday, she was strong enough to venture back to work. They had made a pact that this would be their problem to conquer, together in their own way.

Despite his composed appearance and ability to make important decisions, inside David was fighting a fierce battle. He may have appeared put-together to most people, but deep down he was struggling. His inner turmoil was not as obvious as his outward strength portrayed.

Chapter 11

Trouble in the Air Force

A few weeks after Jeanette's bout with heroin withdrawal David received word from home that his grandmother was visiting from Bermuda. He wanted to see his grandmother but after asking his Commander for permission to leave the base for the weekend he was told,

"Request denied!"

The 'NO' he received resounded with such force in his head that he was blinded by anger. David hadn't realized what effect of being denied this request had on him. He didn't question his behavior, instead he just reacted, and usually without thought of the future consequences and this was how he managed when being turned down for leave by his commander.

David fumed as he left the commander's office. The anger bubbled up inside him until he could barely see straight. He stomped across the base and into the dorm, not caring who saw his rage. That's when he spotted a guy he worked with named Jimmie. An idea formed in his mind. Before he could think twice, David knocked on Jimmie's door and in seconds it was open.

"Jimmie, my man, how's it going, dude? Everything okay?" Jimmie had a surprised look on his face when he saw who it was. David and he weren't exactly friends. David hardly said a word to him before and no he was acting as if they were old friends.

"Hey...David right, your name is David, you work at the engine shop, well we both work at the engine shop, but we rarely speak I kinda thought you were a little stuck on yourself there, but hey that's what happens when you prejudge right?" A weird silence entered between them. "What can I do for you, Dave?"

"I wanted to ask if I can use your car. Just need to get something from the store off base. Promise to be back quick, and I will definitely drive carefully. Please, can I borrow it, Jim?" Jimmie looked down at the ground, silent, in thought, and then he turned and walked back into the room.

"Hey look here. That car was a gift from my parents. I have let no one drive and have never considered ever doing this, so I must trust you. I can trust you, right?"

"Absolutely." David placed his hand over his heart. Jimmie handed him the keys.

"Take care of my baby and please hurry back."

Jimmie accepted David's story as truth and trusted him with his lovely little Fiat sports car.

David nodded as he slipped into the driver's seat. He turned the ignition, and the engine roared to life. As he pulled out of the driveway, he could feel the power of the car beneath him. This was going to be fun.

David drove through the countryside, winding through narrow back roads flanked by rolling green hills. He reveled in the car's agile handling as he took the turns fast and tight. The little Fiat was made for these roads.

The night sky stretched out above him, a vast blanket of inky darkness studded with millions of twinkling stars. In the heart of the Mojave Desert, there were no city lights to obstruct the view, allowing every glittering speck to shine brightly. The desert itself seemed almost otherworldly, with its rugged terrain and sparse vegetation.

During the day, the sun beat down relentlessly, leaving no respite from its scorching rays. And at night, even as the world around them cooled, the heat lingered in the air like a heavy cloak. Yet despite these harsh conditions, David drove confidently through the four-hundred-mile journey. The wind whipped through his hair as he commandeered someone else's car without a hint of remorse. It was a reckless act, but at that moment, he couldn't see anything but his grandmother.

In less than eight hours, David pulled up in front of the family's house. He walked to the porch that led to the front door; the lights were on in the Livingroom and through the shear curtains he could see everyone sitting around talking, even his grandmother. In that moment, while he stood on the outside in the dim light fluorescing through the covered windows, a mixture of thoughts ran through his mind, an amalgamation of guilt, shame, and the pretence of how he would present himself.

Strangely, he knocked on the door instead of just walking in, as anyone would be part of a family. Instead, he walked in as if he had just returned from an early evening out. When he had requested the leave from the Commander, it was under the pretence that his family would expect him, somehow; David thought a familial explanation would add a bit more sincerity, but it hadn't. He used the same tactic whenever he wanted to make sure his requests were approved. He was unaware that the feeling of being denied anything was called rejection.

"Hey mom, hey dad, GRANDMA! How nice to see you! I drove all the way from the base, eight hours, just to see and hear you." He kissed his mom and grandmother, shook his stepdad's hand, and sat on the two-seater on the other side of the room. Only weeks ago, David had been called into the Commander's office,

"David, I had a call from your mother. She says you have not contacted her since you enlisted in the Air Force some four months ago. Is this correct, and why?"

"Well, sir, I don't know. I just haven't felt like contacting her and besides I didn't think it mattered much."

"I am ordering you to call your mother today, and to write her as often as you can, no man should treat his mother this way. That is a disgrace, dismissed."

So here Davis was, treating his mother in a most jovial demeanor, but it had the foul smell of something underhanded.

Back in the house David was full of smiles, while the whole time he was deceiving everyone, especially Jimmie who had loaned him the car.

"I tell you the military is a lot of work." He fumbled for something useful to say.

"What kind of work do you do? Are you going to war anytime?" asked his grandmother.

"No grandma, there isn't a war going on involving the Americans, all I do is work on the jet planes, I remove the engines from the plane and someone else fixes them and then when the engine is repaired, I put it back in, boring."

"How did you get here tonight? What time did you leave the base? Did you get permission to leave the base?" My mother asked, "You know you can get into a LOT of trouble for leaving without permission. I hope you are not in any trouble, David."

"I got permission *mom*, that's how I got my friend's car to drive here. Stop worrying about me, everything is fine, I swear mom." But everything was not fine, and every minute he sat there chatting away made him think of the shit he was in.

"I'm not staying long because I have to be back by morning. You know I'm risking everything for this, the long drive to see grandma, because this was the only opportunity I have." He kissed his mom and grandmother. His insides were all twisted up, and he knew it was all because of guilt. Every time he did something wrong, he did it, knowing he would feel like shit. David would feel guilty and then to get rid of that feeling he would have to unload those feelings by telling the truth, confessing to anyone.

Only a fool would risk something big to win something small, but that was David, the guy who jeopardized his freedom, reputation and military pay for a few hours of instant gratification, not even gratification, he wasn't happy about what he had done, there was a voice in his head controlling everything he did and the only thing it wanted from him was pain.

The early morning light cast a soft glow over the base as he arrived. Saturdays were a welcome respite from wild Friday nights, with everyone resting and recovering. The sun hadn't yet risen above the low mountains in the distance, but its warm rays could already be felt in the air. In just a few hours, the relentless heat of the Mojave Desert would cover every inch of land, just as it did day after day. David's mind was filled with anxiety about the upcoming day – the bustling movement of people, the constant chatter, and the unknown inner turmoil building inside him. He could feel all eyes on him, accusing and judging, as if their thoughts were tangible fingers pointing at him. This guilt only added to his delusion and consumed him from within.

Silent as a feather, he parked the car and crept into the dormitory, careful not to disturb the peace with the sound of his shoes. With controlled precision, he slipped them off and carried on barefoot. This was his way of taking charge of a situation that had yet to unfold. He existed in a murky space between fear and pride, knowing he couldn't confront those whom he had wronged but unable to resist his own reckless behavior.

David made his way to Jimmie's room and gently placed the keys at the foot of the door. Suddenly, it swung open and there stood Jimmie, glaring at him.

"What the hell, man? You said you were just going to the store. That was almost 24 hours ago. Where's my car?" Jimmie's voice rose in anger and David couldn't help feeling relieved that he had been caught. It meant this charade would finally come to an end.

"I'm sorry, I really am," David stammered, unable to meet Jimmie's accusatory gaze. "I had to see my grandmother urgently. She's only here for a short time and the commander wouldn't let me go see her."

"You're messed up," Jimmie retorted incredulously. "Who takes advantage of someone else's property like that?" In that moment, David felt a surge of shame rising from deep within him – a molten pit of regret and self-loathing that threatened to swallow him whole. "I reported you to the commander. You're in serious trouble going AWOL. I hope they throw away the key." And with those words, Jimmie slammed the door shut.

David always thought that saying sorry would be enough to absolve him of any wrongdoing, but now, as he reflects on his actions, he realizes how selfish and thoughtless he had been. Some may even say he had no regard for anyone but himself, and though it disgusted him, he couldn't deny that his impulsiveness stemmed from a deep-seated restlessness – the kind that can only be satisfied by chasing after the wrong things.

The Air Force's decision not to Court Martial David for taking Jimmie's car left him feeling conflicted. On the one hand, he was relieved to have escaped severe punishment, but on the other hand, he couldn't help but feel guilty and unsure of where his loyalties should lie.

As if that wasn't enough inner turmoil, David now also faced an Article 15 for leaving the base without permission. This punishment struck a chord with him, as it brought back memories of his mother assigning him various chores and tasks growing up, all while paying him for his efforts. Now, he was being asked to work for free, which felt like a harsher form of imprisonment than any physical bars could provide.

As time passed and his pay was withheld, David grew more and more resentful of the situation. Not only did it affect his relationship with Jeanette, but it also made him question the role that money played in his life. He never realized how much he relied on it until he didn't have it anymore.

His emotions were in constant flux, riding high when his cash was topped up and plummeting when it dwindled. It wasn't until later in life that David would understand how deeply money had defined him, and how his mother's reward system disguised as pay had created this addiction within him. In a way, she had enabled and supported it all along, further complicating David's conflicted feelings towards her.

David's mother was herself a victim of this same philosophy—get a job, any job, and earn your way—but didn't forget to contribute to the household. His grandmother, her mother, always had a complaint about not having enough money. It was like subliminal messages being drilled into your mind to hear the snippets flowing through the air undirected to anyone but received by everyone especially her two sons, his uncles who he believed were driven to drink by his grandmother's dominating force, which was falsely smoothed over with a veneer of Christianity.

To make matters worse, David sensed a quiet force being exerted on him. You see all the Airmen lived in dorms with roommates. The roommates were not chosen by race or color, but somehow it worked out that way or on an availability of space. At this point he had only been at the base a little over two or three months and the room he was assigned came with a Black roommate, but now that he had become a bit of a nuisance, an anti- conformist his Black roommate was moved out and replaced by a white guy.

Jeanette had been willing to accept the rewards of his indiscretions. Knowing he was without pay didn't bother her as long as they were together, but his ego, that thing he hadn't yet come to know, would not allow him to rest.

Sitting in his room one evening, an inner voice began filling the space where clarity shared the muddied thoughts of self-seeking righteousness. David mixed a tequila-sunrise—as was customary in those days—and as the potion began taking effect; his eyes began scanning the tiny dorm room he shared with a new white roommate. As his eyes roamed so too did his mind; and then another sip and soon his intent became clear.

Inhibitions were lifted and soon the tiny voice in his head began offering him suggestions and so he rose from his seat and began rifling through his roommate's belongings. Finding nothing of value, David stood there still, contemplated the senselessness of his actions, and in that moment, he felt the wrong he was about to commit. But he couldn't give in to the righteousness, instead he fell to the low side and began pulling on the doors of his roommate's locked locker. The locker was six-feet tall and padlocked, so he pulled on the doors and noticed that they gave way enough for you to reach into the locker from above. David pulled up a chair which gave him enough height to stand where he could look down into the locker from the top, and there inside on a shelf was a wad of dollar bills, a temptation so beautiful that he believed it to be the answer to his problem.

As he clutched the stolen money in his hand, the wave of guilt grew taller. He knew this feeling all too well – it always followed the wrong deeds of his impulsive actions. Stealing and lying were not things he was proud of, but they seemed like the only solution to his problems. The conflicting emotions of guilt and satisfaction gnawed at him as he tried to justify his actions.

But now, he had to focus on covering his tracks and hiding the evidence. He frantically staged the room to make it look like a burglary had taken place before hastily leaving. With the money, he went out and bought a large amount of marijuana, hoping to use that to make back the pay he had lost. But just as quickly as it came, his plan crumbled when he was later arrested for possession. In that moment, he couldn't help but feel anger towards the government for taking away his source of income. Yet, deep down, he knew this was all his doing and he couldn't escape the consequences of his own actions.

David sat in the cold, bleak confines of the Military Brig, his mind consumed with bitterness as he watched Jeanette approach. She wore a summer dress that flowed around her in a blur of beauty, but all David could feel was resentment. He wanted to tell her to leave, to hurl cruel words at her until she despised him and walked away forever. But when she cried, all of his anger dissipated. In that moment, she was all that mattered.

He knew he would never see her again, even though his sentence was only six months. But anything could happen in that time; she could find another man or realize that staying with him would only lead to heartache. As they spoke through tears about their uncertain future, there was no comfort or reassurance that could erase the looming reality of their separation.

This was David's first experience with love, and he was lost in it. When their emotions overtook their words, Jeanette pulled out a pipe and aromatic tobacco from her bag for him. It was a small gesture, but it meant everything to him.

"What is this?" he asked incredulously. He had only ever smoked cigarettes.

"I got it for you because I think you have class," Jeanette replied with a smile. "I'd rather see my man smoking a pipe than choking on cigarettes."

In that moment, David saw a deeper love in her than he thought possible. But he couldn't shake off the overwhelming sense of loss. He had made reckless decisions with no consideration for himself or others, and now he regretted them deeply. He wished he had understood the weight of the consequences.

David looked into Jeanette's eyes, seeing the pain and longing reflected there. He knew he had hurt her deeply with his thoughtless actions. If only he could go back and make different choices. But the past couldn't be undone.

"I'm so sorry," he said, his voice thick with emotion. "Please believe I never meant to cause you this pain. I was selfish and scared. But I understand now how much you mean to me; how much we could have had together."

Jeanette reached out and took his hand, lacing her fingers through his. "It's not too late for us," she whispered. "Our love is stronger than the mistakes we've made. We can start again, if you're ready this time to truly commit."

David pulled her into an embrace, tears stinging his eyes. Here was this incredible woman offering him redemption he knew he didn't deserve. But maybe that was the point of love – too

The guard tapped on the one-way window to signal that their visit was over. At that moment they embraced even harder, trying as they could to interlock their souls to keep them as one.

They didn't want this moment to end but knew it was useless to allow frivolous emotions to dictate what they couldn't have; the harshness of reality showed him that love was only as good as the control you exerted upon it.

Following his sentencing by the Summary Judge, he was sentenced to six months at hard labor. After a month in solitary confinement, David was flown to Lowry Air Force Base in Denver, Colorado, where he enrolled in a program designed for individuals with sentences shorter than a year. The program was called The Retraining Group.

The Retraining Group was just as the name inferred; it was a place devoted to behavioral modification for those who had violated military law. There was group therapy and private sessions with a psychiatrist, there was also art therapy, and several other educational programs designed to make you more fit for the military again. This was how he viewed it.

When David first arrived at the program, he rushed toward a bank of pay phones outside the housing area and called Jeanette. The number began ringing and after four rings he wanted to hang up but then someone answered, it was one of the other girls who occupied the same dorm.

"Hello, can I help you?" the voice on the other end asked.

"Can I speak to Jeanette? This is David, her boyfriend, calling long distance?"

"Please hold while I see if she is in."

In the brief moments that the girl was away from the phone, he began thinking that he may be an unwanted welcome. He had never been in love before and even though he was telling himself he was in love; he didn't know if he really was.

How do you know when love enters your life? Is it something that all people experience in the same way? These were some thoughts that ran through his mind while waiting on the phone.

Everything that was happening, the trouble he was in, the court, the stealing, and finding someone he cared for then destroying that all in one fell swoop. David didn't see any of this coming. He didn't know how to weigh the damages against his actions; he didn't understand the real meaning of the consequences.

"Hi," the single solitary word resonated beyond his simple plane of thought.

"Hi, how are you?" He replied.

"I'm fine, I miss you very much," and the tears began to collect and fall and the words that they passed back and forth were useless because they couldn't understand what they were both looking for. At least David couldn't.

David was nineteen, and Jeanette was twenty-six when they met. She was far more sophisticated than he, and David didn't know that there was a level of elegance that two people who claimed to be in love could exert.

There was a long silence followed by the chaotic twisting of words which made their conversation a tedious competition, they spoke only to be hearing each other's voice and so the conversation was not the fulfilment of lonely moments, but a gathering of two empty people seeking resolution.

Calling her became his daily ritual. He needed to be needed by her; it was the only way he felt he could stay sane throughout this separation. It was as if he were trying to control something that he had no control over, and he couldn't convince himself of that. Instead, the phone calls gave him a sense of false hope.

David was now three months into his six-month sentence. The days were not moving fast enough and though he had the phone calls to keep him going, he couldn't help feeling that something was not right. A week had gone by, and he hadn't called her. He thought what he was trying to do was lessen his dependence on her, but after a week he gave in and called.

The phone rang several times and then a female voice came over the other end, "Hello dorm 407. How can I help you?"

"Can I speak with Jeanette Hardy? Please tell her it's David?" The phone went silent for a few seconds and then the voice spoke.

"Jeanette is no longer in this dorm. I'm sorry is there anything else I can help you with?"

"What do you mean she is not there? Has she moved to another dorm?" He asked, while feeling something strange well up inside him.

"I don't know, sir; all I know is that she is no longer in this dorm. If you want more information, contact the worldwide locater."

"Where is she?" He screamed, "when did this happen?" He asked, "did she leave a message?" He said in a defeated tone.

The silent aspect of absence was the answer; he had resigned himself to believing this was all part of a plot orchestrated by the Air Force. Jeanette was gone, and no one knew where. David tried the Worldwide Locator service. This was a branch of the military that had the locations of every person in the service, but that turned out inconclusive.

David was no one special enough to warrant this type of cover-up, perhaps he had failed her, *or that this was all too much, and she had returned to drugs again and didn't want him to know,* these thoughts and more ran through his head, but then he had prepared himself for just such a tragedy.

After six-months of psychological reconditioning, weeks of private consultations with his psychiatrist, hours of group therapy, art therapy, educational therapy and God knows whatever else kind of therapy; the staff found him sound enough;

they said that he was a very intelligent young man, but then isn't that what they're supposed to say, make you feel better than you already feel about yourself so that a trust can be established? Anyhow throughout it all David was recommended for clemency, to be returned to active duty, only now he wanted neither. David wanted out, and he wanted out with an honorable discharge.

He had become so disillusioned with the Military and Government to where his opinion of serving a government that cared little for the small man had been confirmed; he wanted out. David had served his time, had a block of memory removed from his mind. And so, they provided him with a plane ticket back to California and his psychiatrist presented him with these last words that would cling to him forever.

"From this day forward, you shall fail at everything you attempt." An affirmation he would repeat most of his life.

Chapter 12

Returning Home a Failure

It was the scorching summer of seventy-six when David finally returned home to his family after a tumultuous time in the Air Force. Court Martialed for possession of marijuana; he spent six months at Lowery Air Force Base before being released from active duty. The experience landed him in a military rehabilitation program, designed for offenders with low-level crimes. But it wasn't until completing this program that David realized he wanted nothing more to do with the American government. As an option, he was discharged under honorable conditions, but deep down he knew that behind the cryptic numbers and fine print of his DD214 form, he would always be labeled.

Once back home in Richmond, he quickly found a job as a salesperson for a retail tobacco company at the new Hilltop Mall. And it was just shortly after getting this job that he ran into Lilly, an ole flame that he never quite gave the title of girlfriend. Lilly was now living with a new boyfriend and together they had a young son.

David was sitting on the front porch of his parents' house when Lilly strolled by and stopped in her tracks upon seeing him.

"Hi David, I heard you were back from the Air Force. You never said goodbye when you left...that was pretty cold," she whispered, giving him her usual bright, toothy smile.

Trying to play it cool, David replied, "You know me, Lilly, always jumping on opportunities when they come my way. Sometimes there's just no time to say goodbye." But deep down, he knew that wasn't the truth. In reality, he had never been that interested in Lilly and still wasn't sure how he felt about her now. However, since he was back home alone with no prospects for a date, having a friend like Lilly might not be such a bad idea. Who knows, there could even be potential for something more between them again.

"What have you been doing since you got home?" she asked as she looked at the ground. She was the same shy Lilly, she had no confidence, but somehow, he found her attractive with her homely appearance. He had always admired pretty girls and even enjoyed being with them or partying with them, but he didn't want one as a girlfriend, not yet plus, he felt safer with a woman that was not overly hunted by other men, this was a selfishness or insecurity he had.

"Working up at the mall, just a little something till I find something better." He told her. "What about you? What have you been up to since high school? You still see Charles Kirk?"

"You are crazy, I ain't interested in Charles Kirk, never was you were the one who introduced me to him, it seemed like you wanted me to be with him, don't know why." Lilly replied with her same country accent, you could tell she was not dazzling, but as a person she was cool to be with, at least that was what he remembered.

"I got a baby now and living in San Pablo with my boyfriend, Ronnie." "A baby! You got a baby, Lilly. I would never have thought that. How old is he or she?"

"He, Little Ron is what we call him, but his real name is Ronald after his father, but not a junior, just little Ron. He was a year-old last week."

"Wow, you were busy with a new baby and a new boyfriend. Any more news I missed out on? Where is Ronnie now? Suppose he drove by and saw you sitting here with me? What would he do?"

Lilly slapped David playfully on the shoulder and laughed without answering the question and then she said,

"He works nights and sleeps in the day, so he's looking after Little Ron now. You want to come by one night?" Lilly asked.

"Are you crazy, so your boyfriend can walk in and catch me? No, thank you. I don't need that in my life."

But they started seeing each other away from her house. Sometimes she came to his parent's house, or they would meet up at his job. Sometimes she even brought her little boy. He didn't like the kid in the beginning. Lilly grew on him after a few months of clandestine meetings. He liked her more than he expected and one evening she invited him over and he came even though he knew this was against his rules.

Lilly acted as though she was not happy anymore in her relationship and looked at David as the possible missing piece of excitement from her life. David didn't know how women operated down deep inside, but he knew they had a greater power over men than men had over women.

David was leaving his teens and moving into the twenty-something and up to this point the only sort of relationship he had was with Jeanette in the Air Force.

Being with Lilly always filled David with a mix of joy and fear. As he spent more time with her, he couldn't help but wonder if he was falling in love. But how could he be sure? He had never been in love before and didn't know what to expect or how it would feel. Was it the constant desire to be near her, or the way his thoughts were consumed by her that signified love? He couldn't say for certain, but the intensity of his feelings made him believe it must be love.

Despite their undeniable connection, David couldn't shake the guilt and unease that came with being involved with someone who was already in a relationship. He knew that what they were doing was wrong, but he couldn't resist Lilly's magnetic pull. And deep down, he hoped her boyfriend would never find out.

But as expected, the truth came spilling out when Lilly's boyfriend unexpectedly returned home one night to find them sitting close together on the sofa. David's heart raced with fear as he saw the fury in the other man's eyes. He knew he was no match for him - physically or emotionally. But even at this moment of panic and danger, David couldn't bring himself to regret being caught up in this messy affair. Because when it came down to it, all he truly wanted was to be with Lilly, even if it meant breaking all the rules and risking everything for her love.

David froze the moment Lilly's boyfriend walked through the door, the look on his face was a mixture of pain and hate and at that moment David was surprised, he could have taken him down, but he just walked past them and into the bedroom and slammed the door. Lilly and David both sat looking at each other without saying a word and then minutes later, her boyfriend shouted from behind the closed bedroom door,

"Lilly, come here." And she looked at David with horror in her eyes.

From behind the closed doors, David heard a loud thud. Something hit the wall. He got up and walked to the front door, shouting as he turned the doorknob,

"I'm leaving now," and with that David walked out and closed the door behind him. No one followed.

The next day, Lilly showed up at David's. He was sitting on the porch, in the sun as usual. He didn't know at that moment if he wanted her there or not.

"Look what you did," and she pointed to a black eye she had received the following night from Ronnie, her boyfriend.

"That must have been the sound I heard when I was sitting on the sofa." He laughed a little, and she joined in.

A couple of weeks later her boyfriend Ronnie packed up to leave for Los Angeles, he knew it was over between him and Lilly, but before he left, he stopped by her apartment to say goodbye to his son, David was there, and so Ronnie offered him some advice.

"Hey man, I don't really blame you for any of this it was coming anyway, that's Lilly is, but can I ask that you take care of my boy for me," he asked with tears in his eyes, "she is gonna make you miserable too."

The following week I moved in.

This was uncharted territory for David - the first time he had ever lived with a woman other than his mother. He couldn't help but feel uncertain and inexperienced in this new role, unsure of where he fit in or what expectations were placed upon him. It seemed like everyone around him had successful live-in relationships, but he couldn't find any set pattern to follow for his own. It was like trying to navigate through a maze, blindfolded.

Lilly was on welfare and didn't work, so a major part of the bills was taken care of by her. David assumed he didn't have to invest much of his earnings towards the monthly household expenses, instead his money was used on their entertainment and other things such as clothing, alcohol, and marijuana. He was crazy about Lilly, and he realized more each day. He bought her gifts, flowers, perfume and lingerie, he desired her every day, David couldn't keep his hands off her and it seemed she felt the same way, but how do you know what is going on inside another person beyond what they tell you or lead you to believe and so in a short time after they were living together Lilly found a job.

It seemed appropriate at the time as they both were desiring a better life, a better place to live a home of their own and cars, but these desires soon became apparent that this was more for the sake of impressing other people, "Keeping up with the Joneses'."

Lillys' first position was as a secretary with a black law firm in Oakland; Broome, Cooper and La Brie. This transition from being a stay-at-home mom changed the whole dynamics of life for them. Mornings were now becoming more hectic in that time schedules had to be met. Her son Ron needed to get to the nursery. They had gone from a quiet little family to a couple of working-class people with demands and constrictions.

Prior to her taking a job their weekends were mostly spent lying in bed all day watching old black and white movies and making love, or they'd go for drives to Walnut Creek, Moraga, the Oakland hills, looking at houses and dreaming of one day having a life that included their home, Lilly and David were both dreamers, or he was the dreamer but he knew inside his heart that dreams could be made manifest with a little work, money and desire. But all that changed, and she was not part of that dream anymore. She was part of her own dreams whatever they were, because David had no clue.

Lilly stayed with the law firm for about a year, and then she became pregnant with their baby, a boy he named Maurice. She then took a job with one of the law firm's clients, an architectural firm owned by two ambitious Black men one David knew who went by the name of Sid, short for Sidney.

David always thought of himself as a good-looking guy. Looks seemed to have been a generational thing, something that was important to Black people. And Black women especially had this thing for their children to be attractive, pretty, or good looking, and so the women would take to a mixed raced man to bring forth children. The offspring usually came out very attractive. David was influenced by this way of thinking when he was a child. Instead of caring about the child's education, moral and ethical values, children like David—when he was a child—was led to believe that looks were everything, looks was going to carry you through life in your success, but such a stupid statement like that angered David.

Lilly admired Sid based on his education and business accomplishments, and so now David was not a favorite in her eye's, and he could feel it when she spoke of this man. Until that point, David gave little attention to developing himself with a higher education, like the crowd he grew up with and the life his family had brought into, David was lost, but had ideas for small business that he felt might help regain the respect of Lilly again.

An occasion arose several months after Lilly had been working or Sid, she came home and announced to David,

"I'm going to Washington D.C. with Sid on a business trip."

"Why does Sid want you to come along on a business trip? What would he have you do, you know, why you?" she thought about this, "besides you are too stupid to be of any value. I didn't mean stupid in that way. I meant you aren't an architect."

The swirling thoughts inside his head sounded like rational philosophy, but then, if it was rational why was he feeling angry and showing it through his abrasive remarks?

Still, she remained quiet, and the silence was bringing forth a stronger certainty that David's suspicions were right. David felt he may have been correct in thinking that Lilly was having an affair with Sid, but he couldn't be certain. All the things leading to this moment went unrecognized. It's hard to see something as quiet as infidelity coming. The last thing he wanted to know was that something like this could happen to him.

"Don't expect me to babysit your son. I will look after Maurice, but I won't be looking after Lil Ron while you are in Washington fucking Sid."

"I already knew you would say that, so I asked my mother to take care of him."

David was so angry he wanted to kill her, get rid of her so that this could go away and never come back but then he would be missing her because he loved her.

Lilly left for D.C. as planned and David was left in the small apartment feeling like a fool. He paced around the tiny apartment as if it were a prison cell. The hours she was away from him coincided with the increased thoughts he was having about her and Sid together in D.C., soon the night grew darker and colder and the thoughts that moved through his mind more unbearable to manage, he needed to release this unwanted feeling and so he thought he should call her even though it was now three in the morning there in Washington.

He sat on the side of the bed facing the wall where the bedroom window opened out into the parking lot of the apartment. He sat there and stared at the phone sitting on the bedside table, and asked himself: *should I weaken myself by calling her? Should I be strong, a man, her man who trusts in everything she does?* After all, she loved him and a woman who loves someone cannot see anything in another man, but he didn't believe that at all, so he reached for the phone and dialed the number she had left.

"D.C. Hilton, reception how can I assist you?"

"Hello, hi, I am trying to reach my girlfriend who is staying there. Her name is Lilly Barnes?"

"One second, sir, and I will connect you to the room. You realize it is after three in the morning and your party may be sleeping."

"I know it's late, but I am calling from California. It's about our baby." He said and wondered why he was explaining this to the receptionist. Soon the phone started ringing, and David felt afraid and didn't know what to say to her, but not trying to speak with her was worse. He was having a hard time making a choice.

"Hello," a man's voice answers, and in that moment, he felt as if his heart had been ripped from his chest. Quickly, he hung up the phone. Frozen in the spot he was sitting; he couldn't comprehend the kaleidoscope of feelings changing colors within him. After a moment, he called back,

"Hello,"

"Lilly, who was that answering the phone in your room a minute ago, and don't lie?"

"Oh, that was Sid. We were having a business meeting."

"A fucking business meeting, at three in the morning Lilly, you must think I am the biggest fool on earth Lilly. What the fuck is he doing in your room this time of night?" David was growing angrier by the second. He wanted the truth, and yet he didn't know what he wanted at all.

"I can't believe this Lilly, I swear to god Lilly if you don't get back here as soon as possible I am going to kill Maurice, I fucking mean it." And he hung up the phone.

Surely David wouldn't kill his own son, not for any reason, but he couldn't think of any other way to upset things enough to get her back home. After he hung up, she must have called her mother, who called David.

"David, this is Mrs Goree. Lilly just called and said you were going to kill Maurice. Now don't be crazy and don't hurt the baby."

"Mrs Goree, I will kill Maurice and kill myself if Lilly is not back here in the morning and that's all I have to say."

Lilly came home later that day and resumed her part in their relationship, but it was over without being made official. In a brief time, she had moved Sid deeper into her life, and David moved out. The guy before David was correct when he left, saying that Lilly would make him miserable, too. There was an extensive list of things she had done to David, and he was just as guilty because, when he thought she was cheating on him, he began cheating on her. Lilly made him feel love and hate, rage and jealousy and before long he just didn't know how to be in the relationship. Everything had just dried up. There was no more love or life left between them, so David ended things and took his son Maurice with him. She was happy about the decision.

Chapter 13

Susan

David had come full circle, navigated an uncharted course without purpose; it was this place in life where he had intended to escape and now; he was back again. Lilly and David had broken up. David moved back into his parents' home, and left Maurice with Lilly until he could find a place of his own and then he would come back for him.

When he enlisted into the Air Force, he created a break in his education, and all he was left with was a simple GED and so now that he was back in civilian life, he still only had a GED. David was stacking up a mountain of half completed attempts at life. His military career ended with a Court Martial leaving him with limited job skills. He attempted a relationship with Lilly after the Air Force, which ended with nothing positive to take into the future with, except his son Maurice. And so, David had no choice but to fall back on the only things he had; intelligence, youth, looks and the Gift of Gab.

After settling into his parents' home, he knew it was time to figure out his next move. He couldn't stay where he had always been trying to get away from. Living with Lilly gave him a sense of security and freedom, and he must admit so did the Air Force and so did his parent's home, but beyond that he didn't have a clue about taking care of himself.

It didn't take long until he started a plan to liberate himself. He picked up the San Francisco Chronicle and scanned the classifieds for jobs; there were always jobs, hundreds of jobs for people like him, people without education or skills and so after eliminating: Professional, Medical, Secretarial, Administrative, The Trades, Executives, Accountants and Chefs, the choices were narrowed down to: Retail, Warehouse, Kirby Vacuum Cleaner Sales, and Sales he saw where he most fitted in; nowhere!

However, there was an ad from a temporary agency, Kelly Girl, for a light industrial role. This role was as a mailroom worker in Berkeley, with Educational Testing Service (ETS). He signed on with Kelly Girl and received his assignment.

The first day of the assignment was great. David thought how great it was to be working in an office building filled with pre-middle-aged women. It was nice for once to see women in charge. All day long was the coming and going of females, they were buzzing about in an entomological rivalry liken unto a field of ants going nowhere yet soaring to the same summit.

Things were going well at the job and David was, in fact, enjoying all the attention from an older group of women. Then one day, only weeks into his assignment, this uncontrollable boyishness was broken when a woman—not a beautiful woman, handsome, but he was certain she had never lacked for male attention—entered the mailroom.

She worked on the sixth floor, and her name was Susan. Susan was in her mid-forties, with coarse black should length hair, the yellow skin of a China man, and features of someone between Black and Filipina.

She waltzed in on air as she entered the mailroom carrying a stack of interoffice envelopes, which struck David as odd, for there was a scheduled pickup on the sixth floor by one of the mailroom staff.

"Good morning!" she said. "It's becoming a chore staying chained to that desk of mine." She looked around the cluttered mailroom as if for the first time and then at David.

"And good morning to you," he responded, "and what brings you down into the mailroom? We don't get many people from the upper floors in here?" and she laughed.

"This is my daily routine," she answered, yet over the past two weeks, David hadn't seen her here. He began thinking it was because of him she changed her routine.

"It's not too often I have time to exercise, so coming here takes care of my daily walk if I don't plan walking after work, which today I don't." She smiled that same goofy smile again and then handed him her outgoing mail. She caught his eye; he was slightly attracted to her. She was older, but not too old, thick-boned, but not too fat. She appeared shapely in her snug fitting dresses; her bosom and rear-end were providing a view that turned his head every time he saw her.

"How are you finding things here? Are you happy with the work?" She continued talking.

"It's too early to tell, but overall, the people seem nice enough, so that might make up for the work being a little monotonous. Overall, it is a nice place to work. Honestly, I have had little work experience behind me, so this is an acceptable starting point."

After a brief period of silence, she looked down at her shoes, and then gripped the edges of her dress in each hand, fanning the material like a Flamenco dancer.

David smiled, amused that a woman of obvious age would resort to something so coy. He found it delightful, refreshing, and genuine. She was flirting; an uncustomary ritual brought to the surface the interaction between them both. After an exchange of several words, she turned to walk away.

"Wait!" David called out as she turned to leave. He wasn't ready for their encounter to be over so soon.

She paused, looking back over her shoulder with an arched eyebrow. "Yes?"

David scrambled for something else to say to prolong the conversation. "I, uh...was wondering if you might like to get a coffee sometime?" He winced internally at how cliche it sounded, but it was the first thing that came to mind.

Her eyes widened slightly in surprise before a sly smile spread across her painted red lips. "My, my, you are a bold one. I haven't been asked out for coffee in...well, longer than I care to admit." She studied him (appraisingly) for a moment as he held his breath. "Alright," she finally said with a nod. "I accept your invitation. Shall we say tomorrow after work, I know just the little cafe."

David exhaled in relief, unable

When she was gone, David envisioned her seated back at her desk, drifting into a reverie of tantalizing self-deception, a too long extension of thought shaken into reality by the ringing of her phone. She struck him as a woman who had become lost in the absence of love, one entranced by discovering the awakening of something that had long been asleep.

When they met, David was twenty-three, she was forty, the year 1979?

Susan was a widow in her seventh year of mourning.

David had come to understand that relationships were not a defining aspect of this woman's life. Marriage had been a brief experience for her, one that she had never been able to replicate again. Her days were filled with obligatory social events and gatherings with family and friends, lacking any sparks of creativity or passion. There were no intimate dinners or clandestine meetings over drinks; her life was dull and unremarkable. But sometimes, in her quiet moments, she would find herself lost in daydreams of romance, constructed from the pages of novels she had read.

Tucked away on Masonic Avenue in Albany, Susan's rented house sat nestled between well-manicured lawns and tidy homes. The neighborhood was a quiet oasis, populated by an older generation enjoying their retirement. The air was often filled with the soothing scent of liniment, a reminder of the slower pace of life here. However, amidst this idyllic setting, Susan's house stood out like a sore thumb. Its peeling paint and overgrown lawn were a stark contrast to the neighboring houses. Despite her best efforts, she couldn't seem to keep up with the maintenance and landscaping, leaving her home in a state of constant disrepair.

Life was a monotonous cycle of meaningless tasks for Susan. Each day blended into the next, devoid of any passion or purpose. Her existence lacked both emptiness and fulfillment; it simply was. The only solace she found was in her three dogs: Lady, PeeVee, and Gidget. They were her children, and as they grew old and neared death, so did she. With no hope of ever having children of her own, Susan lived vicariously through her beloved pets, desperate to fill the void of motherhood in her barren life.

In just three short weeks, David had become the talk of the office at ETS. His infectious smile and laid-back demeanor were like a fresh breeze in the stuffy halls of the workplace. The women, accustomed to their mundane and routine lives, were instantly drawn to him. They saw him as a reprieve from the monotony - he was not a model or a society beauty, but a charming and relatable young man.

Even amongst his male colleagues, David stood out as someone they could connect with and open up to. He wasn't trying to impress or boast about his achievements like he had done in the company of wealthy men before. As he made his daily rounds delivering mail, he couldn't help but notice Susan on the sixth floor. She tried to appear nonchalant, but her fidgeting and nervous glances gave her away - she liked him. Her regular trips down to the mail-room just to glimpse him showed she would break through social barriers for him. It was a reminder of their different backgrounds and how she would defy those conventions for him.

David clocked out of work and snuck out of the building, eager to catch Susan watching him. He had planned this game of cat and mouse with her for weeks now. As he exited the office and walked onto the bustling street, he looked around in both directions until his eyes landed on the silver Cadillac parked across the street. He knew she would be there, sitting in the driver's seat, pretending to adjust the sunroof as a cover for their secret rendezvous.

They both wanted to see each other without being seen, so they played this game every day after work. It was their way of keeping things exciting and secretive. David ran a hand through his hair, making sure it was perfectly styled, and lit a cigarette as he strutted down the sidewalk towards the train station. He couldn't help but smile to himself as he thought about what Susan may have on her mind about him at this very moment. This was all just a fun game of hide and seek for him.

Dating an older woman was an exhilarating experience for David. He had never felt such a rush before. And even though they didn't exchange any acknowledgement as he passed by her car, he knew she was smiling too. It was their little secret that brought them both joy and excitement. As he hopped on the train and headed home, David couldn't wait for tomorrow's game to begin again.

As the train chugged along, David's mind drifted into a void where he could contemplate all the things he wanted to do with Susan. Not just sexual things, but simple moments between a man and a woman. It had only been a few months since his break-up with Lilly, and already he felt alone and yearning for companionship. David despised this hollow emptiness that came with being single; in relationships, he found a sense of self and purpose.

He was a solitary man, burdened with the responsibility of raising his son alone and living under the suffocating roof of his parents. The thought of improving his own life never crossed his mind; rather, he obsessed over finding a surrogate mother for his son and a lover for himself.

But some things in this universe cannot be understood or explained, no matter how many questions we ask. And there are forces beyond our control that can twist and distort our desires, draining us of hope and grace. Here were two souls yearning for similar things, yet only finding fulfillment when they could glimpse the unseen and intangible bond that unites people in service of something Higher!

David couldn't shake the feeling that Susan was always somehow watching him, even when they weren't together. It made him uneasy, but her persistence and subtle manipulation kept him coming back for more. He knew she wanted something from him, and he used it to his advantage.

Susan was drawn to David's quiet strength and simple way of living. She didn't care if she had money, in fact the less the better or if he had status; she just wanted someone who could understand her upbringing and values. But David saw an opportunity in her, someone he could control and mold to fit his desires.

Their relationship was built on a flawed foundation, driven by their personal agendas rather than genuine love. David's child from a previous relationship was a pawn in their twisted game, with Susan vying for a motherly role while David pitted her against his son's biological mother.

Despite this toxic dynamic, Susan saw something special in David beyond mere physical attraction. She had a rough exterior but craved simplicity and authenticity - traits that she found in David. He represented a way of life that she respected and longed for, coming from humble beginnings herself. But little did she know how dangerous it would be to fully immerse herself in his world.

David stood outside the building, surrounded by a group of women who were all laughing and chatting with him. It was a rare sight for Susan to see such genuine camaraderie between a man and women. David seemed to blend in effortlessly with the group, his calm smile and relaxed posture making him appear like one of them, a vital member of their brotherhood and sisterhood.

He often thought that women had a special connection with each other, one that men could never truly understand. Men were too consumed with appearances and constantly comparing themselves to others. They were always on guard, afraid of being perceived as unmanly if they showed any sign of vulnerability or affection towards others. This fear held them back from experiencing genuine connections with their fellow men.

But on this day, the usual distractions of his entourage faded away as David's eyes landed on Susan. He couldn't bring himself to look away, even as the girls chattered on him without noticing his absence. There was an intensity in Susan's gaze that spoke volumes, her intentions clear even without words. As the other women finished their meaningless dialogue and went their separate ways, David found himself drawn towards Susan, unable to resist the pull of their unspoken connection.

"Are you waiting for someone?" David's voice boomed through the car, his eyes scanning every detail of Susan and her classic car. She shifted in her seat, revealing the sharp contrast between her honey-colored skin and the dove grey leather seats.

David's gaze lingered on her thighs as she nervously adjusted her dress, causing it to inch up with each movement. "Just going over some papers before heading home," she replied, trying to maintain composure under his intense stare. "And you, where are you off to?"

"The BART Station, just up the street. Just heading home," he replied, unable to tear his eyes away from her.

"Where do you live?" Susan asked, a hint of authority in her voice that only a woman of her age could exude without sounding demanding. "Hop in and I'll give you a ride home. Unless you have other plans." Her offer sent a wave of excitement through David. He had always found older women to be more alluring - their demands were simpler, their needs easily fulfilled with physical attraction. They didn't care about his position in life or what he did.

The twelve-mile drive was a blur of comfort and stimulation. Susan seemed to delight in every moment, laughing and engaging him in intellectual conversation. As they approached his destination, he instructed her to pull over and shut off the car.

"This is where I live," he said, pride swelling in his chest as she took in the neighborhood with keen observation.

They chatted for a few more minutes before Susan had to leave. But as soon as she drove off, David's mind was consumed by a thousand different thoughts, each one racing through his head like blueprints for a plan that would ensure their future together.

As the sun rose over the bustling city of Berkeley, the West Coast Division hub for College Board and Princeton, a steady flow of applications for Federal Student Aid poured in. Each form was like a beacon of hope, representing an eager young mind hoping to secure their place on the highly coveted pie chart. The offices at ETS Berkeley were a flurry of activity as mountains of paperwork were processed and meticulously organized into neat microfiche files by the thousands. Down the hall, the phones at Testing Services rang off the hook, with over a thousand calls flooding in each day. Amid this chaos, Susan worked tirelessly, her years of experience shining through as she expertly juggled the growing demands while maintaining an air of professionalism in the chaotic office. Her colleagues often marveled at how she seemed to thrive under such high-pressure conditions, her calm demeanor and efficient work ethic making her an invaluable asset to the team.

As David entered the room, he couldn't help but feel intimidated by the presence of intellectuals all around him. Their formidable character and superior knowledge made him feel like he was in a society of great immortals, the likes of which he had shunned in his personal life for fear of not meeting their high standards.

He couldn't help but wonder how these individuals, who seemed to exude confidence and intelligence, would view him. After all, he had always felt inferior and never gave himself a chance to be weighed by others. Yet, as he mingled with them, he was surprised to find that they took a strong liking to him. He didn't quite feel an equal to them, but he felt a sense of tolerance on their behalf. It reminded him of moments from his youth when he felt accepted and valued.

One particular memory stood out - his first visit to Durant Avenue Presbyterian Church in Berkeley. It was unlike any other church he had been to before. Rather than simply imparting words from the Bible, this community practiced its teachings with a *genuine passion for morality and the betterment of humankind.*

On that day, David and his sisters were dressed in their best Sunday clothes, an endearing sight as they sought favor in the eyes of the Lord. It was their mother's firm rule to take them to church every Sunday and entrust them to the hallowed scholarship of Christianity. Despite their modest upbringing, she wanted nothing but the best for her children.

In time, David and his siblings became central figures in the youth expansion of the church, once dominated by adults. They were a joy among the parishioners, taking part in various church functions and events. Their presence was especially adored by Sarah Miles, a Missionary who had represented the church all over the world, and Hazel Egget, an amateur naturalist who frequently took them on trips to Mt. Tamalpais to explore and learn about nature.

Although David's sisters may not have enjoyed these Darwinian expeditions, he found them to be stimulating and enriching experiences. In retrospect, he realized these moments spent with his family and the welcoming community at church were some of the happiest memories of his childhood.

Looking back on those moments reminded David of how much he had yearned to be a part of that life again; and now the excitement that once held a little boy's heart is now different, and without embarrassment, he can say: *it's not that different needing to return to something that once brought pleasure meaningfully.*

At two o'clock, the phones in Testing Services returned to normal, and Susan took a walk to the mailroom, thinking she had some good news.

"Hi there!" she exclaimed with a subtle excitement. "I don't know about you, but...we...have...been...swamped, the phones have been ringing off the hook, it seems everyone waits till the last minute to get their applications in, it's sickening and to top it off Heather, the girl from Ireland I told you about last week, returned to her country, leaving us one person short," she took a breath and looked about to make sure we were the only one's listening, "Durrell has asked me to look for a replacement and I thought of you."

"Hey Susan, how are you to?" He spoke.

"I'm sorry, how thoughtless of me to dump on you like this." She said, "How are you, things okay here today?"

And the fragile moment was strengthened by dispensing the useless formality of superfluous rhetoric.

David could always gauge with some efficiency the true nature or intent of a person just by the length or content of impertinent dialogue.

"You know Susan, I have always been honest with people and sometimes find myself just saying things to satisfy the other person. This is my way of not being honest."

She looked about the room and then smiled as if she had just realized what I said.

"You can be yourself around me, Susan." She looked into my eyes, smiled, and said,

"There's an opening in my department, one of which I know you'll fit, and yes I thought of you because I enjoy being around you and I thought if I could help you, I would, is that honest enough for you?"

Susan's inference to 'enjoying' his company took him aback. Deep down, he had hoped something of this nature would happen; only he hadn't expected it so soon. Here now was the prospect of advancement; this would mean a parting with the temporary agency and taking on a full-time position with the company, the likes of which would mean a steady intercourse between her and David and if the matter reached a level of intimacy how would he contend both with equal zeal? Though the contemplation concluded more logically, as was befitting his nature, he doubted that the possibility of achieving a standard on his own merits would suffice, and so he concluded with a tincture of mischief.

Susan was the person who would use this moment much like the way she used her car and other things to attract the object of her affection. Though there would be some genuine exchange of human values, the core however would reflect the opportunistic predation risen from the formation of employer/employee, the new position.

"So, what do I do, talk to you about the job?" I asked.

"No. What I'll do is tell Durrell you're interested and that I think you would make a fine addition to the team."

"When are you going to do this?" I asked.

"As soon as I get upstairs," she replied and left me standing on a floor coated with sugar and for once, I felt as if my life was moving in the right direction.

The rift between logic and emotion seems to exist unsubstantiated and its lack of understanding disturbing, yet somehow, he always yielded to the latter. David interviewed for the job and was hired. Should he not have expected this?

The small workspace known as Testing Services had several desks. His desk was directly in front of Susan's. It was as if she could now monitor him throughout the day. It was a busy area, and he was happy to be a part. He didn't know then where his life was going. You never know what direction your life is moving until you are confronted with situations.

Three months had come and gone. Susan had offered David a chance to rent a room from in her home and he took her offer. The room was in the back of her house and because of this opportunity he also brought his son Maurice, who fell in love with Susan and she with him and there her make- believe family was formed.

On Saturday of every week, it was implicit, though not ordered, that David accompany Susan to Transitions, a chic San Francisco hair salon where she would receive a color and style and would most often indulge him as well.

Following would be lunch and then shopping - always for him. She had enrolled Maurice in a bilingual French/English Pre-School and unbeknown to David the implications, purchased for Maurice many gifts satisfying his every whim, but soon David became concerned as well as angered at how his son was taking to this lady and moving further away from him.

The lengths of which she gave were unending and effective in maintaining her illusion of the happy family. She had insisted that David save his pay checks while she managed all the financial responsibilities. This was how she controlled the situation, and David couldn't see it coming. It was her intention to render him dependent upon her and as he further withdrew himself, refusing to accept gifts, she shifted her focus with greater intent and emphasis on his son.

They had started out as lovers, a relationship built on the falsity of love, but David soon discovered that she was not the one for him, he wanted a relationship with someone his age, or unknowingly to him he discovered that there was a difference between infatuation and love. He retracted and pulled away from Susan, and he was sure she could feel the difference in his attitude towards her, but she didn't confront him about it.

Instead, she moved forward, using the only thing she could to manage the situation: money.

Unrequited love ripped through the interior of her soul; the complexity of such an existence baffled her. The romance, which was short-lived burned out. It was not much of a romance as much as it was a one-nightstand over a period of several nights.

From the beginning of their acquaintance, Susan had everything under control. She was an older woman, manipulative, and persuasive at both, and she knew his weakness, or the weakness of any young man his age, trying to start out in life.

The feeling she found in him revealed the relationship she had with her husband, and for once she could see above the illusion of chastity and the convolution of Catholicism, all the years of their marriage, the diversions here and there nothing more than a ruse to cover a loveless marriage.

It pained her to know that within her barren womb also lived the knowledge that she didn't know what true love was. This was the closest she had ever come to fulfilment, a family, one she could call her own and though she realized without a doubt that she was hurting David; she couldn't let him go, nor let him leave. In time, their relationship became a simple friendship, a role which should have started in that manner.

If outsiders believed that what they saw resembled an authentic, loving family, then Susan was happy. And as David saw this to be the case, it gave him an edge and a belief that he had the power to make or break the illusion, keeping a semblance of self-worth and individuality. He couldn't excel in the company because of his lack of education, and so he quit working and enrolled in college.

Chapter 14

Finding His Life in College with Elzora

While still working for ETS, David had made quite a few friends there, including one Doug Clack, the head of the Budgets Department. Doug liked David for many reasons, but one reason stuck out more than the others and that he was his love for poetry. Occasionally Doug would head to the UC Berkeley campus' student union building where on Thursday nights there was a poetry reading. On one of those nights David was there and up on stage reading his poetry, Doug fell in love with David's writing.

An opening in Doug's department came up, and he thought of David, "David, an opening in the Budgets Department has come up, and I thought of you. I feel you will be a great asset to the team and so I am inviting you to apply, and David don't stop writing poetry. I love it."

"Doug, as much as this position would change my life for the better, I have to turn you down. Come on, Doug and I barely have a high school education. What would do in a Budget department? I can barely count to ten."

"Don't worry about that. You can learn as you go. I assure you it will be fine. You will be fine. Just give it a chance."

"Sorry, Doug but I have to turn you down. I can't do that type of job."

David was hurt by this opportunity he couldn't have. He needed to talk with someone about this. He wanted some advice, to hear something that he had never heard before and so he went to the Head Psychologist, Rose Pyan.

"Rose, thank you for seeing me. I just want to tell you something that happened to me today. Rose Doug Clack offered me a position in his department, and I had to turn it down. I don't have the education for that. What should I do Rose?"

"David, all I can say is you have to get your education. You are still young enough to take advantage of the schooling you need; you will never climb the ladder without a proper education."

Elementary Algebra, Chemistry, Geology, Biology, Tennis and College English were the courses that kicked off David's Chemical Engineering Major. David didn't have SAT scores, well he had SAT scores, but they were so low that he didn't dare mention them. His educational level was that of pre-high school or lower, so all he had was a GED and a desire. He was not university material, which meant he had to begin his college career from the ground up, meaning doing his lower division work at Merritt College, a community college in Oakland, California.

Enrolling in college gave David a great feeling inside, a new sense of pride, or the sense of pride for the first time. Merritt College situated high atop the Oakland hills provided a panoramic view not only of the surrounding Bay Area but also of the ineluctable reality that soon he would find his place here on earth. Within a few weeks after registering, he received his first check from the Veterans Administration, a monthly allotment of $800 awarded as part of his being a discharged Veteran of the armed forces. How lucky he was to have just made the cut-off for benefits after such a sketchy and short-lived career in the US Air Force. The rules stated a person had to serve 180 days to qualify for full benefits unless, of course you ended up with a dishonorable discharge and then you got nothing. David served 181 days.

With his first check cashed, he walked into the campus bookstore and purchased books and supplies, a new book bag, a tennis racket and other school junk. He was now a full-time student. It enlivened him, this newfound independence, this setting of goals, this moment of broadening education made real by the simple function of doing what one sets out to do. David felt closer to being part of something he had always yearned, something along the way he had forgotten.

The days of childhood, growing up in the Estuary, then Berkeley, were the beginning of the discovery of his love for knowledge. The world, science, animals and writing were some of his favorites, but along the way he replaced these desires for plain survival, the act of blending in with the crowd for fear of being himself.

Susan took the news of him registering for classes with a delight, she was all for education and though the relationship failed in terms of what Susan wanted, she still loved David as family and wanted most desperately to see him succeed. Susan had a respect for education and any effort at uplifting one's standards she was for it.

Three weeks had passed since David received the call to meet with his course advisor, and as he stepped into the conference room, he braced himself for any news. His heart thudded in his chest as he sat across from his advisor, who looked up at him with a serious expression. It took a moment for the words to sink in: he had been awarded additional funding and financial aid for his studies. And one of those grants was work study; a government-paid job on campus.

With instructions to report to the EOPS (Equal Opportunity Program Service) department and ask for Ms. Elzora Kaufman, the director, David's mind buzzed with excitement as he left the meeting. The following morning, after his tennis lesson, he made his way toward a set of prefabricated buildings near Administration. As he walked up a wheelchair ramp and opened the door, he couldn't help but feel grateful for this opportunity.

Inside, he approached the counter and asked for Ms. Kaufman, feeling nervous but also determined. The receptionist greeted him with a bubbly smile and informed him she was currently in a meeting. But before he could leave, she ushered him through a small half-swinging door into the bustling office.

The small bungalow was filled with students coming and going, all seeking guidance and help. David couldn't help but feel inspired as he watched an Asian girl no older than eighteen confidently recite a pre- rehearsed script to a prospective candidate in need of services. A sense of pride swelled within him as he realized he would soon be part of this team, working to serve the underprivileged.

As someone who himself came from a minority background, David felt a strong connection to this cause and was suddenly filled with a wild spirit to become part of the beat in the educational pulse of the community.

Several students came and left within a matter of an hour, and then there was nothing. Suddenly the door opened and there stood Ms Kaufman a bright beam of light entering the room. She was a woman–not a student–as she bounced in on feet made of springs. The place came alive with just her mere presence.

Ms. Elzora Kaufman was a vision of femininity, surpassing the average young woman with her stunning beauty. Her features were not those of a supermodel, but rather reminiscent of a prototype from years past. She exuded an energetic and playful aura, paired with a genuine affability that made her irresistible. As she moved, her long, French braided hair decorated with seashells swayed gently and emitted a soft tinkling sound like wind chimes in the breeze. Standing at a petite five-feet-four, her body was elongated and slender, draped in caramel-colored skin that seemed to fit her facial bones perfectly. A perpetual smile graced her face, never fading but revealing the inner joy that radiated from within. Her eyes were like two Asiatic orbs, always seeking light and life with their phototropism, a constant duel of two planets vying for the same breath of brightness. Trying to sum up her physical characteristics in simple adjectives and verbs would be an exercise in futility, as they would have to be reassessed daily to keep up with her ever-changing beauty

"Hi, I'm Elzora, and you must be David, am I right?" Her words were a viscous blend of honey and caramel, and David came to attention, rising from his chair as if it had sat on something hot. With an arm extended, he positioned his palm against hers and felt the meaning of life, like Morse code being tapped out among the nerve endings in his hand. They greeted.

David couldn't believe his luck. After months of struggling to find a job, he had landed a position in the EOPS department at the local community college. As he sat across from Elzora Kaufman, the head of the program, he could still hardly believe it was real.

"Pleased to meet you, Ms. Kaufman," David said nervously, trying not to fidget in his seat.

"Please, call me Elzora. It's the last piece of my youth I can hold on to by dispensing with formality," she replied with a warm smile, motioning for him to sit down.

As they chatted, David noticed the tennis racket leaning against her desk. "You're a tennis player?" he asked with interest.

"Yes, I belong to the Claremont Tennis Club and live in a condo association called the San Leandro Racquet Club. We have courts there too. It's safe to say I love tennis," Elzora chuckled.

"I'm just learning myself. It's one of my classes here at the college, but I am really enjoying the game, even though I suck at it," David admitted with a self-deprecating laugh.

Elzora reassured him, "Don't worry, with practice comes improvement. Maybe we can hit a few balls together sometime."

As they moved on to discuss the details of his job and the mission of the EOPS program, David began to relax and feel more comfortable around Elzora. During lulls in their work, they exchanged life stories and formed a friendly bond. However, David was careful not to reveal too much about himself, as he wasn't sure how others would react to his past struggles.

Elzora was an interesting character—a relic from the 60s with a hint of Angela Davis in her appearance and beliefs. She often spoke passionately about her desire to return to Africa, which she considered her true homeland.

As day turned to night, the luxurious facade of western civilization began to crumble around Elzora. Despite her comfortable existence among the affluent, she felt trapped in a dreamlike state, yearning for something more real and raw. She was notorious on campus for her rumored affair with the much older Dean of Students, Dr. George Herring. But as they strolled through the Claremont Country Club together, a striking couple with their contrasting features - her youthful beauty and his silver fox appearance - it was clear that they were both drawn to each other.

One Friday afternoon, just weeks before Christmas, Elzora invited David out for lunch. They hopped into her vintage burgundy BMW and drove to Montclair - an upscale suburb known for its preppy delis and posh residents. As they sat beneath a towering tree at the far end of campus, enjoying their takeout sandwiches and iced teas, there was an undeniable tension between them. Each pause in conversation was filled with the electricity of unspoken desire, as if their eyes could physically touch.

And so, he broke the spell.

"I have a class, Elzora." David said, and that was that.

In the days to come, Elzora announced a Christmas party she would have for her small staff, at her house, just the EOPS crew. David informed Susan of the party and asked if he could use her car.

Susan had helped David buy a Jaguar, but he ended up returning the car to her. The connection between the car and Susan had become too complicated, almost suffocating for David. At first, it seemed like a great idea - he had saved money for a down payment but needed her to co-sign because of his lack of credit. However, Susan took advantage of this and got the car in her name only, leaving David feeling like nothing more than a user. He was hurt and angry when he found out the truth, and wanted nothing to do with the car anymore.

But as time passed, and they continued their relationship, Susan couldn't let go of her illusion of their love being perfect. She couldn't accept that David had his own life and interests outside of her. So, when he asked to use her Cadillac to go to a party with his coworkers, she reluctantly agreed, but couldn't help making snide remarks about him having a date.

As David got ready in his suit, Susan looked at him like she was seeing him for the first time. It stirred conflicting emotions within her - pride at how handsome he looked, but also jealousy that he would spend time with other people instead of her.

She tried to prolong herself by giving him the keys, wanting to hold on to what little control she felt she had in their relationship. But eventually, she handed them over with a mix of guilt and resentment towards David for not needing her for everything.

In that moment, David felt both guilty for causing Susan pain and frustrated with her childish behavior. He closed himself off emotionally and left for the party, determined not to let her ruin his night or take away any small moments of happiness from him.

The air outside was frigid; a dense black emulsion painted on an invisible canvass seemed to encase the earth in an outer shell. On his way to the party, he stopped at an all-night convenience store and bought an inexpensive bottle of champagne and a bouquet of wildflowers, something of lesser ostentation that would delight, rather than devastate. At the porch of Elzora's' condominium, he stood there for a moment before knocking, trying as best he could to plan a convivial demeanor that would disguise this nagging guilt he was feeling. Susan occupied a space in his head, and he carried her like baggage everywhere he went.

Standing there that evening on Elzora's porch his mind drifted as it often did, to the morning he had awakened in Lilly's bed. It was time they tried reconciling. This was the true reason David had given the Jag back to Susan:

David had just taken ownership of the Jaguar, much like a man who was trying to do the right thing he had saved two-thousand dollars for the down- payment, but his lack of credit caused him to ask Susan for a favor, only he hadn't realized that this favor was in fact a means whereby Susan could get the upper hand on him and so she did by using his money as a down payment and her credit as the securing factor, after all the person with the credit would be the one responsible for the car and so that person's name would bare in large clear letters on the contract, he hadn't thought this far ahead yet.

Well, David had the car believing it was all his, and he thought that if he could show up at Lilly's with a fancy new car, she might want him back. He arrived at Lilly's shouldering strange feelings that someone was watching him. In fact, the burden was inspired by guilt a guilt that he didn't have to feel after all because he wasn't in a relationship with Susan, so It wasn't like he was cheating on her, so why did he feel that way every time he tried to escape or find love of his own?

David was in some small way afraid for the car being detected and giving away his location, so he decided not to park close to Lilly's place in case Susan saw the car and found out where he was. Living with this constant piece of guilt attached to himself was agonizing for David, but he didn't know how to escape it. He was into deep with Maurice and the relationship he had with Susan, his new mother.

David was feeling happy in the morning that he and may have solved all our problems and could soon be back together again. He left Lilly's and walked the several blocks away to where he had parked the car, but it wasn't there. He looked everywhere thinking that he might have parked it in a different spot, but that proved ridiculous as he was very keen about every aspect of that car; it was his first car.

He came back to Lilly's and called the police. After the report had been taken, he boarded a bus for home. He walked the short distance from San Pablo to Masonic where they lived and there in the driveway was the car, parked in front of Susan's Cadillac.

At first, he was happy at the fast response the police had made in recovering the automobile, but then another, more sinister twist emerged, it was Wednesday, a workday for Susan, but her car was there as well, parked behind the Jag.

"How'd the car get here, Susan? Did the police bring the car? I reported it stolen just a couple of hours ago?" He asked calmly.

"I brought it here myself," she said cooly with a hint of arrogance, like this was a normal event.

"How in the fuck did you get the car here in the first place?" He charged with the likes of an unscrupulous litigator. And as if what *she was about to say was her right, she recounted the details with puffed-up pride.*

"At the beginning I drove the jag three blocks walked back and drove the Cadillac three blocks ahead of it, I did this all the way home; took me awhile, but I accomplished it." She recited.

He was beyond anger. The anger he felt dissipated until he felt nothing but contempt for her and everything associated with her. David took the keys and threw them at her and then he spat on the ground, "Keep the motherfucker, you bitch, I hate you!" And everything seemed back to normal.

David snapped out of his daydream that was happening at night and returned into the moment. After a sharp rap on the door, Elzora opened it with a lit smile and an overheated welcome. Behind her stood Rakim. Rakim, who thought he and David were in competition for the hand of Elzora, he greeted David at the door with a toothy grin while looking over Elzora's shoulder. Rakim was a native of New York and a few years older than David. He was still recovering from a broken marriage back home and had hidden his pain behind a new identity of Black Power. He wore the Dashikis and a Beret and talked the talk, but underneath it all he was just Karim from New York.

Once inside, the music and laughter from the others helped to erase the remaining thoughts David had left on the doorstep. He moved towards the living room, which was a subtle latitude evocative of a young Black woman's space. She had studied Psychology, that polemic inspiring discipline that most radical Black people chose back in the sixties and seventies as a lunar expedition into a changing sociology. The African carvings, raw and feral, exuded a symbolism so intrinsic in the feminist movement, especially the feminist movement among Black women. A fern here and there, a creeping violet; a room designed to promote photosynthesis; it was her space.

Caught in a moment of intense scrutiny, I brought myself back to the surface.

"These flowers are for you; however, the champagne must be shared by you and your special someone," he smiled, and then looked away. That special someone he was refereeing was Dr Herring.

"Thank you very much, I mean it," and she kissed him on the cheek, lingering a little longer than he expected, "Can I get you a drink...some food...anything?" and with shyness he nodded.

Elzora was good with people. David enjoyed watching the way she interacted; it was almost theatrical. At thirty-five, she had the spirited nature of a teenage girl, and at her suggestion we all played word games, danced, told jokes, ate, drank, and laughed as the chilling Christmas air outside grew colder.

A gentle frost collected on the windows as logs crackled amidst a blazing fire. The buzzing Christmas spirit began a slow descent as empty glasses declined, refilling. One-by-one everyone found an individual reason to leave and soon there were only myself and Rakim remaining. A *Mexican standoff of sorts*, he thought.

David began collecting glasses and plates. "Don't worry with those," said Elzora, but he shooed her off, motioning for her to rest as he took charge of tidying up, and in a shorter time than expected Rakim took his cue and left. With the last of the dishes in the washer, David dried his hands and sat on the sofa next to her. As he sat, she rose, and headed into the kitchen, and returned with two crystal flutes and the unopened bottle of champagne he had bought, which was now chilled and she asked, "Will you please open this?"

"I thought I made myself clear that this was to be shared with your favorite someone," and as he popped the cork, she remained silent; he could see that she was doing just that.

It was his intentions not to seduce or be seduced, and in all earnestness, he remained true to that conviction, but the sight of her made this limpid resolution less sacrosanct. It was not a sexual proclivity, not even a foretelling of love, it was more a wanting to be part of a mood that he felt conducive with, an inner yearning for growth outside the boundaries of a distasteful life that had encased him in a set of false beliefs.

David wanted to be part of her world, only he didn't know if he wanted it, including her. The choices became obfuscated, though logic spoke most clearly, deducing without argument how lamentable an endeavor like this would be if chosen under false pretenses. But like an illicit narcotic whose function is to relieve pain and or make you feel good, you now must take it not to feel bad. A sort of ambivalence occurs.

Her words became an animated silence, she thought to herself: *'how beautiful this man is, he has an ease about him that beautiful people develop, though he doesn't boast it as if it were an embossed calling card.'*

Each prolonged stare sent electrical messages to special nerve endings in those certain areas of her body, and there a pulse is produced, or a movement. A hand placed here, a foot sliding there, warmth between her legs that caused them to flutter as wings on a slow-moving bird. These movements witnessed by onlookers as nervous gestures were the language spoken through the body as the translator of the mind.

In a moment of incertitude, which agonizing tremor that comes with indecision, David kissed her, though not a long confident kiss, one that answered a question, and she asked,

"Can you please do that again, only longer?" And he did, and it was longer, and she felt this was where she wanted him to be.

"It's late and you have a long drive, if you like, and there is no obligation. You can rest here and leave in the morning," which in its ambiguity sounded sincere, however he declined with an explanation.

"I can't do that. Knowing myself as I do and at this moment being here with you and liking you as I do, I wouldn't rest." He paused for a moment, "I don't want to wake up fulfilled and dismayed, therefore I'd rather get to know you, and though this charge I'm feeling right now makes me feel to want more, I'd rather leave just feeling that, rather than to leave not wanting to return." Which made little sense at all.

She was blown away, and he can't emphasize that this is not said of conceit. This was how things were, and he found it strange that in declining sex he was strengthening his hand. He was ensuring a possibility with her. In the morning, just after sunrise, she phoned asking him if he would like to drive with her to Fairfield to deliver Christmas presents to her brother and his family. The idea sounded wonderful to him and agreed to go.

She arrived later that morning; he was waiting near a window where he could see her coming so she wouldn't get out of her car; he didn't want her and Susan bumping into each other just yet, something he was uncomfortable with even though he was not doing anything wrong.

He had warned Susan of this morning's event with Elzora and the nature of their outing. Though Susan was a big part of his life, he felt the need to clarify that she was only a part of his life, not his life, and to continue trying to keep him imprisoned through her own self-pity would prove nothing more than a swifter amputation of what little friendship already exists.

Susan sat motionless in a chair that afforded her a grand view of Elzora and his getting into her car. He watched Susan's expression as Elzora removed herself from the driver's side of the car. Susan watched with vehemence, so deadly, for a moment there he thought she would strike. Susan was becoming a little hotter beneath her skin as she took note that Elzora's car was the same bright maroon color as the Jaguar and in her eye's, he could see her thinking, *'he's just replacing one item for another.'* This sort of shallow thinking kept her the Dragon at the gate, guarding a fortress of impenetrable emptiness.

The meeting with Elzo'a's family was a success, and Elzora specifically mentioned how her seven- and ten-year-old nieces instantly warmed up to him and displayed their charming flirtatiousness. It's the behavior that young girls exhibit when they find someone affable.

As they left her brother's house, the day was still young and the air about was chilled. The traffic on return was light, something that made life seem domestic that time of year when home became more than a mere dwelling and the dropping in on friends and family less an imposition and though their entourage–separate yet endearing–left them standing on opposing shores facing a blankness between them, he diverted their route and drove to the coastal beach town of Guerneville.

Parking in an undesignated space near the beach, they stepped out into a grey void that blanketed the sky in a woollen fleece. Other than the watches on our wrists depicting time, the sun couldn't be calibrated to any planetary position; time of day became an illusion. The fine crystals of silica beneath their feet were damp and soggy, mixed with the alluvial deposits of clay and silt; the beach appeared as nothing more than an enormous field of mortar.

To one side of the crescent beach a huge promontory stood like an ancient sentinel and beneath its northern aspect, where granite superimposes beach, its point of intrusion, lay a rookery comprising hundreds of migrating seals and sea lions, the likes of which appeared a vast grazing of black maggots upon a rotting sandy carcass.

He took her hand and found comfort in the warmth of her touch. They walked as the fog eddied around them in a mystifying spiritual dance; the chilly air had borne an additional weight upon the ocean's surface, bringing it to heel under a powerful climatic trance. As the surf rolled in and out, they moved about exchanging glances; the words being tossed back and forth were more than mere incantations; they were sounds slicing the hollowness of nowhere, affirming the interplay between two souls. Whenever an emotional cord was strummed, she would tighten her grip on his hand and lean her head into his shoulder.

"Don't you find it strange how a moment like this can just come from out of nowhere?" She said and looked at the sand being displaced by her steps.

"I don't know how to explain this," he said, "but I will try. My life is a mess. A father to a small son. A student with a goal. And I'm sharing a space with a woman, and I am falling in love with you."

She looked at him with a sort of amazement and decided not to respond customarily, but let his words find they were not too alarming, and that neither of them was alone in this.

"My life too is a mess, if you call it that. I am not happy with my job, I cannot have children, I am with a man with whom a relationship has no definition, and I too am in love with you."

"What do we do with these lives that are in such a mess?" He smiled. "Bring them together as one and all, but the love will fade." It was not a question, but a statement.

She again looked from her feet to my eyes and again wondered how a moment like this could come from out of nowhere.

Chapter 15

Confusion Between Elzora and Susan

Life began taking shape for David; the empty spaces had now found a source of renewal. The remaining drive home was bringing him closer to some form of happiness and with each laugh and gentle exchange of word; Elzora somehow brought to him a world with new meaning.

Why were women playing a significant role in my life? This question surfaced; later, it became a weighty piece of confusion.

He believed most boys moving toward adulthood find themselves busy with preparing for that phase of life, focusing on the cardinal virtues associated with the alignment of adulthood, but he somehow had his priorities out of kilter.

"What is it with you and Susan, anyhow?" Elzora asked. "What do you mean?" It was not a question.

"Well, you live with Susan, but you say there's nothing between you two," Elzora spoke as she watched the rolling scenery move behind them as they drove. "I'm a woman and knowing how I feel about you; Susan too must be feeling something strong, otherwise why would she let you stay with her? It doesn't add up?"

"We are like family; we have a mutual understanding." He offered.

"A mutual understanding, what kind of understanding could a woman who loves–."

"Susan doesn't love me the way you may think. It's not that kind of relationship, and it's too much to explain. Let's change the subject."

David too, had often wondered why he clung to situations he would normally shy away from. It is almost unnatural to sleep on one side of the bed and dislike the other. Why not just get a single bed?

There was no logic to this unseemly dependency on Susan. She had given David everything he wanted, never bitched about his failing business attempts, sporadic work habits; it kept his life in some semblance of normalcy; he had to remain in a disordered life.

"You can't continue to skirt the issue. It's gonna affect other aspects of your life," Elzora said, "other aspects of our life. The very things that trouble you, those things you say are not what it seems to be, are gonna jump up and bite you in the ass."

"It's not what you think it is," he said with a chuckle amid his frustration for this line of questioning.

"Then tell me what it is!" she snapped. "Be honest about your feelings and your life. What are you hiding from?"

It bothered David deeply when someone tried to analyze him or dig deeper into his life, especially when they were hovering close to the truth. Never had he been confronted like this before. He felt naked, exposed and rather than deal with it to a peaceable resolution, he brushed it off as if it were nothing. Watching her as she moved into the kitchen,

"You want a drink?" She asked. "Please." He spoke.

And he rose to assist her, taking the break in tempo as an opportunity to divert the subject into another direction. David had become accustomed to trying to control every situation, yet with Elzora he felt as if he had reached a deadlock and couldn't sway her suspicions.

"Look here baby," he said, taking her by the shoulders, turning her so that they could be face-to-face. "I never said I had it all together. It's obvious in our discussions, but I will take whatever steps necessary to smooth these rough edges. I want nothing to come between what goodness we have right now."

She softened.

With gentle movements, he pressed his lips to each of her eyelids, lingering for a moment before moving on to the tip of her nose. He traced his way down her cheeks with feather light kisses, pausing at her earlobes to leave soft nibbles. Finally, he leaned in and kissed her on the lips, their breath mingling as they melted into each other's embrace.

In that moment, all sense of time and place disappeared. They were lost in each other's touch, the outside world fading into nothingness like a ghost in the air. Sensuality was his go-to remedy for avoiding tough conversations or revealing too much of himself. And as always, it worked its magic.

But this time, instead of using it to escape, he wanted to savor every moment with her. He didn't want to let go.

But as their entanglement grew deeper and more complex, he couldn't help but retreat into his usual patterns and tactics. He used emotional warfare to create distance and maintain control over the situation.

And three weeks later, they were standing at the altar, bound by vows and promises made in the heat of passion. Little did they know, these ties would prove to be harder to unravel than any mess they could have created.

Susan took the news badly of his upcoming marriage to Elzora. She tried in every way possible to make him change his mind; she tried using every trick she had available to her, but he was determined that marrying Elzora was what he wanted, he believed this to be the surest way of getting Susan out of his life, but when you look closer, he was only trading one problem for another.

Chapter 16

Marriage to Elzora

Hidden away in the breathtaking beauty of Lake Tahoe, Elzora and David exchanged vows in a semi-secret ceremony. The snow had flooded the entire state of Neveda, so they were trapped for a night there amid majestic mountains which bore witness to their love, as they pledged themselves to each other with simple yet meaningful words.

With only fifteen dollars for a marriage certificate, the couple easily secured their union without the requirement of a blood test. It was simpler than David had ever imagined, but then again, he had never been married before or anticipated such overwhelming joy in his life. After the wedding at the small chapel, they made their way to the luxurious Hilton hotel, accompanied by Elzora's brother, his wife, and two daughters, her friend Carolyn, as well as her mother who David would meet for the first time that day, excitement and nerves bubbled within him. The suite they were given was grand and spacious, but with all their family present, David and Elzora selflessly gave up their bed for the others and instead spent their honeymoon sleeping on the bathroom floor. In those intimate moments together, surrounded by love and laughter, David knew that this was where he truly belonged - beside his beloved wife in this new chapter of their lives together.

The land of Nevada lay buried under a thick blanket of snow, the cold air sharp enough to slice through skin and bone. As

David stood among the barren landscape, tears streamed down his face, each drop a symbol of the raw emotions surging through him. The exchange of vows meant everything to him - a sacred bond between two souls that nothing could shatter. But despite his innocent, idealistic view of life, he had been a destroyer of hearts, leaving behind a trail of broken promises and shattered dreams.

The day after the wedding came and went as if nothing had happened. Elzora, David, and her friend Carolyn squeezed into the cramped confines of Elzora's little BMW. David gripped the steering wheel tightly, his knuckles white with tension as he navigated through a blinding blizzard. The roads were slick with snow and ice, causing cars to slide and swerve dangerously. Elzora's frustration grew with every slow-moving vehicle in front of them, her hands clenching the armrests until her nails dug into the leather. She cursed under her breath, wondering why she had agreed to drive in this treacherous weather. David sat quietly while Elzora mysteriously transformed into another person, leaving behind the woman with whom he had just married.

After what felt like an endless drive, he finally pulled into the familiar parking lot of their home. But as he turned off the ignition and took in the surroundings, a sinking feeling settled in his gut - he had made a mistake. The air inside the car grew heavy and thick with tension, and a heavy silence settled between them like a thick fog. Instead of following through with the planned celebration of their marriage, David sought refuge in the Racquet Club's rec room. Perched on the edge of an empty pool table, he brooded over the events that had transpired. What had gone wrong? Was it him or her? These questions swirled in his mind as he struggled to make sense of it all.

At twenty-five years old, David was plagued by questions that seemed to have no end. They swirled in his mind like a tangled web, never giving way to any logical conclusion. Instead, they were fueled by raw emotion, an unfriendly specter that sought to dominate the goodness in his life by distorting his conscious thoughts. No matter how hard he tried, he couldn't grasp onto these elusive questions or connect with their meaning. He pushed them away, storing them in the only safe place he knew - his mind. But even there, they lingered and taunted him with their unresolved nature.

Elzora allowed him a moment of speculation until her own sense of impending doom pushed her in search of him, and there in the empty club house she found him pushing balls across the pool table.

Her voice was filled with concern as she asked, "Are you alright? Why don't you just come home?" He remained wordless, knowing that his silence would only fuel her anger. She was not one to be shut out, and yet he couldn't bring himself to open up. If only he had known then what he knows now, maybe their marriage could have been saved. But deep down, he questions if it was ever meant to work.

"Ever since we left Tahoe, you've been a storm brewing with every step. I didn't expect this from you." She accuses, her words laced with bitterness and disappointment. But he knows he's not the only one at fault here; her mind is a labyrinth of twisted thoughts that he can never fully understand. Yet somehow, it always seems to lead them to moments like this - where everything good becomes an illusion and their love is just a fleeting mirage in the desert of their tumultuous relationship.

"Didn't expect WHAT, that your sudden change in tone would open me up to question," he snapped. "Well, it did. It took me by surprise. Here we are newlywed and already we're having our first fight."

"I wouldn't call it fighting. We're experiencing a misunderstanding," she said and pushed a few balls across the table. "You're being trivial, sensitive towards an issue that amounts to nothing."

But to him, it was not a trivial matter. It held weight and significance, an issue that he couldn't simply brush aside. Until the day of the wedding, Elzora had been a gentle and compliant person, her delicacy and poise alluring to him from the start. He believed that a woman with such grace and refinement must be his perfect match. Her every movement, like the flutter of a butterfly's wings, captivated him and drew him in deeper.

"Elzora, I can't help believing that when a couple has their argument so close to the beginning of their life together it's not just a representation of a one-sided issue, it's an indicator of where things are headed," he looked her in the eye.

"An argument regardless of the content strips away a layer of the foundation and in future arguments, which I am sure there will be, further layers are stripped until the foundation weakens, until there is nothing left but hate." He went silent and began walking around the clubhouse.

"You're so right David, I'm sorry. I don't want this for us. I love you. Let's go home, please." And she nudged him out of his foul mood with a smile that calmed him, and they held each other and kissed. Yet beneath the surface, he held tight to his belief that things were gonna get worse.

By the laws of the universe, time moved forward and so did he. College became a full-time endeavor. Whenever he was not in class, he divided his time between labs, library, and work, all of which took him into the evening before he could even think about going home. Elzora, in her dutiful role as wife was always waiting, jumping on him the moment he walked through the door, never in his life had he been greeted with such eagerness, sometimes he'd wondered: *did she do something wrong and knowing she hadn't been caught by him brought her relief so overwhelming that she jumped for joy at the sight of him.*

Lately she had been talking about quitting her job at the college and becoming a flight attendant. After discussing it one evening, he let her know he was all for it.

"Why a flight attendant, so you can rendezvous with your lovers posted in every city of every country?" He jokingly asked with a smile on my face. "Now that's a great idea," she contemplated, and then laughed. "It would be good for you as well, give you more time alone to study."

"Oh yeah, how thoughtful. Make it look like it's all for me. You can't fool me. I know your moves." He looked at her from the corner of his eye with a smile. And three-weeks later she came home with a check for ten-thousand dollars and the announcement that she did it, she quit her job.

Everything seemed so premeditated even though we had danced around the notion and reached a mutual agreement about her quitting, only I didn't think she would do it so soon.

"Have you given this matter thoughtful consideration, Ellie?" He asked, and she became defensive.

"It's what I want," she snapped at him. "Merritt College is not what I call my future."

"What's with the check?" He asked.

"It's what's left of my retirement. I pulled it out to use until I secure another job."

Elzora goes on a spending spree, buying clothes and furnishings, leaving David to undergo the responsibility of paying all the bills. In just a few months, their marriage deteriorates, and they both set out to file for divorce.

This was nineteen-eighty-three, he was twenty-seven.

In a year, the marriage proved too great a burden on him. He was a student studying chemical engineering. He was left with loads of bills to pay, Elzora also left owing thousands in back taxes. His GPA had fallen, and he found himself on academic probation and so after two years with a good GPA, all of this and a divorce was too distracting and so he dropped out, sold everything he could and moved back in with Susan.

Piece by piece, David sold off the last remaining assets that marked a life of attempted individuality, stripped himself bare so that Susan could put him back together again. It was the engine that drove her existence.

During this reunion, the entire spectrum cast a different light, not that it swayed from its intended course, rather a new one created to enforce the original lesson.

In time, David became addicted to cocaine. The addiction somehow made staying at home more bearable; and no one knew. At least he thought no one knew. Being in the same house with Susan brought him more pain than before, but like the woman who sacrifices love and happiness for the sake of her children; this entire redevelopment was more for the sake of my son Maurice.

The absence of intimacy and the shared life with a woman he felt no love, waxed frustration the likes of which could only be tolerated as an acceptance through orgasm.

He began immersing himself—with pride and affection—in his son's education and social development by participating with him in local scholastic activities, volunteering several days per week as a teacher's assistant and somehow Maurice enjoyed this because the other children found his dad a joy to be around, thus grew a sense of pride Maurice had never found in him.

David became a stay-at-home-father, cleaning, and cooking meals of which he and Susan enjoyed; they were now both happier than he could ever imagine being. Where Susan once shunned the domestic aspect of life, she now took on a complementing role alongside him. There was no rigidity or harshness, only laughter for her and Maurice.

There now were many children from the neighborhood coming around to the house. Maurice enjoyed sharing his home and his father. The kids all considered him cool. In time, other parents began showing a greater interest in their own children's activities. This made for a community balance, and they even enjoyed his status as house father and trusted most freely the safety and welfare of their child in his home.

All this fierce conviviality, this doing of what he thought was the right thing, was robbing him of his place in life. He didn't want to seem cruel in his assessment of how his life was, after all it involved the coming into happiness of other's and perhaps, he should consider the welfare of them before he considers his own life, but somehow, he cannot seem to accept that he should go without love.

Chapter 17

Wadie Amar and Jail

It is now 1986, and David is 30 years old.

On one of his solitary afternoons, three years after a failed marriage with Elzora, David sat alone in his living room, the sunlight casting long shadows across the floor. The emptiness of the space matched the emptiness in his heart. Suddenly, there was a knock at the door - it was his Aunt Lynn, her warm smile and kind eyes bringing a glimmer of hope to David's gloomy state. She insisted on taking him for a drive to meet her good friend, Wadie. As they drove through winding roads that led up to the plush El Cerrito hills, David couldn't help but feel like he was ascending into the clouds. The sun shone brilliantly against the blue sky, but as they continued to climb higher, it vanished behind a sea of fluffy white clouds. It felt like they were flying above the world.

Finally, they reached Wadie's house - a stunning home perched atop the sprawling hill. The entire area where Wadie lived was enveloped in swirling clouds, giving off an ethereal and almost otherworldly aura. As David stepped out of the car and followed his Aunt Lynn towards the entrance, he couldn't help but feel like he was stepping into a different realm altogether.

Over the past year, David had partnered with Gene, one of Susan's male friends who also lived in the El Cerrito hills. In his room, David had begun a self-study of all the aspects of real estate finance and development. Gene, who visited Susan frequently one day noticed David in his room and the floor of the room covered in papers and blueprints. He called his company DGG Development.

It was lunch time When Lynn and David arrived at Mrs Amar's, as David preferred calling her. When she invited them in, she was preparing lunch and drinking a cocktail at all at the same time. Wadie was a dowager two times over. She was also only a high school graduate who hadn't time for college, raised four children and did it all while moving through the ranks at the Chicago Title Company where she had retired at the early age of fifty-five. It was the connection in real estate that opened her initial interest in David.

Wadie was hard to describe. Brightly stunning and well-dressed even for the afternoon at home in the kitchen. A politely vulgar charm, and she spoke of her first husband first.

"Ira, my first husband was a pimp." She offered freely, "But he had a mother who was actually in charge of everything Ira did." She sipped on her drink. "Forgive me, can I offer you Lynn a scotch?" They all had drinks now. "Yes, he was a pimp, had girls coming and going in the house but his mother thought that pimping and selling pussy was cheap so she invested his money in liquor stores and so the two of them his mother and he lived well, I left only after a few months, no room for two mothers."

Regardless of this past, unsavory as it may have been, she wore it well and had somehow mellowed into a life of dignity, some wealth, and scotch. She loved drinking Pete Dawson and Ginger Ale.

That day she wore a tight-fitting skirt of woven knit that fell below the knee and a matching top, and when she walked, David thought she reminded him of a Geisha.

Her strawberry blonde hair was coifed in a conservative style and the lines stressed a face that hinted a touch of make-up.

The smells emanating from the kitchen were heavenly and it amused David to watch as she busied herself in the kitchen, oblivious to their presence, but aware at the same time somehow this all seemed uncoordinated for a woman this beautiful.

The three of them sat unanimated, talking, and laughing as if they all were all old friends. Wadie set the table for lunch and served everyone, including herself to a hearty lunch of moussaka. After lunch they moved to the front room which had a panoramic view of the San Francisco Bay. They all slipped into a light repose mixed with drinks and useless banter. For a moment David had excused himself and when only a few steps away he overheard Wadie say to his aunt,

"Lynn, he is gorgeous, why haven't you brought him before?"

"Girl it never dawned on me, I just happened by his house today and wanted his company."

"I see why," said Wadie, and then David reappeared.

Lynn and Wadie caught up on some old gossip while David listened and smiled at Wadie and every once in a while, he caught her looking in his direction.

"Wadie, excuse me Lynn, can I talk with Wadie in private?" He asked and she led him into the kitchen, "Wadie, can I see you again, alone?" He asked.

"I would like that very much." She replied with a naughty smile.

"Lynn, if you are I am ready to go."

"Already, just like that?" Said Lynn. Wadie stayed quiet, not interjecting at her company's early departure.

After Lynn dropped him home, he felt himself a bit more drunk than he had realized. He wanted to return to Wadie's house that evening but he didn't have access to a car and if he did, he was not in shape for driving. David called his new business partner Gene:

"Gene, I hate to bother you, but I was wondering if you might give me a lift up the hill by your house, I met this nice lady and I want to go back to her house?"

"Who is she, I know everyone up here on the hill?" said Gene. "You might know her, Wadie Amar."

"Excuse me, but yes I know that bitch, and she is a bitch so you better be careful, maybe you can get her to invest some money in the business, she certainly has it."

In a matter of minutes Gene showed up, he stayed in his car and frantically blew the horn.

Gene dropped me at the curb of Wadie's house, "Don't forget to ask about money tell her you need fifty-thousand, she can afford that."

"I'm not a Gigolo Gene and you are acting like you, my pimp." and he walked up the small set of concrete steps that led to the front door of Wadie's house. After ringing and hearing the doorbell sounding off inside the house and getting no answer David looked around each side of the house, and all the lights were off. He knew she must still be home because the Cadillac was still in the driveway. So, he pressed the bell a few more times and when there still was no answer he walked around to the rear of the house where he saw a light on in a room that had sliding glass doors a balcony.

David assumed this was her bedroom she was the only person living there. He began to rehearse the things he would say and do, and then brushed this notion off as something stupid, just be spontaneous, he thought. And so, he picked up a ladder that was lying on the side of the garage and placed it up against the balcony and climbed. After hoisting himself over the balcony's railing he stood there quietly for a few moments thinking if what he was doing was cool, weighing one thought against another when suddenly the door slid open forcefully, and standing there was Wadie with a wide toothy grin on her face.

Wadie stepped out onto the balcony, her grin growing even wider. "I've been waiting for you," she said, her voice low and sultry. David froze, unsure what to do or say next. Before he could react, Wadie grabbed him by the shirt and pulled him into the bedroom, shutting the balcony door behind them.

She pushed David down onto the bed and straddled him, leaning close. "You're cute when you're nervous," she purred. David's heart was racing but he didn't resist as Wadie began unbuttoning his shirt. Her hands were soft but strong and she explored his chest eagerly.

"I've had my eye on you all day at lunch," Wadie murmured. "These last few hours were torture while I was waiting for you." She slid David's shirt off his shoulders and kissed him hungrily. He responded kindly, all hesitation gone. As things heated up between them David stopped.

"I tried ringing the bell."

"Oh, that stupid thing, you can't hear it this far back of the house, but I do like the way you handled the situation, the ladder on the balcony is priceless."

Our hands fumbled frantically, tearing at each other's clothes in a frenzied rush. With every piece of fabric discarded, our emotions heightened, and our desires were unleashed. And then, after what felt like an eternity of enthusiastic exploration, we lay spent and fulfilled on the rumpled sheets, basking in the aftermath of our intense encounter. The air was thick with the smell of sweat and desire as we caught our breath and reveled in the raw connection between us. It was a moment that would be etched into our memories forever, a recklessness born out of youthful passion and unbridled desire.

"Are you okay?" He asked, lost for anything worthwhile to says. "Yes, never better," she replies. Suddenly fraught with shyness.

"I can't believe this happened," He said, but then it was what he wanted, what they wanted, "I feel like a little boy who's just done something wrong." "I do too," she said, "a little bad girl." And they both laid in silence staring into the ceiling when she jumped up and rushed into the bathroom muttering from the other side of the door, "You've got to get dressed!" she said, "I'll drive you home."

"Is something wrong, did I offend you in anyway?"

"No, just get dressed, everything's fine, it's just that I haven't spent the night with a man in a long time, I feel self-conscious about breaking my solitude."

David noticed how Wadie's hand instinctively reached for her face, fingers touching the bare skin where makeup should have been. She spoke softly, almost apologetically, about her appearance that evening without the aid of beauty products. He couldn't help but feel a twinge of guilt for seeing her in this vulnerable state.

As they grew closer, they opened up about their pasts. David learned that Wadie had always admired beautiful people and things, and saw aging as a vulgar and undesirable process. Growing up, she was the "pretty one" among her three sisters who had all gone on to pursue higher education and successful careers. But Wadie had chosen to focus on maintaining her looks, using Maybelline foundation to create a flawless facade.

In sharing their memories, they discovered that Wadie's oldest sister Mrs. Williams (whom David remembered as the yard teacher at his elementary school in Berkeley) had been her favorite. It was a small world, and through these connections they found comfort and understanding in each other's pasts.

Life has a strange way of following you around, always reminding you of its presence; even though sometimes playful, often cruel, but when you come to learn that its reaction to you is your reaction to it, you find a soothing point that makes life less a chore.

As flamboyant as she was, she was quite content in the lesser role of homemaker, Wadie even expressed how she enjoyed it even more now that he was around, she delighted in her simulated wifely duties. If his visits extended into more than a day, she would prepare elaborate meals that complimented morning, noon, and night, ensuring never to repeat the same dish. Her need for out-of-house socializing was simpler than he had expected; she went to the grocery store, church, and an occasional funeral; [church and funerals] provided the evocation for snappy dressing with older black women; with her it was always a flashing debut when she attended these events.

Her last husband Walter, who hadn't died a physical death like the other three, was her fourth. Though all the others were what you had considered men of the trades, Walter was a slick city councilman in Sacramento. After discovering he was a philanderer, and a fake, they were divorced after his botched attempt at taking out a mortgage on her home. He was the kink in the ebb and flow of ended marriages.

As a compliment to what she had accustomed herself, David began taking an interest in areas of the home that were in disrepair. he painted, re- landscaped the front yard with plants and flowers he had collected on long walks in the mountainside. Remodeled various areas inside the house, kept the Cadillac clean and was like a loving husband. Her friends adored him, and this made her proud, more committed to their relationship, the opinion of her friends was important to her.

In a fleeting moment, the perfection he saw in their relationship began to crumble, giving way to old insecurities and manipulative tendencies. These traits that he had worked hard to overcome suddenly reemerged, threatening to sabotage the love and peace he had found. It was almost as if there were two sides of him at war, one wanting love and the other always focused on money and its impact on his relationships. No matter how much his partner loved him, this issue would always be a barrier between them, causing constant conflict and doubt.

David knew how much she favored drinking without thinking she might be alcoholic. He attempted to match her drinking prowess, a futile undertaking which only fortified his own drinking problems which caused him to release all inhibitions, through which, he became abusive and then he would blackout waking some hours later feeling deep chasms of guilt and remorse for a situation he had no memory.

They would break-up and he would return to the house where Susan lived and then after sobering would find that he wanted Wadie more than ever, they would make-up and then everything would repeat itself again and again. Little by little the relationship wilted from misguided passion into a simple friendship. David started back using drugs, crack cocaine which was brought on when he drank. The relationship with Wadie was strong but he was a fool to think he could outdrink a woman who spent all her waking hours with a cocktail in hand and then at night right before bed scoop the ice cubes from the glass and leave the remaining potion in the refrigerator until morning when she'd refreshen and start again.

Wadie was losing respect for him as quickly as he was losing respect for himself. She did like being with a younger handsome man and of course the sex always overruled any sensibility. The drugs changed him into a monster who cared about nothing but drugs and where he could get the next high and he didn't know what to do except try and fuel this desire. David was new to cocaine, a late starter compared to all his old friends who had rotted in a cesspool of drug addiction and trying as best they could to pull him in with them.

On one occasion when David was spending time at the crack house in North Richmond, he spent all his money and began craving more than ever. He got a cab to Wadie's, but she was not home. He asked the cab driver to wait while he went into the house, and he did by entering an open side window. he scratched around the house looking for money but couldn't find any and so he left the house through the front door just as Wadie pulled into the driveway. He ran to the cab and left thinking she hadn't seen him.

David had sobered up and had been home for the last several days following the incident at Wadie's when there was a knock at the door. It was David and his son Maurice at home when David opened the door and saw two men in suits standing there.

"Morning, can I help you?" David asked.

"Are you David Parker?" one of the men asked. "Yes, what can I do for you?"

"David, do you know Mrs Amar?"

"Yes, I do she is my girlfriend when are not breaking up, what is this all about?"

"We have a warrant for your arrest." The officer said matter-of-factly. "A warrant for my arrest, I don't understand, a warrant for what and what does Wadie Amar have to do with this?"

"We are arresting you for first-degree burglary." Maurice was standing behind David clutching his leg, scared as to what was happening to his father. As the officer started putting him in handcuffs, he could hear Maurice behind him.

"Leave my dad alone!" Maurice shouts.

And as he was put into the back seat of the car, he could see Maurice in tears and him in shame, wondering more about what the neighbors might be thinking.

The next day he was arraigned in Contra Costa County Court. The judge bound David over for a preliminary hearing to determine if there is enough evidence to go to trial.

The courtroom was buzzing with anticipation as Wadie took the stand, giving a small knowing smile to David before she began her testimony. But David's heart sank as he watched her unfold a sheet of paper, a list of stolen items that he knew nothing about. She confidently read off each item, an extensive list that seemed never-ending. As she finished and calmly explained how she had reported these items to the insurance company, David's mind raced with realization - he was not only being falsely accused, but also a victim of an elaborate insurance fraud scheme. This was all part of Wadie's plan, she just needed one more thing - a conviction. And now, as he sat in disbelief, it seemed like she might just get it.

David spent his time on the Contra Costa County Farm, where he started attending drug rehab and awaiting his trial. He even called Wadie who kindly accepted his collect calls. Every few weeks or so he would be shuffled to court to hear a plea deal that the state was trying to achieve but his attorney told him:

"Sit tight, this will all be over soon, and you will be released, they don't have a case, and the evidence is in your favor."

The thought of sitting in jail longer was driving him insane. This was his first time as an adult being locked away like this and though he was not sentenced yet he still found it disturbing just to be inside. At that moment, his attorney and the prosecutor had a side bar and then she returned to David:

"The prosecutor has offered you time served if you plead guilty today, but I say no because in time they will dismiss this case, which is why they have gone so low in the terms." Said my attorney.

"So, if I plead guilty today, I can leave today, I can go home today is that what the deal is?" He asked.

"Yes, but you should understand that if you plead guilty to this you will have a felony conviction on your record and that will not look good in the future."

"But I can go home today?" He asked again and then he accepted the deal.

Upon his release he went straight to Wadie's house, and never mentioned a word about what had taken place between them. She got what she needed, and he got what he thought he wanted but, in his haste, to be released he failed to consider the future implications, this was only the beginning of an eroding life.

Chapter 18

Search for Self

David was not beginning a journey through life; his journey had already begun long before he knew it. Suddenly—at the tender age of 30—he realized that a very subtle relationship between his mother and father occurred. Also, there was a relationship between himself and his stepfather, between himself and women, and then himself and God; these are some things he had found along the way.

His son Maurice continued to grow taller by the week, and though he was aware, his son was not as inclined as he had hoped. He didn't let it become a marker between their friendship. Having a child does not cause love to exist magically; love develops when a friendship forms between two people over time, which also does not guarantee that you will come to like each other. Maurice and David were friends, but Maurice and Susan loved each other, and so he accepted his failure as a father and remained a father under the auspice that in time he would come to see that David loved him both as a son and a friend.

David's cocaine habit erupted again, disrupting his personal life beyond repair, and so when Maurice was just seventeen, it was 1996, he decided to leave the house completely decided it was time to find himself and make sense of this life he was wasting. David had no idea what this would entail; he had become so accustomed to living in a relationship with someone and the thought of going it alone frightened him, yet somehow, he knew he couldn't remain in this paralyzed state of existence with Susan any longer.

It was a day in nineteen-ninety-six, but the sun's rays were soft and gentle as they fell upon his face. He walked out of the house, determination flashing in his eyes as he claimed the open world as his new home. With no solid plan in mind, only the clothes on his back to accompany him, he set off towards a familiar recycling center on Gilman Street in Berkeley.

Susan had always been fanatical about recycling, her passion for saving aluminum cans filling their garage to overflowing. David used to feel embarrassed accompanying her to the recycling center to cash them in, but now those memories flooded back with bittersweet nostalgia. He couldn't deny making a good sum of money from those cans though. As he walked, he couldn't help but notice the countless homeless individuals hauling their own loads of cans, glass bottles, and plastic containers. It was this peculiar sight that pulled him towards the center, a strong compulsion pulsing through his veins.

Despite his tireless efforts and determination, he ultimately succumbed to the temptations of drugs and alcohol, cutting short his dream of becoming a broker in San Francisco. He had worked tirelessly for this opportunity at McLaughlin Piven & Vogel, the prestigious bond trading company that he had admired. But after only a month on the job, the allure of cocaine proved too strong, and he was defeated in the battle for his dream career. The fast-paced city life and constant pressure to succeed had taken its toll on him, leaving him broken and defeated in the end.

To David, the other underlying fragments that had chipped away from the mould, those pieces of self, left him feeling incomplete, robbed him of the totality of life, and set in motion the forthcoming events.

He awakened early after a restless night of adjusting to the primitive conditions of outdoor living. What appeared natural to most homeless people was a crude form of self-denial and conditioning. And though the longing for conventional comforts became a monumental desire, where once it was a given, now a pleasant memory.

The morning sun had taken its post, casting a warm and golden glow over the bustling city streets. The awakening of life translated into a new energy, a sub-dialect within the same context of everyday routines. David felt like a fish out of water, his entire existence stripped down to its very core and now being reshaped to fit into this new society into which he was thrust.

As he made his way through the busy streets, the metallic sounds of shopping carts clanging echoed in his ears, a jarring reminder of the consumer-driven culture that surrounded him. It was a world that he found hideous and loathsome, filled with unnecessary waste and garbage heaps that seemed to pile up on every corner.

But he knew he had to adapt, to blend in and become just another face in the crowd. Like everyone else, he took his cue and rose with the rest of the people, preparing for another day of assimilation. As he walked, he couldn't help but notice the run-down areas where people were no longer seen as individuals but rather an arm of some greater entity. Where drug addiction offered temporary relief from the harsh realities of life and cries for justice fell on deaf ears.

Yet even in this dark landscape, there were glimpses of hope and resilience. The system may not be perfect, but it still offers a safety net for those who need it most. And perhaps someday, with enough perseverance and determination, things could change for the better.

David's eyes scanned his reflection in the grimy storefront window, taking note of every crease and wrinkle that marked him as a tired, aging man. He couldn't escape the feeling that he was a soldier in an endless battle against time, his clothes serving as a uniform of exhaustion and decay. Disgust rose in his throat at his own pitiful image, but he had no time to dwell on it - he had to focus on maintaining appearances for now.

This façade was necessary to blend in with the sea of wandering individuals, all searching for their next fix. David's addiction was not the problem; it was merely a temporary relief from the unknown disease that consumed him.

Amidst this bleak existence, David found solace in Ernie, a former civil servant who had fallen into homelessness and addiction. Ernie took David under his wing, teaching him the ways of recycling to survive on the streets.

Under his guidance, David learned the routes and customs needed to avoid drawing attention from angry residents who despised the presence of homeless people rummaging through their recycling bins on garbage day. With Ernie's help, David adopted the role of scavenger as both a means of survival and a form of rebellion against society's rejection of those like them. He took up his shopping cart and followed the same daily route outlined by Ernie. It was a tour of duty that would take some five-hours to complete and yield upwards of fifty to sixty dollars, with this David would buy food and other items to cure the pain and in time he expanded his route, coming in with his cart so full it looked like a pack mule, and the pay increased to a hundred dollars and more.

In time he befriended those recyclers who drove trucks, exchanging his knowledge and labor for a ride in their trucks and with this the route was further expanded and the income increased to where he was making up to eight-hundred dollars a month. His nights were restless ones and so he worked at night and played during the day and on this one occasion, he encountered the police.

"What cha doin' son?" asked a local police officer who had been patrolling the area.

"Getting bottles and cans, sir," he replied.

"I can see that; you got any ID?" and with that he pulled out his wallet and handed him a driver's license.

The police officer called in for wants and warrants, there were none, and then asked," Where do you live?"

"Up the street, on Masonic," he said. Still using the address of the house where he and Susan once shared.

"What the hell are you doing out here this time of night with a shopping cart if your homes around the corner, you on drugs or something?"

"No sir, just making some extra change." He lied.

"Well, we don't like people roaming through the town at night, gives people the wrong impression, if you know what I mean, so finish and don't be seen out here tomorrow night." He spoke.

"Yes sir, you won't." and he felt relieved feeling his first encounter with what he called the anti-homeless association.

When the cart was draped in bags filled with recyclables, and almost impossible to push he headed in, but he didn't stop there instead he unloaded and headed to Berkeley where he knew the local law was more tolerable of the homeless and there, he filled the cart again and then called it a night. In the morning, Ernie was surprised to see that David had amassed so much, which caused him to decide to take the day off and rely on his resources. He didn't mind, as it was my way of expressing gratitude to Ernie.

This became David's habit of walking and work at night and scouting for more during the day. In time he rented U-Haul trucks and hired other addicts to work the area's he had mapped out, he had quite a system going and before long had employed between ten and twenty people, from the small area of West Oakland they called (Dog Town) where David had found a recycling center that catered to the homeless, no questions asked.

In a year's time, David had earned close to a hundred-thousand dollars, which would have seemed impossible for a homeless man, and for once he felt alive again. But the money was short lived, he spent it on expenses, salaries, food, accommodations, and drugs. Being homeless proved to be more expensive because the money had no discernible boundaries.

As the days passed, David found himself increasingly drawn to daydreams of his past. He fixated on what he called "cold cases," unresolved moments in time that still haunted him. In the solitude of his thoughts, he replayed these events over and over, searching for solutions that always seemed just out of reach. It was as if he were rearranging puzzle pieces in his mind, desperately trying to make sense of the chaos and disorder that had consumed him in those moments. And in these quiet moments, he couldn't help but wonder how things would be different if he were to see those people again - the ones who had played a role in those pivotal moments of his life. He imagined finding a way to make amends, to right the wrongs of the past and find peace within himself. But deep down, he knew that some things could never be fixed, no matter how hard he tried.

With homelessness came other aspects of the 'underworld', the continuous confrontation with the law. And so, David starting amassing multiple arrests for petty crimes like trespassing, entering abandoned buildings, possessing stolen property, and driving with a suspended license. Soon, a sentence of ten days, turned into thirty, then thirty into ninety, ninety turned into six months, and then the big ONE year: twice, two times in a row. He luckily was allowed by the court to spend both of those years serving time in the Salvation Army Adult Rehabilitation Center for drug and alcohol abuse.

David tried as best he could to make use of what the Oakland ARC program was trying to give him, but it was during a time when his drug addiction had taken a hold on him in that crucial time when he didn't understand what was happening and the implications to come. He wanted far away from the maladaptive life he was living, but it was only something he told himself over and over with no change to support his desire for change.

David was running out of time, salvaging the remaining shreds of pre- mid-life was closing in on him, he was now entering his early forties with nothing tangible to show for his years of living; except a son, but even leaving him a legacy would be a joke in terms of pride for a father who contributed little or nothing to the world.

It was a quiet Sunday afternoon in the desolate streets of Oakland. As David rode with a friend, they stumbled upon a horrifying sight - a crowd gathered around a man brandishing a metal pipe at a woman on the ground. She begged and screamed for mercy, but the man's threats only grew louder and more violent. Suddenly, David felt an urge to intervene in this domestic dispute, not knowing if the two were lovers or strangers. He had to make it stop; he had to save her from the wrath of this madman. In the next moment David grabbed a piece of metal from the back of the pickup. With the piece of metal clutched tightly in his hand, David approached the man cautiously. He could see the woman cowering on the ground, shaking, and crying. As he got closer, the man turned and snarled "Back off!

This doesn't concern you David!" David stood his ground. "Please, let her go. Violence isn't the answer." He kept his voice calm but firm. The man laughed derisively. "You think you can stop me, motherfucker?" He swung the pipe menacingly. The woman screamed. David took a deep breath. He had to end this, now. In a flash, he swung his makeshift weapon, connecting sharply with the man's neck. The pipe clattered to the ground as the man howled in pain and rage. David positioned himself between the assailant and the woman. "Leave. Now." The man spat curses but backed away, clutching his injured hand. David watched him until he disappeared down the street.

Her name was Pam, a tall slender Black woman, with the close-cut haircut of a man. She had huge buck teeth, not pretty at all, but had a smile. He unknowingly befriended this woman Pamela; was a year older than he, an addict who saw no future beyond the present situation. Pam followed David everywhere he went, and helped with everything he did, it was her way of ensuring he would take care of her and her addiction and in return she took care of him.

The life of a homeless man had become an exhausting, monotonous cycle for David. He longed to return to the comfortable normalcy of his previous life, but he knew that simply returning making no changes would not lead him in the right direction. Pam, his companion on the streets, was becoming more of an addiction than the drugs they shared. Despite multiple attempts to seek help together, they always fell back into their destructive habits. David realized that the only way to save himself and break free from this downward spiral would be to distance himself as far as possible from Pam and their toxic relationship. Every time he looked at her, he could see the familiar glimmer of longing in her eyes, and it broke his heart to know that he couldn't save them both. But he also knew that he needed to prioritize his own well-being before it was too late. The streets, once filled with excitement and adventure, now felt suffocating and suffused with a constant sense of danger. David yearned for a fresh start and a chance at redemption - anything to escape the constant grip of desperation and despair that engulfed him every day.

It was 2002, and David, like most criminals seeking a better life, wanted to make one last score on his way out the door. He had taken a couple of guys on a mission to steal a commercial generator from a construction site; it was to be his last escapade before hanging up the life.

The evening of the planned theft at the construction site, David had warned Pam,

"Pam, I don't want you with me tonight it is too risky and if we get caught, I'm afraid I can't help you out of this one, it's too serious based on the amount the generator costs, so please just stay away from me for a bit."

There had been occasions when David and Pam had broken into construction sites and locked containers on construction sites. They had also broken into scrap metal companies and stolen metal, as well as stolen vehicles and if David was ever caught, he would tell the police,

"Look officer that bitch is just a strung-out crack head who doesn't know the difference between today or yesterday. She had nothing to do with this; this is all on me, so don't waste your time on her." And that was how David protected Pam from going to jail.

Pam didn't want to be away from David because she knew he was her key to the finances needed to buy crack and he was good at providing those funds, better than any other homeless man in the Oakland area who stole or recycled for a life on drugs.

David fought her off with everything he could, short of physical violence. There was no greater way he could stress the severity in what was going to happen this night, but Pam saw this night like every other night, and if she were to allow David to make off with these two guys chances would be that she would lose out on the prize. He finally got rid of her, picked up the two guys who were helping, and off they went to the construction site.

This was a simple piece of work for David,

"Look guys, Clint, you get out and cut the lock on the gate. When I drive in be sure to replace the lock with our lock and lock it from the inside." And clint got out of the truck and fetched the bolt cutters.

"Gene, just drive the truck. Nothing more. Just drive the truck over to that generator with the long pole attached that has those bright lights on it." Gene nodded his head and took another drag on his crack pipe. "Gene! Put that fucking pipe down and concentrate just for a few minutes and this will soon be over, and you smoke till you die."

After Clint cut the lock, David moved in and went straight to the generator where he dismantled the pole that had the lights connected to it.

"Gene, back the truck up slowly to the generator so I can hitch it to the truck." And like that, the generator was hitched, and the gate unlocked again, and they moved the truck into the dark street of Dog Town and secured everything while off the construction site. They drove the generator to Victor's.

Victor was a Jamaican who lived in Emeryville. He was the big guy around there and he bought stolen material related to construction and shipped the items back to his hometown where he was building a large homestead. Victor like David, and always bought what David was selling because he knew David always brought him the best for the money.

When they had finished the work and collected the money, David paid Gene and Clint off and then drove the truck to the back of an abandoned factory where there was tall overgrown grass and plenty of darkness and he sat there and smoked his crack and drank from his bottle of White Port wine. David sat in the shadows of the building, his mind swirling with conflicting emotions. On one hand, he was proud of himself for pulling off another successful score and rewarding himself with drugs and alcohol was his usual way of celebrating. But deep down, he knew this lifestyle was destroying him. He was a sensitive and caring person, but as an addict, he became ruthless and controlling. His relationship with Pam was complicated - she had been in this game longer than him and knew how to manipulate him through their shared addictions. Sometimes it felt like she had a hold on him, like a slave master. David had rescued her from a beating, but in reality, she had just found another person to use for her own gains. As he sat there in the dark, David couldn't help but wonder if this was truly the life he wanted for himself. Deep down, he knew it wasn't, but breaking free seemed impossible.

David's addiction to Pam was all-consuming, more potent than any drug he had ever experienced. He would do anything for her - even resort to using his ingenuity and resourcefulness to supply her with the drugs she craved. But Pam was not solely responsible for David's downward spiral; she was just a small player in the dangerous game they played. Without her, he would have succumbed to death long ago, as surviving on the streets was no easy feat. The constant struggle for food, shelter, and safety was like a never- ending game of survival, and Pam was his only lifeline amidst the chaos.

The night dragged on for David, the darkness surrounding him like a suffocating blanket. He glanced at his watch, noting with desperation that it was nearing 2AM, the cruel hour when liquor sales came to an end. His eyes flicked to the nearly empty bottle of wine, a lifeline that was rapidly disappearing. Without it, he knew he would be consumed by a madness of agony and despair.

As the clock ticked closer to two o'clock, David's sense of urgency grew. He raced to the nearest local liquor store, determined to get his hands on some cigarettes and wine before the alcohol curfew kicked in. When he returned to his truck, he found Pam sitting in the passenger seat. Her appearance was a stark reflection of her self-esteem - low and unkempt. Despite his countless attempts to help her turn her life around, she remained entrenched in her destructive lifestyle. It was as if she couldn't see or didn't want to see the potential for something better. Deep down, she seemed to love the chaos and recklessness more than anything else.

"What the fuck are doing in the truck, Pam, after I told you I didn't want to be bothered with you tonight?" She didn't answer.

"You know Pam, I really hate you. You know I pray to God every day, don't you?" she turned her head and looked at David with sorrow in her eyes.

"Do you know what I pray the most for?" And David waited for an answer from her, but nothing came. "I pray to God each day asking him to take you out of my life." And still no words from Pam.

"I hate this life Pam, I hate the drugs, stealing, living like an animal outside in cardboard boxes and taking care of your ass, I cannot do it no more I want out which means I need to get away from you Pam and I am."

She cried and for once he thought he may have got through to her, but still she was unmoved, and he knew that this couldn't be love. He tried everything to get her out of the truck and then he said,

"You are black and ugly and ever since I've been with you my life has turned into shit. I have been jailed a dozen times, my driver's license is suspended, my family can't stand me around them because they are afraid, I am going to rob them blind. I eat from the garbage bins, sleep in mud and water if it rains, in cardboard boxes, or just out in abandoned cars or trucks and to top it off I hate you so much I wish you were out of my life so I could return to a normal life." The words spat from David's mouth like venom, each one hitting Pam with a sharp sting. She could feel the weight of them, heavy and suffocating in the confined space of the truck.

The air was thick with tension and desperation as they sat parked in the liquor store parking lot. Outside, the world was dark, wet and silent, a stark contrast to the turmoil brewing between them.

Pam remained motionless, her body stiffened in fear and shame. She couldn't bring herself to speak up or defend herself against David's cruel accusations. With each passing moment, she felt smaller and more insignificant.

David's frustration boiled over, his hands gripping the steering wheel with white-knuckled intensity. He knew he had lost this battle - no amount of pleading or yelling would make Pam leave the safety of the truck. In defeat, he put the vehicle in gear and drove back to his spot - an abandoned building off Wood Street in West Oakland.

As they pulled into the empty lot, surrounded by darkness and decay, David's mind raced with thoughts of how his life had spiraled out of control since being with Pam, even before Pam. He expertly maneuvered the truck off the street and into the field pregnant with overgrown grass and weeds. He eased the truck towards the loading dock attached to the back of the building. It provided a sense of safety and security hidden away from prying eyes. But even here, in this secluded spot, David couldn't escape the weight of his toxic relationship with Pam.

Even though the building sat in a dark spot, from that darkness you could see the few lights that illuminated the adjoining freeway some hundred feet away. It was his plan to sleep there in the truck and begin working in the morning. As he pulled up, with the front of the truck facing the loading dock, in the lights of the truck, Pam saw what she thought was sitting on the loading dock. Through their association and the work, he did with scrap metal, she knew they were onto something valuable, and in her greed, she became entranced and left the truck for a closer look.

"Let's get it now. Load the metal in the truck." She ordered anxiously. "Tomorrow, it's late," he said and took another sip of his wine.

"No, now, before someone sees it," and like an insistent child, she begged. "I will not load that metal up tonight. It is dark; I already have money and everything else I need. Look here, just take this money and go buy you some crack and leave me alone. I am not in the mood to do this tonight." But Pam didn't want the money. She kept insisting they get the metal that lie in the dark on the loading dock of the abandoned building. David grew tired of her whining and figured the only way to shut her up so he could relax in peace was to give in, and so he pulled the truck backwards and turned so the tail end was facing the dock.

"Move out of the way Pam!" he yelled as he looked over his shoulder, but she didn't respond, instead she just stood there staring at the crates of brass on the loading dock.

"Move the fuck out of the way," he yelled louder and when she didn't move, he put his foot on the brake thinking the glow of the brake lights would signal her and then he put the truck into reverse and when he did that the truck shot backwards at full speed. Frantically he kept mashing on the brakes, harder and harder, but the truck would not stop until it came to a full stop on its own after hitting the loading dock.

Part of him knew something wrong had happened, and another part of him thought it was just a dream. Despite being caught between two uncertainties, he reacted and pulled the truck forward, got out, and walked to the rear. He didn't want to see what he knew was there, but he needed to handle the situation.

There she lay like a baby, in a fatal position, and his heart sank to the ground. A feeling he had never experienced before in his life - a feeling of fear, terror, and hurt overcame him. He lifted her like a baby into his arms and, yet placed her on the passenger seat. Like a madman, as fast as he could, he drove towards Merritt Hospital, which was the closest. He had no mobile phone and with no one else around to help; he did all he could for her on his own. With her on the seat next to him, he drove through the chain-linked fence which led out onto the open motorway and from there proceeded up West Grand Avenue, shaking her every moment and saying,

"Hold on baby, hold on baby, we'll be there soon. I'm driving to the hospital. Just hold on." Comforting her with all his power proved to be a waste of time, but he kept shaking her to ensure she stayed conscious. However, he could only hear muffled breathing coming from her, as if blood had filled her throat and she was fighting for air. He looked at her frail, limp body, and thought of all the horrible things he had just said to her earlier, how he so much wanted them both to move into a better life and if not together then alone for this was becoming a more dead-end than ever, but he didn't want it to end this way, and then a light from one of the street lamps shone on them and he could see more clearly the extent of her injuries, the skin on the right side of her face was peeled back, exposing teeth and jawbone. David continued shaking her and with what seemed hours was only seconds and in the last moment, as he approached the hospital emergency section the last shake only produced an ending gasp of air and the sound of teeth clacking together. It was over.

At the emergency section of the hospital, David blew the horn wildly to get someone's attention and then someone came out and in seconds a team rushed out to the truck and took Pam on a gurney, and a nurse returned to him minutes later.

"I'm sorry, but she is DOA dead-on-arrival." Those were the last words he heard before he went into some kind of silent panic, a shock of some sort. The nurse was speaking, but he could hear no words. He looked at his clothing, and for the first time, noticed he was covered in blood. And so, he walked, going nowhere in particular. He left his truck in front of the Emergency.

That rarefied moment had lifted him into a world of gut-wrenching guilt and soul-crushing remorse. He stumbled away from the hospital in a daze, his mind trapped in a zombie-like trance. Abandoning his truck, he couldn't bear to drive it with the reminder of her blood smeared across the seats like grotesque paint. It had become a cursed hearse to him, only useful for carrying the dead - which it had already done. The reality of her death hit him like a freight train, shattering his thoughts and leaving him reeling in confusion. All the times he had wished for God to take her out of his life now felt like sickening lies, as the weight of his emotional baggage grew heavier with every step. Surrounded by stone walls that seemed to mock his half-life existence, he was consumed by a suffocating grey mist that drowned out all but two emotions: rage and fear. His senses dulled and numbed. He felt doomed to an eternity of futile damnation, just like Sisyphus endlessly pushing his damnable rock up the mountainside.

A block or two from the hospital, in the frost of an evening chill, David removed his blood-stained clothing and walked back to their camp in his boxers and tee shirt back to the little camp under the freeway. Under the repairs of the Cypress freeway damaged in the earthquake of 1989, they had lived in a makeshift cardboard shack. In the scant light of night, among the detritus of many months of foraging, he sat. All the uneven surfaces of life couldn't have prepared him for this ride; he was in shock and didn't know it. No mood-altering substance could be strong enough to dissipate the emotional torture chamber he had descended. From a bucket of greying water, he scrubbed the layers of that day from his skin. Each dousing of the cloth left the water darker until the stars in the sky reflected in the black murky water in the bucket.

Chapter 19

Pamela the Homeless Girl and San Quentin

Pam had been a wife and girlfriend in several abusive relationships. A simple woman and a simple indeed person, so she eluded people into believing. It was her mechanism.

Her first and only certified marriage began in Pittsburg, California, a community of varied ethnic backgrounds, but most certainly a culture of addicts, alcoholics, and criminals. It was where the lowest of Blacks and whites, living together like animals in a zoo. After migrating from Mississippi and landing in Pittsburg, her husband quickly became part of the neighborhood and developed a crack addiction and ensnared his wife, Pam, in the same addiction, exploiting her as a prostitute to get money and more crack. He would beat her, sell her, and use her in every immoral act known to man. He had broken her down.

When David had met Pam, she had been divorced for ten years and into a reflected relationship that mirrored what she had become accustomed to, at this stage in her life she had been so conditioned to the routine that when with David, she found happiness even though she didn't know it. Pam was in love for the first time, tasted the sweetness that came with a kind hand, but in time his hate for the life he was living, combined with the love of the life she was living, made life an abomination.

Though he couldn't make understood the fact intimate love between them couldn't exist, he still gave her a template by which she could use to learn to love herself, the one element that stood between her life and misery.

David had seen enough human suffering to evoke in himself a daily systematic internal search of values. Out of chaos, order would come about, and in certain cases of human suffering order came through death, the Devine edict.

Three days after Pam's death, David felt a great tugging at his soul, a force drawing him towards the purity of absolution. He rose from his resting spot in the camp they once shared, feeling resurrected from a necropolis of undead, and walked into the Oakland police station and poured out my heart; he didn't want to fight this matter. At first, the police were not aware of what he was talking about. It had only been a matter of hours since this had happened. So, they told him that there was nothing they could do and so the police handed him back his driver's license and wished him well.

David walked solemnly out of the police station; the weight of Pam's death was still heavy on his shoulders. Though he had confessed, it brought him little peace. The police may not have understood, but he knew the truth - he was responsible for her death. The image of her face, twisted in fear torn into pieces as if someone had taken a sledgehammer and beat her in the face, haunted him. He didn't love Pam; their relationship was a more symbiotic process developed out of a twisted need to co-exist in a cruel, heartless culture disguised as homelessness.

David had taken her life. And David knew he could never undo that split- second moment that changed everything. All he could do now was try to make things right, though he believed he hardly deserved any forgiveness. With hands in his pockets, David made his way down the busy Oakland streets, back to the world he had been in for almost ten years. The surrounding city of Oakland was pulsing with life while he felt nothing but death inside. He didn't know where he was going, only that he had to keep moving forward even if he didn't know how or why. The gravity of what he had done would forever mark his soul. But David hoped that maybe, just maybe, things would sort themselves out.

As he walked, every police car frightened him. Even though he tried turning himself in, deep down inside he didn't want to accept the possibility he may go to Prison for a long time. He worried what the charges would be, murder, manslaughter, first-degree, second all these things kept running through his mind and so he went inside and hid at a friend's house.

He knocked on the door of Pat, a woman who David knew well, Bicycle Pat. They called her that because she always rode a bicycle. The door opened and unlike Pat she answered with a frown.

"Hi David, I heard what happened. That is so sad about Pam." She looked at him cautiously and stood at the door. "Tell me the real story David, what happened?"

"That is what happened, besides what are you trying to say, Pat?" "That you ran her over with the truck." And she invited him in.

David explained what had happened, and they sat and chatted for a while. "David, I don't mean to be fucked-up, but I am worried that the police will come around and if they catch me with you they might think I'm part of this and Lord knows I don't want to spend even one day in jail, so please I need you to go until this matter gets settled, you understand don't you? Plus, we all smoke around here. That looks bad."

David found his place on the streets again among old friends who looked at him differently now. So, he was determined not to make any new friends nor talk with those he already knew. He reached deep into each of his pockets and hastily pulled out a couple of single dollar bills, mindfully forgetting that his cash supply had run low days before. There wasn't enough to get smokes or a wine, so he walked the back streets of West Oakland until the sun dropped below the horizon, which was just on the other side of a string of railroad cars waiting patiently to be put back in use. As he walked he came across a familiar shopping cart, not familiar in terms of being recognizable as one he had used before, but detectable enough to know what it's value was and tonight that was to retrieve items to trade for money, and so with it he started to recycle.

David rummaged through trash cans and dumpsters, filling the shopping cart with empty bottles and cans. The clinking of glass and aluminum was a familiar sound that took him back to simpler times. He remembered when he was new to the streets, how he marveled at the resourcefulness of scavenging for cast-offs that could be exchanged for a few dollars. Now it felt rote, just something he did to get by.

As David made his way down the alley, the cart bumping over cracked pavement behind him, he spotted a grocery bag next to an overflowing dumpster. Inside were untouched packages of ground beef, only a day past their sell-by date. His mouth watered at the thought of cooking up a real meal instead of subsisting on handouts and scraps. The meat would fetch a good price or could be bartered. He tossed it in the cart, ready to push his haul to the recycling center, when he heard a faint noise, the sound of a woman crying and so he followed the sound until he was upon the road that led to where Pamela suffered that tragic accident, it was only then that David knew he was only dreaming, but as he walked closer to the scene of the accident he stopped long enough to view a pile of discarded items that had been illegally dumped, and as he bent down to pick up a shiny object, a police car came to a full stop alongside him, the sight of which cause him to jump to attention with hands raised in the air and he shouted,

"IT'S ME YOU'RE LOOKING FOR, I KILLED HER."

The two officers conferred with each other then got out of the car,

"Hold on a second there, what are you talking about, we stopped you because we thought you were dumping illegally."

"No officer, I am not dumping anything, I am collecting things to recycle, but when I saw you I thought you were out looking for me to arrest as I am the guy who killed that woman the other day."

"We haven't a fucking clue what you are talking about, but stand there while we call someone."

And in a matter of minutes the area was swarming with cops.

David stood bewildered as more police cars arrived on the scene. The officers surrounded him, demanding answers about this supposed confession. Finally, a tall, imposing man in a suit emerged from an unmarked car. He flashed his badge at David before barking out, "You have the right to remain silent..."

The sound of Miranda rights being recited in his ear sent David into a panic. He started to protest, "No, no, you don't understand! It was an accident! There must be some mistake," David stammered. "I don't know anything about a woman being killed. I was just looking through the dumped trash, trying to find things to reuse or recycle."

The Homicide Detective stepped forward, eyeing David suspiciously. "Then why did you confess to killing someone when the two police officers pulled up? Explain yourself!"

David shook his head, confused. "I... I don't know. It just came out. I think I was remembering a dream..." His voice trailed off as he tried to make sense of it all.

The Detective grabbed David's arm. "You're coming down to the station with us until we get this sorted out. Something's not adding up here."

David didn't resist as the officers cuffed him and led him to the back of a car.

"Sir," the tall man said, cutting him off, "We just want you to come with us downtown for some questions."

In the police station David was escorted to one of the interrogation rooms where he sat for what seemed hours until the same Detective came in and started to question him, but this time David said, "I am not answering any questions until I get a lawyer, I know how you Okland Police are you get a person to talk and next thing you know you're charged with murder."

"Fine have it your way, but I tell you know I am charging you with Vehicular Manslaughter and that carries a sentence of fifteen years." They escorted David to a cell and held him overnight, for court in the morning.

The courts presented him with a lesser charge on arraignment because he was already on felony probation, despite being charged with vehicular manslaughter. The courts didn't waste time with a trial, all they had to do was violate his probation and send him to prison, and that is what they did. The court sentenced David to two years in prison, and his first stop on this journey would be San Quentin. But before going to San Quentin, he stayed in Santa Rita jail for three weeks.

During his free life, life outside of bars and prisons, he had traveled the same forty-mile bus ride many times, and each time, the moving landscape transformed into frames, creating a serene experience. The sky was clear, not a cloud to be seen, a day he would have appreciated if he were free. Though there was calm, there was also anxiety. The unknown elements of a sadistic world would now become his temporary abode, or permanent one, depending on the reception.

Throughout his years of homelessness, many male acquaintances had been at one time a prisoner at San Quentin. Most of them were still on parole. Often, stories shared depicted the intriguing subculture and how subjugation was its primary role in survival, both in and out of prison. As a form of penal anthropology, the subject was quite fascinating to David, only now he would become part of his own study in curiosity. Be careful what you wish for.

The prison bus maintained a steady and unwavering pace as it continued to move along. Passing along the outskirts of Richmond, where David's immediate family would rest in that city. He had left there in 1973 to join the Air Force. He remembered wanting to get away from a life he thought imposed too much order. With each step of his wanting to get away from too much order, he fell deeper into greater order, order was seeking him.

He could see the San Rafael Bridge up ahead, and the skyline of San Francisco. The water was murky and choppy below the San Rafael bridge. David wondered to himself *'how can someone jump from a bridge and kill themselves?'*

He thought about Mr. Parker; his stepfather, who for years David had despised and bore shame because of the man's color and lack of education; a not so flamboyant person whose only primary concern was the welfare of his family. It was weird how his stepfather and he had been at odds for so many years, yet in his closing moments on earth, Mr. Parker, David's stepfather wanted him as his caretaker in place of his own blood children. He knew his children would be around, but David he felt sorry for. After David's mother died, he came to him and said,

"David, here's a couple of hundred bucks, it's not all, just something to get you over for a while. Your mother said I should take care of you."

He knew David had transitioned to the life of a bum and homeless person; he knew because David admitted to him that he was an addict. One day they were sitting out in the backyard talking about the repulsiveness of drug addicts:

"I can't stand those fucking addicts, living off everyone stealing and wasting life." His stepfather William said to him.

"Dad, I'm an addict." He said matter-of-factly. For once, he was not ashamed to confess his sins.

"I was the one whole stole mom's TV. I climbed in the window when no one was home, I needed money to buy crack, crack will make you do almost anything dad to get it so I am going to ask a favor of you, if I ever come by and ask you for money, it won't be a lot maybe twenty or thirty dollars, give it to me because if you don't and this not a threat, I will figure out a way to steal from you and that might cost you more."

"Why didn't you tell me this before I could-a got you help?" William said to him.

"You could-a got me help; you are the reason I'm like this." And at that moment he was the reason for all his problems. David didn't know where else to lay the blame. And so, after William suffered a severe stroke, leaving him in need of constant companionship, he chose David for the job. David was Williams last companion so that he may give and receive the knowledge of love's true intent, a man of morality and ethics, a man of which David would now die for if only he could receive a modicum of his stepfather's character.

In his solitary seat on the prison bus, the chains became such a senseless achievement. The stolen scrap metal that supported an ugly drug habit that kept him prisoner was now a reminder of the extension of metal links that held him restrained.

From a small rectangular window, webbed by pieces of quarter-inch flat bar to preserve the integrity of encapsulation; he caught a view of a medieval fortress that seemed out of place in this millennium; it was San Quentin.

As the bus approached the imposing gates of San Quentin, David felt his stomach tighten. He had heard countless stories about the harsh conditions inside, the rival gangs, the brutal guards. He took a deep breath, steeling himself for whatever lay ahead. The bus eased to a stop at one of several checkpoints; it was there an armed guard checked the manifest against its cargo to make sure it matched. The bus then moved forward about a hundred feet and eased to another stop inside a caged bullpen over a mechanics pit where another awaiting officer checked the underlying section of the bus's hull for incoming contraband. This execution of duties was more than professional, it was amazing how routine could be so flawlessly orchestrated. After all the checks a guard stepped on, and David filed out with the other new inmates. They were lined up, shackled, and led inside to begin processing. The heavy metal doors slammed shut behind them with an ominous clang that reverberated through David's bones. This was it - his new reality. As they were marched down the cell block, David kept his eyes forward, careful not to make eye contact. He had to seem tough, indifferent. Inside, his mind was racing. How would he survive here? Could he stay under the radar, or would he have to choose a side? Join a gang for protection? The uncertainty ate at him. But he couldn't show fear.

After the initial induction and issuance of kits, the likes of which comprised a blanket, set of sheets, pair of towels, soap, toothpaste and brush, comb, and a cup, all of which fitted neatly into a brown paper grocery bag, David had stripped his life to this.

In the last stages of seeing the outside world before entering through the metal doors leading into what looked like a large medieval castle, David noticed in the distance several hundred inmates lumbering about in small herds. It was easy to see that each of several herds (groups) were self-contained within their own ethnicity. The sea of bright orange prison issued clothing was blinding, the groups almost appeared as a single organism.

The day's processing of inmates from Alameda County totalled thirty- five; and there were still buses to come from: Contra Costa, Santa Clara, San Mateo, San Francisco, Calaveras, Napa, Solano, Sacramento, Humboldt, and several other counties that made up Northern California, the flow of flesh seemed endless and new human warehouses were in the working. San Quentin itself was a small city with its own zip code; it had a maximum capacity of three-thousand and if necessary, they would start stacking bodies to maximize space.

Upon arrival, David was housed where every new or returning inmate was housed, West Block. West Block was one of four huge warehouses whose inner tomb was hollow and in the middle extending several-hundred-yards a monolithic block of concrete divided in half by theory only and on each side five tiers with fifty cells on each tier and two men in each cell for one-thousand inmates per block, this was, David thought, where the term [cellblock] came from.

The noise was staggering, a decibel level that drowned all thought. They assigned David a cell on the second tier, and the steps leading there started at the bottom. This design induced shock as he walked past successive cells. Depending on a person's level of perception and intellect, the initial shock would either intensify or reduce to a familiarity of acceptable terms. At the first cell, the thought of a human kennel came to his mind, and in walking deeper, the breeds showed a visible contrast. The odor of testosterone filled the air in a sickening vapor; one-by-one, a cell emerged and within the cells cold hardened bodies forged from penitentiary steel. The gladiators, each dressed in a pair of white boxer shorts, had bodies stencilled with the hieroglyphics of each gang's Magna Carta.

"Yo, homie, who you ridin wit?" asked a brown-skinned youth who may have been in his twenties with a definitive Latin drawl.

"I beg your pardon," David replied, and the tone of his voice answered the question. He was nobody.

All eyes inspected the new guy (David) with deference, looking for telltale signs and markings that would identify his gang affiliation, but there were none. He was a (first termer), a new booty, as they called him, fresh meat, a guy who had never been to prison before.

During classification, they asked you to identify the ethnic group you belonged to, and he claimed [Other] after receiving advice from a seasoned inmate. (Other) was a neutral classification of no affiliation. As a result, they placed him in a cell with a man of the same classification. The cell was small, and its size was shown to him by his new cellmate, Diaz, when Diaz stretched his arms to both walls to show its width and paced off nine steps to show its length. There were two beds and at the rear of the cell was a sink, toilet, and some shelving. Two men would have to take turns walking about, otherwise they would compromise the afforded space.

The inmate spent twenty-three hours per day in the cell, dividing the other hour between the time to go to and from the chow hall for breakfast and dinner. During breakfast, the staff served lunches in a bag. Once a week for an hour, there was yard time. Yard time was where one-thousand men crowded into a space the size of a little league ball field. In the yard, shirtless men lifted (iron) or weights while admiring each other's tattoos. Gang members held board meetings and shot callers, distributed assignments and death wishes. The yard was a place where people traded drugs and currency and settled disputes, he be likened unto Parliament.

The inmates segregated the communal areas by race, huddled together in what seemed like victorious moments, and hugged old friends while offering canteen items as a start or sort of advance until they received monetary support from those on the outside. The convicts enjoyed these cherished moments until they zapped all the money from their supporters.

This was a society dominated by sheer violence, and segregated racial groups, yet there was a moment in the day, always the same hour, at ten o'clock in the evening where chaos became order. Each night at the same hour, each ethnic group paid respect to the other groups through a chant. Each group repeated the chant until the last group finished, enveloping the tomb in a deafening silence and completing the day.

Chapter 20

Release from Prison

Of his two-year prison sentence, David served only 8 months. Unlike what you see in movies where guys do time and get more time added on, this was not the case with him. Quite the contrary. The prison system is not just a place where they house criminals, but also people who have committed crimes. People do things based on many situations. Sometimes it just comes down to plain survival. Though he had been a long-term client of the legal system, David was an infant in terms of State Prison. Most crimes, whether felony or misdemeanor, fall just below the two-year sentence needed to be upgraded from county jail to state prison. David got that upgrade in 2002.

Eight months after entering the prison system, David's time was finally up. He was eagerly looking forward to being released from Pleasant Valley State Prison, California where he spent his time as a low level-1 inmate. Upon release, prisoners receive what they call: [Gate Money]. This gate money has always equated to $200. In his excited and impulsive mind, he didn't see this prison sentence as a lesson and though he was sorry about the way he had gotten there, the awful painful taking of another life, even accidental. No, instead he was more interested in getting back on those streets and resuming his status in the world of homelessness, drugs and scrap metal. He was still an addict who hadn't learned how to be clean.

The day the prison announced he was being released was the happiest day of many happy days like this. To return to West Oakland, his turf, his spot where he could pick up a shopping cart and start living life on his own terms was all he could think about, his mind was salivating. But things had changed while he was in Prison, something very different was going on and so when he arrived at the checkout point at the prison, he received information that the Immigration and Naturalization Service INS had placed a hold on him, and despite going through all the normal processes for anyone being released from prison, this agency trumped all else.

David remembered the interview when he had first arrived at San Quentin by INS, and though they assured him this was all just formality and that nothing would ever come of it, he still believed that promise would come true that day when he was released from state prison. However, he was mistaken and, once again, the fool.

David sat in a holding cell at the prison waiting to be taken into custody by the INS and some hours later; they showed up, handcuffed him, and threw him into the back of a windowless van. He felt like he was continuing his criminal journey to its farthest links.

During his first stop in Fresno, California, where the local INS office was located, the authorities fingerprinted him, took a DNA swab, and performed a facial and retinal scan, and informed him they were starting the process of removing him from the United States. David was put in a holding cell along with dozens of illegal immigrants awaiting deportation, only he was not an illegal immigrant he was a documented Resident Alien who held a Green Card.

David had been in the US Air Force, studied at the University of California at Berkeley, was a father, and spent 48 years of his life believing he was as much a US Citizen as anyone. His mother had married an American, which was how he and she both ended up emigrating to America from Bermuda. And though David knew he was Bermudian, he also along with that believed himself to be American, it was all he ever knew and now that citizenship was being threatened over a minor technicality.

There was so much secrecy. This clandestine journey orchestrated by the American Government was above belief. He couldn't understand how this was happening to him. The American Government orchestrated a clandestine journey, whereby US Marshals flew him from Fresno to Oakland, California, and he was detained at the Oakland Police Department, which had a section for housing Federal Detainees.

David found himself surrounded by a sea of people who were going through the same situation as he, but each for different reasons. These people came from all over the world, but mostly from Mexico. People were fighting deportation. Somehow you had to agree to be removed from the US or have exhausted all legal recourse that no other avenue was open for you. It was said that David committed a crime which sent him to State Prison and that anyone with his immigration status who went to State Prison had his right to live in the US revoked; they called his crimes those of Moral Turpitude. David spent days on end in the law library of the Kern County Sheriff's Department County Jail in Bakersfield, which was another place he stayed from time to time. There was this constant moving from place to place in an effort to disorient and confuse, to wear down the subject until finally he would give in and sign the papers to be removed.

After weeks of studying the law books and looking for a glint of hope, he realized that six months had passed, and he was going nowhere.

They wore him down by moving him to new locations until he finally gave in and asked to be removed from the United States. An Immigration Judge signed the order in a court in San Francisco. David waited another week for a passport, and then they issued him a passport that read The United Kingdom of Great Britain and Northern Ireland. They put him on Continental airlines to New York unescorted, and then in New York he was picked up by more agents and escorted to another jet to Bermuda.

Chapter 21

Deported to Bermuda

A strange revelation to know that he would no longer have any physical contact on American soil. Everything gained, achieved, or owned had been stripped from him. No legal leg to stand on. His tenure in America was only waiting to be disposed of or waiting to be used in a more positive manner. He would like to think the latter was true.

While on his flight from New York to Bermuda, he started thinking about how much less of a punishment this was going to be. Bermuda was beautiful, warm, friendly, and sophisticated in terms of government and finance. People lived very well there and perhaps now it was time for him to give up a life of debauchery in trade for a life of clean living in paradise. Exile suddenly had a sweet taste.

The immigration processing in Bermuda lasted about an hour and then he moved through customs with nothing to declare except a brown paper bag containing paperwork and useless receipts documenting his penal history in America. Looking at it reminded him of all the unnecessary vacancies in his life, but when outside the airport in Bermuda, all the contempt and loathing he felt over the past twenty-years evaporated when he collided head on with a beauty so magnificent.

From the tiny air terminal, he walked to a bus stop he had last remembered twenty years before; there, the background completing the small seascape captured the essence of serenity.

Though this moment in his life was an uncertainty; somewhere in there was a hope for something good.

When David got outside of the airport, he could feel the warmth of the surrounding air. There was a breeze, a whisper, and it felt so oceanic. Everywhere blue dominated the scenery; making it difficult to differentiate where the ocean divided the expanse of sky. A feeling crawled up inside of him as if he were being taken over by another spirit, a refueling that would help carry the journey further. A lot of things had changed in twenty years, which was the last time he had visited Bermuda. the skycaps [baggage handlers] were liveried; the airport itself had undergone a massive transformation, all from that one point standing at the airport felt as if modern technology had transformed the island; even the people were less subservient and had taken on a more ruggedly crisp demeanor; America felt as if she had taken over Bermuda, too.

He climbed aboard one of the many pink buses marked for Hamilton. There were only two directions from this point: Hamilton or St. George's and his destination was Bailey's Bay, toward Hamilton, the island's major city. David exited the bus at the Perfume factory in Baileys Bay, intending to begin his journey where he had left off as a child many years before.

The tiny triangular lot where a small one-bedroom house once stood home to thirteen adults and children was now extinct, evolution had sprouted several larger homes with magnificent landscaping, it was a tableau of interesting articulation, an artistic movement of delicate lines and pastel shading transmogrified into something vulgar.

Also, there once was an old pink house atop the hill, through a small field across from the triangular lot where his mother's sister, his aunt Nell and her five children once lived. It, too, had vanished; replaced by a large condominium complex which now absorbed the magic that once was home. David had a great grandmother who also lived in that pink house atop the hill. What had happened was they somehow spilt the big house into two smaller apartments. It was a rural farm life there with Nell and her children and Tony her Portugues husband, as well as David's nana and her two adult children, his aunt Doris and Uncle Murray. Murray was very much a drinker who lived inside a bottle after working long hard days. Most of the men lived in a bottle after work and on weekends, it was a life filled with drunks, but people didn't see it that way.

From the look at this new resurrection, poverty had been transformed into prosperity. The remaining shreds of his architecture, in retrospect, had always been women; they had survived in and of men, but never with them. The women of his family were the strong shepherds who tended the flocks made of children and the weakened men who used alcohol to eschew responsibility. Not that they were worthless souls, the men, for they had tried each day of their lives to reach a level whereby Ianthe, David's grandmother, would exert some friendly recognition for their efforts, yet she couldn't as if to do so would weaken further what little effort the men were already exerting. The object was not to reward incompetence, even though incompetence was the highest level achieved. If she were to flatter them, the ignorant would interpret the praise as a sign to stop striving and not pursue further aspirations. It was a unique form of emasculation, of retaining the feminine hierarchy.

Men overcompensate the lack of intelligence with violence, women with cunning.

Ianthe, David's grandmother, was a woman who had survived the indiscretions of the man she loved. She had been a victim of his infidelity, and through this tragic twisted love affair she survived, but in her mind, and through this painful ordeal she claimed a different fulfillment through Christ. Interpreting Christ was used to suit the believer, and she used it as a weapon to reinforce her position as a matriarch. Christ was a tool whereby she used as a weapon of promoting guilt and it was through guilt that she inspired submissiveness, the one ace that kept her position tenable.

Most of my old friends—those who I last remembered—had a worn-out look about their faces, an unnatural rapid-aging process brought on by what he would come to learn as years of alcohol and drug abuse, the very things he had left behind in America. The likes of which made him happy to not have fallen too deep into the pit. These old friends survived the abuses of life, the fatigue showed most clearly. Aside from the physical changes, everyone remained the same. They lived in a perpetual state of immaturity, grown no further than when David last saw them.

It was as if everyone had been caught in a time warp, frozen in the same location where he had left them; no one had progressed, not even David. He had taken the long way around to get back to the same location from where he started. But he had brought with him a variety of changes that were beneficial; education, some sophistication, and the life skills most Bermudians lacked.

After a couple of beers at the Baileys Bay Cricket Club, someone who recognized David told him he would find his cousins Cindy and Marty cleaning fish over at the old dock where David's mother had thrown him off to teach him how to swim. David took the short walk and there he found them, as well as several other old acquaintances of whose names he had forgotten. The reconnection wasn't thrilling, but it surpassed what he had expected.

Cindy and Marty were two of David's cousins. They were the children of his aunt Nell. They were a few years younger than him. The last he remembered, Cindy was a teenager, but she now appeared an old woman with hardened skin, and the wrinkles of many worrying thoughts, there as a crudeness about her; the likes of someone who had lived a hard life. There she was, swilling a cold bottle of Heineken beer.

David's aunt Nell's five children differed from him, and the only similarity they shared was their mixed Black/Portuguese blood. However, in this case, their father Tony stayed and married their mother Nell, but the outcome of their upbringing was nothing to be proud of. They behaved like children in adult bodies.

When the fish they caught were all cleaned and filleted, and the sweat had dried on the empty bottles of beer, they gathered everything and drove to his aunt Nell's. David's aunt Nell, or just Nell as they all called her, was happy to see David and despite his situation vowed to help him in any way she could. She gave him a room in her house and showed as equal a love between him and her own children.

"Aunt Nell I promise I will have a job in a couple of weeks, and I will pay you for putting me up."

"Don't you give it a thought because you have always been good to me, never caused me any trouble, not like the others and besides you are my sister's son, you are family."

And in two weeks, he secured a job with a steel company at $20/hour; an amount that he had never achieved in America. The rent at his aunts

$400/month plus expenses and with the residual he bought new clothes, books and his first ever computer, a laptop and begun a savings plan, life was feeling worthwhile again for David, he felt as if he had reached a point of independence without the drugs.

Every Saturday he'd catch a ferry to Dock Yard, a West End community that reminded him of Sausalito in Marin. The serenity in Dock yard offered him a greater clarity into his life. This moment he was living was a pivotal aspect of his new future, though he knew it was far from absolute.

"Can anyone really know themselves?" this was something David thought about often. The puzzling aspect of self was not so much the ability to calculate with clairvoyance, but a gentle knowledge of thoughts, responses and emotional behaviors, a simple matter of paying attention to one's inner truth. Surprisingly, each day turned out to be a beautiful day, not only of climate, but a universal beauty radiated from within. David was happy to be here.

There was always a matter of correspondence. The Saturday mornings he spent in Dock Yard allowed him to write out a few postcards which he sent to friends and family back in the States. He thought that by sending these postcards people wouldn't think his exile was desolate and isolated, so to impress upon those back in the States less familiar with the island; he used photo interpretation as a way of conveying an emotional image that everything in his life was all right.

These innocent moments began speaking of an excessive tranquility, a less harsh term than boredom, yet he was not prepared to give up his little sanctuary and so he began including alcohol. He started buying a couple cans of Budweiser along with the postcards combining the two into one activity, but at the time he hadn't realized that the alcohol was serving as a gateway to other left behind temptations, cocaine, but he resisted as long as he could. Back at the family homestead also lived another two of his cousins— Patrick and Antonio who both were addicted to crack cocaine and alcohol— both of whom were bringing their drug behaviors to David's attention, the likes of which was pressuring him into memories of his days addicted to drugs and so he thought the only way to save himself was to leave his aunt's house. David felt the pressure growing stronger, bending him as if he were a brittle piece of metal. He was growing weaker to his cousin's advances, so he decided he would try to leave Bermuda and head for a place that was like the US. He chose Canada.

The steel company where he worked in Bermuda was called The Mid Atlantic Steel Services, in St. George's. Though the job was a good place to be, it soon was exerting pressure on him because of his cousin's constant reminder of drug addiction back in the States. He was now beginning to feel as if he were in a prison as the world of the old was closing in on him.

One Friday after work, David caught a bus to the airport and bought a round-trip ticket to Toronto. He needed a round-trip ticket in order to look legitimate, but in reality, David was not planning to return. He was thinking of trying to make his way from Toronto to Vancouver and into Washington State and back to California. The next day on Saturday, he asked his aunt:

"Aunt Nell, would you drive me to the airport?"

"The airport. Where are you going? Why didn't you say anything about leaving?" He could see the tears in her eyes as she spoke. "You don't have to leave. I love having you here. You have been a blessing since the first day you arrived."

The emotions swelled inside him. He should have taken her love for him as a sign that he needed to stay, but he had to think of himself first.

"Aunt Nell, I love you and I'm grateful for all the help you have given me, but to be honest Patrick and Antonio—(Snooky and Babes)—as they were known are getting on my nerves with the drinking and you know what else, I know you aren't stupid to what's happening, well I need to be away from that else I am doomed to return myself so I am going to go to Canada and make a life there, so please I need to get to the airport soon."

That afternoon he boarded Air Canada armed with everything he owned in a suitcase, along with several thousand in US currency. The flight was pleasant, lunch the whole bit. Then, when the plane landed and he approached the immigration kiosk, a delicate woman in her uniform asked,

"May I see your boarding pass and immigration form?" The lady looked at the form suspiciously, she spoke again:

"Hello Mr Parker, first time in Canada?"

"Yes, thought I'd come and see what Canada was like."

"I see here in your declaration form you haven't listed an address where you'll be staying. Do you have an address, Mr Parker?"

"I don't, thought I might get a room outside the airport; you know, a motel or something like that." He replied.

"Mr Parker, I am sorry, but you can't just enter the country without an address, we have to know where you are so that we can prevent people from just entering the country and staying without permission, I'm afraid I will need you to take a seat until one of the other officers sees you." And so, she handed him back his declaration form. She had drawn a line with a purple sharpie from one corner to the other of his form and in that moment, he knew something terrible was about to happen.

David sat for an hour until a man carrying a large file folder in his arms showed up and asked David to follow him.

"Have a seat Mr Parker, I have a few questions to ask of which I would like you to reply either yes or no and the sooner we get this over with, the sooner you can get out of here."

David knew he was not going anywhere. They never put you through anything like this and then just let you go. This was the beginning of something worse to come.

"Mr Parker, because you didn't present an address where you'd be staying while here in Canada a red flag went up which prompted us to look further into your identity and we have received more information relating to your criminal background, do you understand what I am saying?" He only nodded in confirmation. "I am going to read out loud the offenses you have been convicted of in the US and in return, I want you to answer yes or no if these apply to you."

"Don't bother asking, let's just get to the next part, I am answering yes to everything, all the crimes you have in that file is me and you know it's me and even if there was some doubt you are going to believe it's me anyway so let's just get this over with so I can know what is going to happen next to me."

"We cannot allow you to enter Canada, Mr Parker, not with your criminal history and also the fact you have been deported from America." David looked at the file and then to the officer, "So this is what's going to happen, you will be deported from Canada and put on the next flight back to Bermuda, do you understand what I am saying to you Mr Parker?"

And with that, they escorted David to a holding facility outside of the airport and placed him in a cell. The next morning, they handcuffed him and escorted him back to the airport. They put him on a plane for Bermuda and he arrived that Sunday afternoon. David felt as if he had just come back from a long holiday.

He sat outside the airport in Bermuda with the sun beaming down on his face, with a bottle of Heineken in his hand. He thought about how lucky he was that he hadn't quit his job, so come Monday he will just continue as if nothing had changed.

He called his aunt Nell. "Aunt Nell it's me, David."

"Well, how is Canada? Are you making out alright?"

"I'm not in Canada, I'm at the airport in Bermuda, I never got out of the airport in Canada, well that's not true I went outside the airport in handcuffs to be locked in a cell till the next day and then put back on the plane and so here I am, can you come get me?"

Chapter 22

Starting Over in Bermuda

The steel company David was working for was an excellent company and the pay was higher than any salary he had received in America and here he was throwing it all away by trying to escape to Canada. He was lucky he hadn't formally quit, and that he had made it back before Monday.

David still had the problem with his cousins, though, and he had reached his breaking point. This setback with Canada made him feel he would be stuck in Bermuda, on 20 miles of sand and rock, forever. When he got back to his aunt's house, everyone was sitting out on the porch. Not that they were waiting for him, but what else do a bunch of people do on a Sunday in Bermuda? David got out of the car and all he could hear was laughter and.

"What happened, bro? That was a quick trip." Said his cousin Marty.

"Change your mind?" laughed Antonella. But the strangest thing was his other two cousins, Snooky and Babes were smoking cigarettes and drinking beer sitting there as if nothing had happened.

"Glad to see you back bro," said Babes and with that David called him aside to whisper into his ear,

"Let's go get high." David pulled out a roll of bills and showed him and, just like that, they were off to the crack house.

David had used the moment of defeat as a moment rewarded by self- destruction. He had no clue why he was acting this way or why he had given in to this temptation. His mind just cleared a path for him. David didn't know it that giving in would at least get this familiar feeling out of his system so that he could get back on his path, a path he didn't even know anything about.

Babes and David spent all day Sunday in Warwick at what they called the Purple House, it was a meeting house for all drug deals and crack addicts, David must have spent all his money and found himself back to zero again and so with his tail tucked between his legs he walked the ten miles back to his aunt's house where he lived. He didn't even have enough money for a taxi; he had depleted his entire savings, and he was feeling like shit. The only thing he had in his favor was his job.

"I will start over fresh tomorrow." He told himself. David took a seat out on the porch. It was midnight; he felt both stupid and ashamed. His aunt came out onto the porch. She looked right at him and all he could do was lower his head and look into his lap.

"You let them get you, didn't you?" she said, and all he could do was look up at her. "You knew this would happen, you told yourself that this was why you wanted to leave Bermuda before all this fell into your lap and now, I bet you don't have a penny to your name, what about work tomorrow what are you gonna do?" He couldn't say much. She got up and walked into the house and then returned and handed him a wad of bills. He started crying, for she had saved him without him even asking.

That Monday David talked to his boss.

David's boss Craig was a small man standing some five feet four inches. Craig was about the same age as David older. It was hard to tell his age without asking as; he had the youthful features of a young teenager and David thought it rude to ask. Craig wore glasses and used the word (fuck) a lot and he always wore the same baseball cap, which was frayed and worn along the edges. He always had a smile on his face, which made it easy to approach him. David never looked at Craig as a boss, but since he was Portuguese, David thought of his own father being Portuguese, and then Craig and their connection became friendly.

"Craig, can I speak to you? I need help in the worse way?" "Of course, my boy. What's on your mind? FUCK spit it out."

"Well, Craig I have been living with my aunt since I came back to Bermuda, and I love it there, but I have two cousins who live there who are on drugs and they are always asking me for money, I need to get out and was wondering if you knew of any place I could rent?"

"Fuck, you are lucky. I have a one-bedroom apartment over in the boatyard." David's face formed a smile.

"I'll take it!" the words sprayed from his mouth.

"I haven't told you anything about it yet." Said Craig.

"It doesn't matter, whatever, I'll take it. How much is the rent?"

"Well, look here my boy, the rent is $800, but I won't charge you a deposit. And then the phone that is in there you can use and not pay the bill as it really is my phone, also the electric comes with the place, all you need is your own cable for TV, how does that sound."

"When can I move in?"

The St. George's boat yard was another business David's boss Craig owned. Craig preferred the boatyard work to the steel company work and so he left the steel business to be run by his wife Donna. The boatyard and the steel company were located only feet apart, making for the perfect situation and conditions.

And like that, he was on his feet, on his own for the first time in 48 years, except for being in the Air Force but that didn't count according to David because it was a free situation provided by the government, this was something he would have to work and take care of.

David hadn't a clue about living on his own and paying his own bills. The entire process frightened him. He realized now how dependent he had become on females in his life and why he was constantly seeking one relationship to replace another.

A sense of defeat came over him after returning from Canada. He realized he was never going to America again. And that he had to live out the rest of his life on a twenty square mile island or find another country to live. The more he thought about this, the closer he was to giving in again and returning to his same old habits. It was his nature to self-destruct when things didn't go in his favor.

Chapter 23

First Ever Place Alone and Lynda Milligan-Whyte

The new apartment was his first attempt at living alone. He was forty-eight and the excitement of his own place made him happy. David had come to a point that he had sought most of his adult life, and now he was feeling like a kid all over again.

Although the apartment was at the far end of the boatyard, which was cluttered with boats and other nautical fragments shrouded by colored tarpaulins, David found a sense of comfort, especially when he walked out onto to a little beach some five-feet long just a few steps from his front door. The months had passed, summer moved out and winter took its place and rain fell everywhere. The small apartment had a very thin roof and so when the rain pummeled the roof, he could almost count each drop as it hit. David stayed home alone most of the time; he felt safer alone, away from all the negative influences he knew would penetrate his mind and his memory.

One clear Saturday, after weeks of self-imposed confinement, he got dressed in a pair of khaki shorts and a tee-shirt and sandals. He hadn't been out on his usual ferry ride in quite a while and somehow felt a strange compulsion to do it now. It was nearing the close of the tourist season and once again Hamilton would come back alive with its own native people.

Sales were being offered by the local shops and a tiny bookstore across the street from the ferry terminal struck his fancy and so he walked there and purchased a dictionary and the book "The Art of War."

With the books in hand, he made his way to the ferry terminal and boarded the fast ferry to Dock yard. On the upper mezzanine of the boat, where seats were exposed to the open air and sun, he took a seat behind a handsome black couple who seemed to enjoy the end of the season as well. Already he had consumed a couple of small cans of Budweiser beer, so he was feeling quite sociable. David liked to drink because he believed it made him more sociable. He wanted to be what he thought people enjoyed about him.

"Isn't this beautiful? I feel so lucky to be a part of this beauty not as a visitor but as a native." He spoke aloud to no one in particular.

"That it is," replied the woman in front of him. "Are you visiting?" she asked.

"No, like I said I am enjoying this not as a visitor but as a Bermudian. I live here. I'm most grateful to be in a place in this world where beauty is not a tiresome exaggeration or cliché." And with that, she turned to look at him.

This woman was not beautiful, she was attractive in a confident way. Her skin was dark, and her hair was long and coarse, with sprinkles of silver dazzling in the sunlight. Had it not been for a perm she might have got away with having good hair, but David knew the difference from growing up around his female family members. Her smile was fragrant, and when she talked, it was not just the voice of a feminine black woman, but more of a person who was above articulation. She sounded intelligent, like she knew everything she was saying.

"What about you two? Where are you visiting from?" He asked as the ferry moved through the restrictive speed zone of the harbor.

"I'm Bermudian as well," she said. "My friend here, John, is visiting from Boston." And John turned to face David, and they shook hands. They all exchanged names, John and David, but the woman only kept her eyes fixed on David. He found it most exciting to be looked at by her. The ferry ride from Hamilton to Dockyard was quick, only lasting some fifteen-minutes, so there was not time to have a proper conversation. As the ferry lined up next to the dock at the terminal in Dock yard, slowing just enough to allow further words between her and David, she said,

"If you ever need an attorney, look me up. My name is Lynda Milligan- Whyte." And she had said that with tremendous pride, as if she were showing off.

"Is that all one word... Milliganwhyte?" He asked.

"No, it's hyphenated Milligan-Whyte." And the ferrymen roped the boat to the dock, and they all went their separate ways. David walked into Clock Tower Mall to a teller machine and withdrew two-hundred dollars even though he didn't need it. Somehow, the feeling of having access to money he had so often squandered made him feel whole again. David purchased several postcards and stamps as usual, two more cans of Budweiser and, with thoughts of the woman he just met, he sat with a smile on his face under the verdure of several palm trees.

David finished the beers and, as expected, his thoughts started wandering. It always started that way, a drink or two, and he suddenly became this creative genius, as if he could take on anything, be anyone, and do with his life whatever he wanted. But not once did he tell himself that it was the alcohol causing this illusion? Instead, he felt as if he were embarking on an important self-discovery that was separate from the booze. David knew it was strange, welcoming an inner voice, but that reflective voice always said what he wanted to hear. As was customary, the slight euphoria caused his thoughts to leave the present moment. In this state of mind, he could travel and visit old friends with a better understanding of what he wanted to let them know. One postcard he found to be more beautiful than the others and so he turned it over and wrote:

Dear Wadie:

In the long years that mark what we call time, I feel sadness in its distance. I often wish that I could have changed the way things were, and yet in some small way I have, only this was not the change I was looking for. I wish you were here with me and that it was us who were writing these cards to some of our envious friends. Take care and know I love you.

David

The last punctuation mark brought on a litany of memories encompassing Wadie and him. People always said: 'leave the past where it is,' but he liked to think those who adhere to such a rigid affirmation are only speaking of the unpleasant terms their past held. Why shouldn't he feel normal in his past? It is a part of him, a collection of building blocks that shape his identity.

Dock Yard was like a tiny Monte Carlo to David; it was nice in its small grandness. There was the Clock Tower Mall constructed from the same material that San Quentin was built from. David associated the two buildings in likeness. Inside were various shops with interesting contrasts. They reminded him of the manifold personalities that had escaped the mundane by allowing everyone freedom of expression. Everything reminded David of something. Like Berkeley, he found a connectedness to this melting pot. As a small boy, Berkeley was the one place where everyone was a piece of the mosaic. He liked that. Also in Dock Yard was a small harbor that sheltered a flotilla of luxury yachts. Opposite was a large berth that accommodated large cruise ships. There were several tugboats and two of the island's largest ferries, the Bermudian and the Coralita, all of which gave Dock Yard its nautical ambience. It was as if you were looking into a child's mind when you experienced what David saw in everything.

If he could but allow himself the discipline that would enable him to enjoy such splendors without useless distractions, he would remain happy in a peaceful sort of way. He couldn't understand why he had to include liquor, its fine for a moment, but it soon produces an anxiety of which he was never aware, and it left him craving cocaine and then the anxiety turns into depression. His attempts to be free of this demon were futile. There was a weakness of which he couldn't understand, therefore unable to confront. It was something beyond a simple anatomical frailty, and it was the mixing of this inner complexity, this elusive partnership which reminded him of who he was.

As his visit in Dock Yard ended, he took the long road back to Hamilton by bus instead of the usual ferry. The winding drive into Hamilton, along the coastal road with stunning views of the ocean, was a longer route, but he hoped it would give him enough time to clear his mind and sober up. Surrounded by the salty sea air and the gentle hum of the engine, David felt himself gradually coming back to reality. When he finally reached Hamilton, he transferred to another bus that would take him on to St. Georges. As they passed through the quaint town of Baileys Bay, where he had spent his childhood in 1956, memories flooded back to him. He remembered the vibrant community full of boisterous people who had welcomed him with open arms. But now, as he looked out at the familiar streets, he couldn't help but feel a twinge of sadness. Most of his friends from back then were gone, taken too soon by AIDS or trapped behind bars because of drug addictions. The once lively streets were now lined with dilapidated buildings and vacant lots, reminders of the struggles faced by this community. Despite this, Bailey's Bay still held its charm and beauty - with its famous Swizzle Inn, now quieter than before, and the Perfume factory which had long since closed down. And, of course, there were the Crystal Caves surrounded by lush greenery. David also remembered Coney Island; a small islet connected by a rickety bridge that was now a sanctuary for birds. As he continued on his journey without stopping in Baileys Bay, David couldn't help but wonder if things could have turned out differently if he had stayed in this picturesque parish. But he knew that stopping there would only lead him back to old habits - something he was desperately trying to move away from.

Lynda Milligan-Whyte, the beautiful woman he met on the ferry earlier that day, was heavier on his mind than drugs or alcohol. When the bus stopped in St. George's, he went into the little grocery store near his apartment and purchased several bottles of soda pop and water. Once back at the apartment, he scoured the phone book for her address as she had instructed him to, and there in the yellow pages he found it, complete with website.

David opened his laptop, searched the web address, and read the site with enthusiasm and found her life exciting. She had served as a Senator in Bermuda, had begun her career as a teacher, had degrees in history, law and English, totaling eleven years of post-graduate work and now she was the senior partner in a corporate law firm, it was the first time he had done his 'homework on a woman.' After reading her bio he sat lost in her picture, conjuring many ideas about the woman while trying to remain calm.

He searched his mind for the past, and somewhere lost between the memories of many relationships he had had, was a critical missing element: compatibility. Thinking about this woman, he saw a quality that he hadn't seen in others, or at least had cared not to see and saw that he had substituted qualities in his other relationships for the simplexes of sexuality, the SUPERFICAL. In the past he failed to incorporate the elements that he should've thought would make for a good foundation, rather he placed no emphasis at all on a woman's innate ability to rise above her physical attributes, he had found them somewhat insignificant and now he sees that the shallowness of himself was a way of covering up his own insignificance, how could he demand qualities he himself didn't possess?

David opened his e-mail to a blank page. And on his left was a dictionary and thesaurus. He was determined to write an introduction that was not suggestive or intimidating. He wanted the right elements that would make for an above proper introduction, and so he began:

Dear Lynda Milligan-Whyte:

Though you had said, on the ferry this afternoon, that if I needed an attorney, look you up, I have. At this moment in my life, I don't require legal advice or legal mumbo jumbo, but I had hoped that behind this armor of jurisprudence, there might be a woman who could benefit from a friend or a spiritual counterpart, and if you are interested, maybe we could have dinner to satisfy any curiosities.

*I enjoyed my day; especially the ferry ride and you,
and I should also thank you for bringing something
beautiful into my life.*

David

For the rest of that day and all of Sunday, he stayed home, ready to reply to her message, but there was none. And like him, he panicked as he did whenever he encountered any kind of rejection. Anytime something monumental entered his life, red flags would go up. It was part of his insecurity, though everyone says they couldn't see it. That evening his panic calmed down, and he returned to the safety of his empty life, *'nothing ventured, nothing gained,'* he thought. All weekend he waited for a reply, but none ever came and so as always, he thought the worse even before he had the answer.

The next day, he convinced he was convinced that Lynda and he would never have a future together. And so, he went to work as usual, with no further expectations. He started working as usual. Gene, his supervisor, and he began work earlier than the owners and then David saw Donna, Craig's wife:

"Morning Donna, you have a good weekend?"

"Great weekend, and you David, anything nice happen over the weekend?" she asked in her general upbeat tone. David couldn't stand.

Donna was Craig's wife. An American who had an annoying way of imitating the accent Bermudians have. She was an attractive woman who towered over her husband, Craig. David had often wondered how their sex life was; he was so tiny, and she was always bitchy.

"Oh, David, you had a dozen messages from Lynda Milligan-Whyte. New girlfriend?"

Donna said, and he rushed to a phone and dialed the number Lynda had left.

"Hello, can I speak with Lynda please?"

"This is Lynda. How can I help you?" She asked in a professional tone. "This is David returning your call. I emailed you over the weekend, but I never got a reply, so I thought you weren't interested."

"You never left your cell number so I couldn't call you, and I didn't know where you worked so I spent hours just going through the phone book looking for a metal company, you said you worked for a steel company then I came across this one, M.A.S.S. is it, the name of the company where you work I called and left several messages, I guess I didn't realize the place isn't open on the weekend, shows how desperate I was to get a hold of you." And before anything could be said, "Do you have a cell phone?"

"I don't have a cell phone." David replied.

"You must get a cell phone, nothing like a blackberry."

"Would you like to meet for dinner here in St. George's?" David asked. "Why don't I call you later from my landline, and I promise to get a cell phone as soon as I can, but here, take this number down and we can talk later."

Somehow his email kept kicking back the message, which was why he hadn't heard from her and all along he thought she was not interested. She called him that night.

"Would you like to meet for dinner tonight?" She asked.

"Not tonight. I would like to get to know you a little better." Was his dumbest excuse yet. David was a man who had prided himself on securing the affections of a woman and now here was playing his cards close to his chest. There must be some other reason.

"Why can't we meet sooner? Are you waiting to be paid?" She asked. "No, that is crazy. I am definitely not waiting to be paid." He replied, taking offense, but not letting her know, "I just thought that it would be better for both of us not to have to worry about rushing to work the next day," which of course was a lie he told her to cover up the fact that he indeed needed to wait for payday.

David didn't have the luxury of coming and going when he wanted to. He had a job, and he needed every cent of his money to survive and though he knew he was stretching it trying as he was to involve himself with a lady of this much wealth and power, he couldn't help it. He liked her.

"That's ridiculous," she said. "I decide whether I want to get up. It's my law firm and besides, I want to see you now," she insisted.

"Okay, how about tomorrow evening at eight at the White Horse in St.

Georges, I'll meet you there?" He said, and the date was set.

He wanted to see her as well, but he couldn't say with absolute knowledge why money brought about this apprehension. It hadn't been a problem in the past, at least not to this magnitude, and for some strange reason, he was uncomfortable about it.

The next day after work, David went into St. George's to do a little shopping. At least if he didn't have a million dollars, he could try to look like it. After shopping, he walked into the White Horse Restaurant and made the dinner reservations for two; he thought if he went into the restaurant in person, he might better secure a pleasant spot for them on the veranda overlooking the tiny canal. That night, David arrived at the restaurant early to ensure his spot. He then ordered a Heineken to bring on his social side.

Being shy drives him crazy, but at least being shy was better than making a fool out of himself. Now, in that moment, he understood the pattern of alcohol use where he hadn't before.

That night, he seated himself at a small round table that was strategically placed towards the entrance of the restaurant. His heart was racing with nerves as he waited for her arrival. He couldn't help but fiddle with the silverware and glance around at the other diners, trying to distract himself from the anticipation. And then suddenly, she appeared in front of him.

His breath caught in his throat as he took in her appearance. "Wow!" he exclaimed, trying to lighten the tension. "You look absolutely stunning, Ms. Milligan-Whyte."

A smile tugged at the corners of her lips as she replied, "So do you, Mr. Parker." In one swift motion, David stood up and offered his hand to guide her to her seat.

Lynda had been wearing glasses when they first met, but tonight she had opted for green-tinted contacts that gave off an enchanting aura. Her normally brown eyes now gleamed a vibrant emerald color, adding to her already alluring presence. As they chatted over dinner, David learned Lynda was actually four years older than him, placing her age at fifty-four. Despite their age difference, David found himself drawn to her fierce sensuality and youthful energy.

In the past, a first date would have served as an opening for sexual encounters if things went well. But as David looked at Lynda across the table, dressed elegantly yet casually, thoughts of sex didn't even cross his mind. He realized that such vulgar intentions cheapened the genuine connection he felt with this sophisticated and captivating woman before him. Lynda was not a woman to be cheapened by anything or anyone; she exuded grace and refined taste in everything she did.

"Would you care for a pre-dinner libation, my dear?" David's voice was smooth and inviting, his eyes dancing with excitement as he motioned for the waiter to approach their table.

"I think I'll have the steamed mussels," she said, her words rolling off her tongue like notes in a symphony. "And a glass of Pinot Grigio."

David couldn't help but be impressed by her choice of drink. He had been afraid she would order something extravagant and costly, but as he remembered the commercials boasting about this wine, his fears melted away. It had been so long since he had been on a date that even the simplest details, like wine selection, seemed to elude him.

As they waited for their food and drinks to arrive, David found himself captivated by the woman sitting across from him. Her every word was like a song, weaving together a beautiful melody that he could listen to for hours on end. She was easily the most fascinating person he had ever met.

Their dates continued, and she made a conscious effort to introduce him to the finer things in life. As her student, she shared with him the knowledge passed down to her from generations before. Despite living in a male- dominated society with deep-seated chauvinistic ideals, she excelled. Her sharp mind and charming manner far surpassed any man's, yet after years of competing, she found herself yearning for more than just success. A simple moral code mixed with the search for love became the two driving forces that shaped her definition of a fulfilling life.

After two weeks together, she invited David to dine at her home. He assumed this was his chance to finally make love to her. She was a woman accustomed to lavish dinners out, but being with David as the one leading the date proved to be more than just financially taxing - it was draining his credit limit. So, a change of venue to her own home provided a sense of comfort for both of them.

For David, physical intimacy with a woman was his only means of securing their love. In his mind, using sex as a tool was necessary to distract them from all his flaws and shortcomings. Over the years, he had become quite skilled at manipulating women through physical affection.

As a boy, David had no worthy role models other than his stepfather, whose presence he constantly rejected. His mother's lover, James Logan, was the only person whom he truly looked up to and admired, but as David grew older, feelings of resentment festered within him about James Logan. So, he yearned for the strong and assertive qualities of his stepfather, but it took him too long to realize their true value.

During their evenings at home together, Lynda would cook extravagant meals for them to enjoy, but David couldn't help but think that her cooking was still far superior. Even after dinner was finished, they would continue to spend time together playing cards and talking while listening to music. The hours seemed to pass by effortlessly in their company. As the night wore on, David felt conflicted about how the evening would end between them. In the past, he and his dates had always predetermined whether they would sleep together, and so he wondered if Lynda would want him to stay overnight. But in that moment, David didn't want any distractions from their genuine connection. He just wanted everything to be right between them without the pressure of physical intimacy looming over them. And suddenly she stood up and said:

"I'm going to take a shower," and David believed he felt a hint of playful sexuality floating through the words. "See you in the room."

With that, he went to the spare bathroom and showered, making do with some toiletries that were for guests. When he finished, he went into the bedroom; she was still in the shower at this point. He slipped beneath the quilt, now cooled by the flow of the air conditioner. David had expected her to wear something slinky and seductive, but she arrived in bed as if we had been long-time husband and wife.

She emerged from the master bath wearing an oversized t-shirt and flannel pajama bottoms. Her damp hair was pulled up in a messy bun and her face was freshly scrubbed free of makeup. Slipping under the covers, she turned to him with a serene smile.

"I hope you don't mind. I wanted to get comfy," she said.

He shook his head, charmed by this relaxed domestic side of her. As she snuggled into his arms, he caught a whiff of her shampoo - something clean and botanical.

"This is nice," she murmured against his chest.

He had to agree. There was an easy intimacy between them that felt far more meaningful than any late-night rendezvous. As they lay together in the dark, he realized this is what he had been longing for. Not a fleeting thrill, but a deep sense of belonging. With her breathing slowing beside him

Lynda and David's night of passion was both beautiful and tumultuous. As they held each other tightly, they tried to find solace in the connection between their bodies. But as the morning light crept through the windows, David's sudden need to leave filled Lynda with confusion and sadness.

"Why do you have to leave so soon? Don't you want to be with me?" Lynda's voice trembled with hurt and disappointment, but David couldn't bring himself to admit the real reason for his early exit.

"I have some work to catch up on. It's important," he lied, feeling guilty for not being honest with her. But deep down, he knew it was more than just work that made him want to escape back to his own space. Being with her made him painfully aware of his age, his lack of money, and the truth about his deportation and time in prison.

He didn't want to burden her with these truths, but he felt like he was robbing her of the chance to make an informed decision about being with him. The conflict within him grew stronger as he drove away from her house, torn between his desire for her and his fear of revealing his past.

David had always taken the easy way out when it came to handling his problems - drowning them in alcohol and drugs, waiting until his courage returned before attempting to find a solution. This pattern of behavior had become second nature to him, and he saw no reason to change it.

However, after not calling her back that evening and being bombarded with constant calls from her, David's nerves were on edge. Despite this, he refused to answer her calls. In the middle of the night, the phone finally stopped ringing.

The next morning, David rose early and hastily dressed, hoping to slip out of his apartment unnoticed in case she showed up. He called for a taxi to take him to the Baileys Bay Cricket Club. As he rode towards his destination, he couldn't help but notice her car pass by going in the opposite direction towards his apartment. It was as if fate was taunting him. Arriving at the club, David took a deep breath before ordering a drink and making his way out onto the balcony that overlooked the sprawling cricket field. With trembling hands, he dialed her number and waited anxiously for her. As the phone rang, David's pulse quickened. He wasn't sure if she would even answer after the way he had treated her.

"Hello?" Her voice was tentative but had an edge to it.

David paused, suddenly unsure of what to say. "Hey, it's me," he finally managed.

"Oh, so you finally called me back?" The hurt in her voice was palpable. "Listen, I'm sorry about last night. I got scared and handled things badly,"

David said.

"Scared of what?" she asked.

David looked out at the emerald-green cricket field stretching before him. "Of this...us. I really care about you, but this is all new for me."

She was silent for a moment. "It's new for me too," she whispered.

David smiled slightly, hope rising within him. "I know, and I want to do this."

"Hey, where are you?" He asked, knowing that he knew where she was. "In St. Georges, looking for you, I was worried when I hadn't heard from you," she said.

"WHERE ARE YOU?" She demanded. "Bailey's Bay cricket club," he replied.

"Didn't move! I'm on my way." And in a matter of minutes, she pulled into the dirt lined parking lot. David waved at her from the balcony, and then rushed inside to order her favorite wine, and he watched as she made her way up the steps.

"Where have you been?" she asked again. "I've been calling you all night. I guess you were with your other woman." Right then, he took her in his arms and kissed her.

"This is not how a person who loves someone acts, David, you don't just disappear without saying something." How profound that statement was. In the past, always in the past, it had never dawned on him how many unwarranted absences spoke of being unloved. For once, he had accepted the blame for something he had been doing his entire life.

It never occurred to him before that all these silent trips and clandestine movements sang out a deceit that he thought no one would hear, but others could hear it. The absolute sense Lynda made right now was an awakening. When they cleared the air of these unfortunate circumstances, he took her by the hand and started walking towards a small cove on Coney Island (Coney Island was a little islet, like many little islets in Bermuda). It was there, as a child, his mother and the rest of the family picnicked on hot

Saturday afternoons. The beauty and the seclusion surprised Lynda; all her years here in Bermuda, never once had she seen a place so enticing and he was pleased to introduce her to something he knew she might appreciate.

They climbed down a short, rocky path onto a small sandy beach that was only a beach when the tide was low.

"Let's go for a swim," he said.

"I don't have a bathing suit," she laughed.

"We'll go in our underclothes," he said, and they began undressing. "No one will see us. No one ever comes here." And she followed his lead. They swam in each other's arms, and talked, and laughed.

"I have done nothing this spontaneous, ever in my life." She laughed like a child, and it pleased him to know that he could bring a small amount of happiness to someone who had been so accustomed to having to spend money just to have fun.

They caressed each other's body using the sea water as an ointment, delighting himself in the softness of her skin. David felt so alive, so normal, and thrilled to be human; for once, he embraced the simplicity of being human.

They sat upon a patch of sand, drying their bodies using the warmth of the sun. They then dressed and strolled back to her car and headed to her house. These precious moments they shared were always most essential to David. They were the summit of love for him, and for her as well, and though he longed to keep this secret to himself, he knew it would be a matter of time before things all went sour.

Love was a strange indulgence. David could have and enjoy all the rapture that people could receive, but as in life, this opening portion must yield to reality and inhale the other aspects of life that live under love yet lose pieces of its fervor with the movement of time.

David could sense the end of this relationship nearing. As in most of his romantic endeavors, he had reached a level where he could go no higher. Many would choose to believe that there is not stratification where love is involved, yet there is. Love is a series of stages only achieved in one relationship and its stratosphere reached when the relationship ends and transcends the empyrean, beyond the adolescent stages of love, that period when love is at its highest peak based on certain physical and emotional fulfillment, he couldn't transcend. He was trapped in the beginning stages and didn't know how to progress further in the relationship; he could have fought for a richer evolution, but then that would have required more of him, and he hadn't been willing to make those sacrifices and instead kept hidden this selfishness, behind behaviors associated with drugs and alcohol.

Taking his cue, he descended below the level of love he had created. He couldn't end the relationship and couldn't also face bringing to the surface the failures of his life, those aspects that have caused him to fall so far behind. He couldn't see then that he could change all that by starting today what he didn't do yesterday.

David was so caught up in his past and after meeting Lynda, his past had a deeper meaning that he had made it his present and his future.

They were lying in bed one morning after making love and David became distant.

"What is it now? Don't you think we have a wonderful relationship?" She asked in an agitated state, "I'm tired of this emotional rollercoaster you're on, you see me, I never waver, I'm always the same, but you, you float in and out, can't you just be happy with what we have?"

"Lynda, I need to say something to you."

"I knew this was coming," she retorted. She threw back the blankets and grabbed her clothes.

"No honey, it's not that, there's something about me you must know..." and he began crying. He explained to her the truth about his returning to Bermuda, how he had killed Pamela in an accident, and how he ended up in prison and then deported.

"I worried about losing you if you'd ever found out about my situation in the States and so I was trying to buy as much time as I could by not telling you, but I can't take the secrecy anymore, I can't make this choice for you, which is why I have been acting the way I do."

From that moment, he felt a profound sense of relief; it was not just this moment, but many moments before. All his life he had held one secret after another, compounding the few into many, placing upon himself a void filled with empty questions and decisions all put on hold hoping that one day they'd all find a place, and so he overflowed with useless secrets that amounted to a life of lies and it's no wonder why he'd felt so treacherous towards himself.

When the tears had cleared and she'd assured him they'd work through this, he knew then it was over; it had to be over because any revelation brought into a relationship after it started was an admittance of betrayal and he couldn't live believing another human being could give him absolution, life didn't give such things.

Their lives continued as if nothing had changed, but something had changed, and its impact was being felt daily. It was in the behavior, the movements, and the apprehension. The easy flow of things became heavier, thus slowing. One day he stole from her, fooling himself into believing it was easier this way to end it. It was what he wanted, but he didn't want it this way. He was so confused and trapped in his own problems. He believed that by committing such a despicable act, he could force her to leave him, thus resolving the problem.

David loved her more than anything; she was the only woman that showed him the importance of truth, that oh so elusive term that never seems to be where he wanted it. It ended and there was no pain in the break in his heart. He tried calling from time-to-time and when that failed; he tried e-mailing, but his words no longer had any power, he had reduced himself to its lowest terms, a solution that would save him all heartache, and though it did, it also created greater pain by shattering what little character he had. Without her as his focus, his life declined further. He had increased his drug and alcohol consumption, took on meaningless jobs to support his habit, further pushing himself into the abyss.

Chapter 24

Homeless Again

In 2007, after his breakup with Lynda Milligan-Whyte, David became homeless again. He quit working at (M.A.S.S.) the metal company. Nights of drinking and crack cocaine made it too difficult to maintain a normal life. He started stealing from his job and soon the guilt became too much. He couldn't stand looking everyone in the eye each day, not knowing if it was he they suspected of these thefts.

His group of upstanding friends no longer had a value in his deprivation. He had replaced them for the lower unwanted bunch of people; those individuals who would rather see him going when he was clean and coming when he was not.

It was difficult for him to maintain any type of employment while once again on drugs and alcohol, and not being employed was becoming something he had become accustomed. And so, because of his addiction and the onslaught of homelessness, he began engaging in petty crimes, which resulted in his first conviction in Bermuda after being deported back to Bermuda. The charges were for: (trespassing and willful damage) and he served two years on probation with the condition he would not drink alcohol and that he would receive a psychiatric evaluation to determine whether he had a personality disorder; it turns out he didn't have a personality disorder.

His first job under the probation order was with the Bermuda Creamery in their production department, switching the valves that transferred the various liquids from one vat to another; he hated that job with a passion and resented being yelled at by a forty-year-old high school dropout who was his supervisor. And so, after Christmas, with only three months on the job, he quit and went into a better position with a company called Treecon, installing doors and windows and doing service work. The pay was better, and he got to travel around because the company gave him his own van.

A coworker, Adam, who was from Canada, let him share a four-bedroom house in Spanish Point with him. He purchased a new laptop after a relative had stolen his first one and sold it for drugs. Then he bought a new television and gloated in his new bedroom that was the size of a one-bedroom apartment. Once again, he was feeling normal and in control of his life. He went to AA meetings once a week and minded his own business and kept close to the few friends that were of value to his life. But in a matter of time, he began feeling a sense of complacency and instead of filling the void with positive activities; he reverted to drinking alone and then back to Bailey's Bay where all his troubles started.

Marty, one of David's cousins, was a drug dealer. He had David act as his accountant frequently and often entrusted him with sizeable sums of money to which he often had David wire to Jamaica for him. On one such occasion, before Marty's departure to Jamaica, he left David with two-thousand-dollars that should have been waiting for him there, but David took the money and partied for two weeks.

The people at his job with Treecon had become so overly concerned with his disappearance that they notified the police. Now he had placed himself in the awkward position of having to explain his undocumented absence. David used his age, and the death of Pamela back in the US, and his drinking as a triumvirate, forming the ultimate excuse for his absence, and when the air had cleared and excuses evaporated, he felt too ashamed of the weakness he had projected and so he quit.

Bermuda's a small island, some twenty-one square miles, as he often mentions, and so by now every employer had known him. This sort of behavior was a trend with David, get clean, find a job and then fuck up.

"Had it not been because I was personable and had charm, along with education and decent work ethics—which I was losing sight of, but a rarity in the Bermuda job market—I would have exhausted my chances long ago." David thought to himself.

A week later, after his foul-up with Treecon, David took a job with A.F. Smith; a local office and furniture supplier, installing office systems. That job lasted him three to four months; he told himself *it had lost its charm the first day.* No job advertised in Bermuda was as it said. David was growing tired of laborious, non-thinking jobs that had no upward mobility, and so he moved again to another job with a company called D.E. Mortimer as a sales associate; another dead-end job paying a few hundred dollars a week.

David was blind to the fact that his constant job-hopping was fueled by his addiction to drugs. Each new paycheck from a job was immediately spent on paying bills and then indulging in a spree of Crack Cocaine. The drugs were slowly consuming him, but he couldn't resist their hold. When he stumbled upon a large sum of money in a lockbox at D.E. Mortimer, where he worked as a keyholder for opening and closing the building, he saw it as an opportunity to fund his habit even more.

He broke into the company after hours, using his own keys to enter and leave without any signs of forced entry. Inside, he found a few thousand dollars in cash and made it look like a burglary had occurred. But his half-hearted attempt at covering his tracks only led straight back to him. It was like déjà vu from his time in the Air Force.

For weeks, David lived it up on booze and cocaine, thinking he was living the high life. But inevitably, the money ran out and his popularity at the crack house fizzled away. He went from feeling like he was on top of the world to hitting rock bottom. Before long, he was arrested - something that always happened at the end of these trysts with drugs. He knew how to destroy his life, but he also knew how to rebuild it. These terrible situations were just part of his journey towards redemption.

His actions landed him with a one-year prison sentence. But during that time, another charge surfaced, leading to an additional three years behind bars for receiving stolen property. At first, David was shocked at the amount of time he would spend locked up. But deep down, he felt relieved that his life had finally come to a halt - without him losing it completely. He was tired of constantly wandering aimlessly and self-destructing, so in a strange way, defeat became a welcome friend.

How did he become so numb to life, drifting without a purpose? He had lost touch with himself and didn't know how or where to start looking for answers. Growing up, he carried the weight of his interracial identity, constantly feeling out of place in both worlds. And when his mother remarried and left his biological father, David blamed her for sabotaging their relationship and leaving him without a father figure. For years, he held onto this resentment towards his mother, not realizing that it was destroying him from within.

It was 1985, and David, a 27-year-old divorcee, had retreated to Bermuda to heal from his failed marriage. One night, he found himself stranded on Blue Hole Hill after running out of gas while riding a friend's Triumph Tiger cub motorcycle. As he began pushing the bike towards his grandmother's house in Bailey's Bay, a man pulled up next to him in a Volkswagen Bug. The man was built and bald, with a friendly face that seemed out of place in the small car.

"What's wrong with the bike?" the man asks, seeming unusually friendly with someone out so late at night.

"I ran out of gas. It's not my bike, so I need to return it safely to the owner," David replied, eyeing the man and his car curiously.

"It's no trouble at all. Let me give you a lift into town to get some gas. What else do you have to do this time of night?" the man offered with a mysterious smile.

David hesitated, wary of the stranger's intentions. But ultimately, he took the risk and hopped into the car.

"My name is Richard Bell. What about you?" the man said as he extended his large hand.

"David Parker. Thank you for offering to help me," David replied cautiously.

As they drove towards Hamilton where the one gas station opens all night was located, David couldn't shake off his suspicions about the man. Who goes out for leisurely drives at eleven o'clock at night? And who stops to help a stranger in need? But he brushed off his concerns and engaged in small talk with Richard Bell.

"That's a nice bike. Can you handle her?" Bell asked.

"Yeah, you caught me walking it back, but I can ride it just fine," David responded with mild sarcasm.

"Where do you live? You're not Bermudian are you? I haven't seen around here before." Bell continued to ask.

"I'm staying with my grandmother in Bailey's Bay, but I actually live in California with my mother and stepfather. Just here for the summer to find some work," David explained.

"Well, I live in Bailey's Bay too, up on Belvic View estates in Harlem. You should come by some time, and maybe we can talk about getting a job at Top Valu a grocery store in the back of town. I own some shares there and could help you land a job in the liquor store. A good-looking young man like you would be great for business," Bell said with a sly grin.

They got the gas and headed back to where the motorcycle was parked.

David put the gas in the tank and handed Richard the gas can.

"Thank you for your help Richard, maybe see you around sometime." Richard and David met again. It turned out that Richard was also the Chief

Immigration Officer at the airport in Bermuda. Along with his interest in the store, it sounded like he was doing well for himself. He had a wife and two children. Richard Bell appeared a respectable man who lived a silent, unsuspecting life, but David was sure that Richard had many friends who knew who David was.

With the gas can in hand, they made their way back to where the motorcycle was parked. David carefully poured the fuel into the tank, his movements precise and efficient. Richard stood by, watching with interest.

"Thank you for your help, Richard," David said gratefully, wiping his hands on a rag. "Maybe we'll run into each other again sometime."

As fate would have it, David encountered Richard again. He soon learned that Richard was not only a helpful stranger but also the Chief Immigration Officer at Bermuda's airport. Clearly, he was doing well for himself, with a wife and two children to support. From his appearance alone, Richard seemed like a respectable man - one who lived a quiet and unassuming life. But David couldn't shake the feeling that Richard had connections; friends who knew exactly who David was.

True to his word, Richard helped David secure a job at Top Valu on Court Street in Hamilton. It wasn't glamorous work - just managing the liquor department behind the counter - but it kept him busy and away from drugs. In those days, money was David's drug of choice; he didn't need any grand plans or goals in life. He simply operated on autopilot, just going through the motions.

To everyone else in the store, David appeared as an intelligent, charming and charismatic young man. It came naturally to him to sell himself to others and fit into any social circle. However, he saw these skills as nothing more than tools to deceive and steal from those who trusted him. It was a lifestyle that he had grown comfortable with.

Then one day, out of the blue, Richard walked into the store and approached David.

"How about dinner with me? In town," he asked casually.

It was a strange invitation from someone like Richard, but David supposed it was normal in the business world that he knew little about.

David hesitated, his gut twisting uncomfortably at the thought of spending an evening with Richard. He couldn't see the real value of a friendship with this man, but he knew he couldn't refuse the dinner invitation.

"Tonight?" David asked reluctantly.

"Sure, tonight would be fine, and I won't take no for an answer. Pick you up here after work." Richard's words sounded calculated, like he had planned everything out beforehand, including picking David up from work as if it were a way to ensure his availability.

After Richard left, David called his girlfriend, Mary Jo.

"Mary Jo, it's me. How are you, baby? I miss you so much," he said softly. "I miss you too, honey. Are you working today?" She asked.

"Yes, I am, at the liquor store. I can't talk long, but I need to ask you a favor," David paused for a minute. "Can you please call me tonight at nine, nine sharp? I'll be at dinner with the boss, and I don't trust this guy. There is something creepy about him."

"Why, what's happening? Is everything alright?" Mary Jo's concern was evident in her voice.

"Everything is alright. Why wouldn't it be? I would tell you if it wasn't, but please promise to call me at nine. We will be at the Lobster Pot. Just call and ask for me. I'll let them know I may get a call," David reassured her before ending the call.

Finishing stocking the refrigerators with beer and serving a few more customers, David kept watching the clock; it was almost eight o'clock and Richard would be arriving soon. There was something off about this guy that bothered David, but he couldn't quite put his finger on it. He seemed too nice, almost too good to be true. Nobody does anything for nothing. Everyone has an angle of some sort. As if on cue, Richard pulled up in front of the store where David was waiting, chatting with Judy, one of the other employees at Top Valu. "Hey, get in," Richard said with a smile as he sat inside his little VW Bug.

But to David, that smile held treachery and danger within it. He climbed into the car nervously, keeping his hands on his knees and avoiding eye contact with Richard. He could feel Richard's predatory gaze on him, like a hungry lion sizing up its prey.

"How's the job?" Richard asked, his deep voice cutting through the silence of the car.

"Great, I like it and am grateful to you for helping me get the job," David replied, adjusting his seatbelt. "But you know the pay is... lacking. I wish there was some way I could earn a little more money." He said this not because the job wasn't paying well, but more to gauge Richard's response.

"Well, you must be patient, one step at a time," Richard replied in his authoritative tone. "You know when I first started working with the Government, I was in a quiet position much like yourself. But over time, I proved myself and the rewards paid off. Look at me now, Chief Immigration Officer."

David couldn't help but feel a twinge of envy as they drove out of Hamilton. The sun had just dropped below the horizon, casting a warm orange glow over the island. As they left behind the city lights and entered a quieter part of the island, David noticed that the tree frogs were starting their chorus. Their high- pitched screeches filled the night air, signaling darkness.

Despite the warmth of the night, David could feel beads of sweat forming on his forehead. He wiped them away with the back of his hand and rolled down his window to let in some fresh air. The sweet smell of flowers drifted in from the fields they passed by, creating a comforting blanket over the island.

"Where are we going, Richard? I thought you wanted to have dinner. That was what this meeting was all about, right? Dinner?" David asked, his voice laced with confusion and a hint of annoyance.

"I'm not starving right now, are you?" Richard responded casually, his tone betraying nothing. "If you are, we can find somewhere to eat or we can wait a bit. I want to show you something."

"Show me what? This time of night, what could you possibly want to show me?" David's frustration was rising.

"Just sit still and relax. I promise there's nothing wrong," Richard reassured him.

They drove along the Harrington Sound Road, the darkness enveloping them like a thick blanket. The air was heavy with the salty scent of the ocean and the distant sound of crashing waves.

As they approached Bailye's Bay, Richard suddenly pulled off the road and onto the Castle Harbor Golf Course. The car bumped and jolted as it made its way across the uneven terrain in the dark.

"Are we going to play golf?" David joked nervously, trying to lighten the mood.

"I want to show you something," Richard repeated cryptically as he continued to drive deeper into the golf course.

David couldn't understand why they were out here in the middle of the night. And then it hit him - Richard's intentions were clear. He was going to seduce him right there in that tiny car.

An uncomfortable feeling settled in David's stomach at the thought of Richard's large hands on him. He couldn't imagine anything more repulsive.

But then an idea struck him, and a mischievous smile spread across his face.

Maybe he could turn this situation around and make it work in his favor.

"I think this is crazy. A man driving another man out to the golf course in the dark, you make me sick!" David said, and Richard went to put his hand on David's leg and when he felt the fat stubby fingers grip his leg tighter, David started convulsing, and having a seizure.

"Are you okay?" Richard asked in a sudden panic, but not worried enough to drive him to a hospital.

David shook and shook, rocking the tiny car back and forth, and still this man was interested in either the thought of fucking David or hiding the truth of his actions from the public. David calmed down within minutes, as if recovering from a full-blown seizure.

"Please take me home." David insisted pitifully.

"Just wait a minute, I'll drive you. Just sit a minute and calm yourself." Richard said.

"Drive me the fuck home you insensitive bastard. I wonder what your fucking family would think if they knew what you were doing right now, so take me the fuck home now. I can't believe this is happening. You actually thought you were going to fuck me or have me suck your dick out here on the golf course as if I was some cheap little male prostitute, well this time you made a big mistake."

From that day forward, their friendship became stronger in that Richard now feared for David's silence. After several weeks of silence, David called him.

"Richard, I need your help. It's important?" David asked. "What is it? Are you in trouble with the police?" He asked. "No, why would you ask if I was in trouble with the police?"

"I don't know. Sorry I meant nothing by it, just assuming when you said it's important."

"Richard, I need to borrow $2500 to pay some taxes back in the states. If I don't pay this, I will be put in jail once I go back to California."

"That's not a problem. Come up to the house tomorrow morning." Richard said.

"Does this mean you'll give it to me?" David asked. "Come to the house. I'll give you the money."

After the phone call ended, Richard rushed to the bank in St. George's, where he withdrew the money David had asked for. Richard ran into a friend on his way out of the bank.

"Dudley, old boy what are you doing here in St. George's?" Dudley Ebbin also worked in Immigration under Richard. Both of them were interested in young boys.

"It's my lunch break. Came to St. George's for food. Anything new on the horizon? We have to get together again sometime?" Said Dudley

"My house tomorrow morning, got a fine young thing coming by, you'll love him even though he might be a little older than the usual boys we meet, but he is hungry for money so that will solve a difficult problem, so come by the house in the morning." Said Richard.

The next day, David walked up the hill to Richard's estate. There were a couple of cars parked on the grass in front of the house. David walked up to the back door, which opened to the kitchen, and knocked on the glass slats that were opened. Richard opened the door.

"Come in my boy, I want you to meet someone," Richard said, and David followed him to the Livingroom where another man was seated, "this is Dudley Ebbin, he works with me and also part owner in the Bermuda Sports Shop, you know the Bermuda Sports Shop don't you?"

Dudley was a squat, small fellow, an overweight man with dark skin. He was almost school boyish in looks with wavy black hair that shined as the sun broke through the sliding glass doors that gave a view overlooking the ocean.

"Beautiful view, don't you think?" Richard asked, and Dudley reached out a small, fat hand for David to shake. David motioned Richard to the kitchen.

"David, why am I here meeting your grubby little friends?" David asked. "You came to borrow some money, and I am going to let you have it. Just wait here a moment while I get the cash." But David went back into the front room where Dudley was seated.

"You're a good-looking boy, I'd like to see you sometime away from here, why don't you call me at the shop sometime and we can set something up." said Dudley. And then there was a loud call out from David.

"Come to the back, just down the hall!" David's voice echoed through the dimly lit hallway. Unsure of what to expect, David cautiously made his way towards the room where he found Richard sitting at the edge of a large bed. In his hand, Richard held a wad of cash that he waved and gestured for David to come take.

As he reached for the money, Richard quickly pulled it away with a sly grin on his face. Anger boiled inside David as he realized the sick game this man was playing. "What kind of fucking game are you playing?" David seethed.

"You know exactly what I want," Richard taunted, continuing to dangle the money in front of him. Suddenly, it clicked for David. This man was offering him money for sex.

"Fuck you and fuck the money," David spat, feeling disgusted by the mere suggestion. "If you thought I would sell myself for twenty-five-hundred or twenty-five-thousand, you're out of your mind. Go fuck yourself, or better yet go fuck Dudley or let him fuck you."

With no hesitation, David stormed out of the house in a rage, but he didn't leave completely. He hid behind some shrubs outside, hoping they would leave soon. Once they were gone, he snuck back into Richard's unlocked house and searched desperately for the money he needed. But all he found was a checkbook.

In a moment of desperation and anger, David wrote himself a check for twenty-five-hundred dollars and left to buy a plane ticket back to California. The money was spent quickly, leaving him even more desperate and alone.

After months had passed, David finally mustered up the courage to contact Richard again. But instead of receiving help or understanding, Richard coldly warned him that if he ever returned to Bermuda, he would be arrested.

"I'm sorry you had to resort to stealing, I would've given you the money if you had just waited," Richard said, his voice dripping with insincerity. "But my wife noticed the missing funds and filed a complaint with the police. You need to be careful."

Deep down, David knew that Richard's concern was merely to protect his own dirty secret. Betrayed and abandoned once again, David could only hope to move on from this traumatic experience.

Six months after having stolen the check and returning to California, Richard for a plane ticket to Bermuda for David.

David was taking so many unnecessary risks, he couldn't for the life of him understand what he was doing, he wasn't thinking at all he was just living, trying as best he could to be in Bermuda, but he didn't have a clue on how to live a normal productive life. David had gone through the motions before, but every time he got close to some kind of normalcy he would self-destruct.

Believing his life was that of a jetsetter, jumping between California and Bermuda, David convinced himself without thought or effort that he could move under any circumstance. The problem was...he wanted to be this mystery person.

David thought he was aiming high, he wanted the good life, the finer things, everything his mother had primed him for, she had once said to him:

"You are my million-dollar boy." And David believed that, but he took it out its proper context. The only thing was she hadn't taught him how to get it, so he improvised, and the results were always short lived, illicit, or immoral.

David landed in Bermuda without a suitcase, he thought he might fill one up on his way back home. Two days after landing in Bermuda David contacted Richard who wanted to see David that very evening. And so, for the rest of the day David just chilled and walked about Bailey's Bay as if he were a sight-seer and then feeling a bit exhausted he took a seat on a concrete wall that separated the street from a dirt road behind him. David had been smoking pot and just tripping all day long when out of nowhere a voice called out:

"David!" a voice from behind him said, the voice was in a Jamaican accent. And David didn't respond. He thought somewhere in the back of his mind he knew what was happening and his first line of defence was to pretend he didn't hear the voice.

"David Parker?" The same voiced called out, and this time David turned to the voice and there behind him was an unmarked car with several plain clothed black men, real black.

"You talking to me?" David asked.

"Are you David Parker?" The man with the familiar voice asked.

"No, my name is John." David said. *How stupid could I think people are, how small could I be in thinking that I could control the outcome of my every action.* Thought David.

"Looks like you man," the man took out a manilla folder, opened it and unfolded a poster size picture of David. "Get in de kar man, give us no trouble there'll be no trouble." Another man held the back doors of the car open and David in and two other men entered the back of the car both on each side of him, they were plain clothes detectives.

"You're going down man, you're gonna do fifteen-years for fraud." And then laughter rang out through the whole car.

David was taken to the Hamilton Police Department and put in a cell. A few hours later David's Aunt Lynn came and bailed him out and told David to report to an attorney which she had hired for him; Charles Vaucrosson.

The following day after his arrest David reported to the attorney's office,

"Mr. Parker, this doesn't look good. For one thing you unlawfully entered, or broke into Mr. Belle's house without his permission, took one of checks and forged his name and cashed it, does that about sum it up?" Said Mr. Vaucrosson who was an overweight man that barely fit into the chair behind his desk. His skin was fair in color with glossy hair that was held into tight concentrical waves.

"Let me tell you something, David Bell is a child molester, he goes for boys, him and his stinking friend Dudley Ebbin and they both tried coming after me, making me promises of money and jobs."

"Well, that has no bearing on this case, it doesn't matter if he is into boys, you can't get away from the fact of what you did."

"The fuck it doesn't, I tell you this, IF I GO DOWN, THEN THAT MOTHERFUCKER GOES DOWN, I will get in court and tell the judge how he tricked me into coming to his house with the promise of money and then when I came to collect he tried to make me have sex with him so if that is how you guys want to play then bring it on."

"Arraignment is tomorrow, I'll see you in Magistrates court at ten."

And David left and headed back to Bailey's Bay where he decided to sit by the water and think about what had just happened.

The next day David showed up in court, the building was small and old, looked like something British Colonist had left over from the 1600's. The Magistrate was elevated up higher than a normal seat most judges sat in, from his spot he could look down onto the court rather than at it. The magistrate wore a regular suit as if he were just another businessman, and over the suit a long flowing black rob open all the way in the front, his name was Archie Warner.

"Good morning, Mr. Prosecutor, and you Mr. Vaucrosson," said the Magistrate, "is the defence ready?

"Defence is ready your worship," said David's Attorney, and he rubbed his hands and turned to the open crowd with a smile on his face.

"Is the prosecution ready?" asked the Magistrate, and the prosecutor sifted through the papers on the desk, looking from desk to magistrate and then said, "Your Worship, I'm sorry but we seem to have misplaced Mr. Parker files." "Then I have no other recourse but to pronounce this a mistrial, Mr. Parker you are free to go, but before you leave can I give you a little advice," the Magistrate paused, clasped his hands together and looked into them then down at David, "Mr. Parker, in America you are a little fish in a big sea, but in

Bermuda you are a big fish in a little sea, do something with it."

David's attorney met him in the hallway and said: "My boy if I were you I'd get on the next thing smoking." David assumed he meant the next jet out of Bermuda, but David didn't have the money so bravely he called Richard:

"Richard, I need a plane ticket." David said. "Where are you?" Richard asked.

"I'm at my grandmother's, I just left the court."

"There's a ticket waiting for you at the airport." And David not having a suitcase called a taxi and found his way to the airport and through customs. There were two men who followed him onto the aircraft and when he was seated they left the plane.

The next day when David was at home in California he got a call from his grandmother:

"You were lucky you made it home because right after you left for the airport the police showed up to arrest you."

Chapter 25

Prison Again

The news hit David like a ton of bricks. Three more years behind bars. He couldn't believe it. Those who barely knew him now looked at him with a mix of awe and pity. He had always strived for success and to be seen as deserving of a higher lifestyle, but now he was just another inmate in Westgate Prison.

His fellow inmates were shocked to see him there. They never would have thought someone like David could end up in this place, let alone for the crimes he had committed. Even the prison officials were baffled, unable to reconcile the person in front of them with the one who had ended up here.

"The average inmate gets what they deserve," they said. "But you, David…what happened? You had so much going for you."

David hung his head, feeling the weight of their disappointment and confusion. He had tried so hard to hide his struggles, to maintain his image of perfection. But now that façade had crumbled, and he was left facing the consequences of his actions.

As he sat alone in his dreary cell, David couldn't help but feel conflicted. Part of him was relieved that his secret was finally out, that he no longer had to pretend. But another part was filled with regret and shame for the pain he had caused others and himself.

Lying on his uncomfortable mattress, David replayed everything that led him to this moment - the pressure to succeed, the fear of failure, the void inside that drove him to self-destructive behaviors. He knew he had let down so many people, including himself. But, just maybe, this time behind bars would give him a chance to confront his demons and start anew with structure and counseling. Could he finally break free from his destructive patterns and rebuild a better life? Only time would tell.

David's mind buzzed with questions, each one more pressing than the last. Why was he here, in this place that seemed so foreign and disconnected from his own life? Why had he come all this way, only to arrive at such a small, insignificant point? And yet, as he stood overlooking the vast expanse before him, he couldn't help but feel a sense of clarity and purpose washing over him. This place was meant for reflection. The stillness and purity of the surroundings offered David the chance to dive deep within himself and unearth his true intentions. It was as if life itself had guided him to this exact moment, presenting him with an experience that would shape his consciousness.

But how did he know this was the experience he needed? Because it was happening right now, in this very moment. The universe had a way of giving people exactly what they needed for their growth and evolution. And as David gazed out into the horizon, he knew this journey had brought him exactly where he needed to be.

The forty-five years he spent living in California would seem like a preparation for this moment. Fate is the development of events outside a person's control, regarded as having been decided in advance; the outcome is not ours to control, but the effort is ours to control. He thought.

Until this point, David hadn't realized that he had control over his destination, that by following and acting upon certain situations he could influence the direction of his path. The situations along the way were the elements that educated him in this course, and the realization of the meaning of all those events combined should have been how he graduated from this course. In the suffocating confines of prison, David's mind was forced to confront its own dark corners and twisted beliefs. With newfound clarity, he finally accepted and even like himself. But as he reflected on his past mistakes, he realized that he had been blind to the simplicity of self-love all along. He had dwelt in his own self-loathing, constantly punishing himself with harmful actions. But now, as he emerged from the depths of his own hell, he knew there was no excuse for continuing down that destructive path. The past was a chapter that could not be rewritten or undone; it could only be acknowledged and left behind. And with this realization came a sense of liberation, as David made the conscious choice to leave behind his old self and embrace a new beginning filled with self-compassion and acceptance.

David was fifty-two when he landed at Westgate, Bermuda's so-called maximum-security prison. It is quite small for a prison, nothing compared to San Quentin. Westgate can house only up to two hundred people where San Quentin can house a minimum of three thousand. Westgate sits on a landfill, overlooking the ocean. To David, it reminded him of a holiday retreat, just a return to the past. The one reason he always hated communal type living was the basic lack of privacy, people had a tendency of pushing themselves into your life, even those whom you would never have associated and for him it seems even worse because everyone wanted to be his friend. Prison everywhere is much the same in that you must contend with so many personalities, so why would he do something that rewarded him with everything he disliked?

Winter was on its way out, and summer was on the rise. It was March the 3rd, the first day of David's sentence and the first time for him at Westgate Prison as a convicted person. David was ashamed of what he had done and being imprisoned in Bermuda was more personal because everyone knew each other, and when you are in court in Bermuda, it is advertised to the world the things you had done to get there. Anyone who listened to the radio, watched televised news, or read a newspaper would have heard the report about: "David Parker convicted for Receiving!" The way they announced it you would have thought they had caught one of the ten most wanted. It was so humiliating.

Bermuda is a small island, so any news regardless to how sensational, was monumental; especially things that affected the community. In the United States David never worried about anything like that, no one cared who you were or what you did as long as you didn't do it to them. But in Bermuda everyone knows you even when they didn't know you, so it is personal.

The man David had never known, his father Frank, had also fathered a child under similar circumstances to David's own illegitimacy. Her name was Sandra, a stunning woman with fair skin and dark hair, ten years older than David. She sought him out, already aware of his existence before he even knew she existed. From the moment they met, David felt an inexplicable love for her, despite the years that had passed and the strangeness of their relationship.

Sandra embodied the proud spirit of most Bermudians, but in the early stages of their newfound siblingship, she was ashamed of David's actions that landed him in prison. Although she did not speak to him during his time behind bars, her silence spoke volumes; it was a language he had become all too familiar with.

Reflecting on the pain he had caused those who loved and cared for him more than he cared for himself, David couldn't help but think about how important he was to these people's lives. He realized that he was part of a community where individuals rely on each other to uphold moral values, and his actions had ripple effects on all those around him.

For years, David failed to understand that his life was intertwined with others', and every decision he made affected them in some way. The weight he placed on himself when choosing to do something wrong directly impacted on those who loved and cared for him. Their affection and completeness were tied to his importance within their lives. Without the love and support of his community – anyone whose life he touched – he would be alone and insignificant.

David's brother-in-law, known as Red to those who were close to him, paid a rare visit to David in prison. Sandra, David's sister, refused to join them but did make the long journey with her husband. Red acted as the intermediary between David and Sandra, a painful reminder of their strained relationship. Despite his best efforts, Red could never fully replace the love and support David received from his sister.

As he sat across from his brother-in-law, David couldn't help but picture Sandra at home, consumed by confusion and anger over his incarceration. He understood her perspective and felt immense guilt for causing her pain. For so long, he had believed that his life was predetermined by a higher power, using it as an excuse for his questionable actions. But now, facing the consequences of his choices, he questioned whether it was really fate or just his own selfish decisions.

The idea of God being used as a justification for criminal behavior sickened David. He didn't want to rely on religion to absolve him of responsibility; he needed to take ownership of his actions and make amends for the harm he caused others. As he contemplated these thoughts, David knew he needed to change his perspective and live according to a moral code based on what he truly believed God intended. He couldn't continue using faith as an excuse for wrongdoing; it was time for him to be accountable and strive towards redemption.

As the sun set on the day that would change his life forever, David's heart raced with fear and anxiety as he stood before the judge. Desperate to delay his inevitable imprisonment, he summoned the courage to ask for a brief reprieve in order to put his affairs in order. To his shock and relief, the judge granted his request, granting him a small amount of time before he would have to face his sentence.

With a weight lifted from his shoulders, David hurriedly made preparations for his journey to prison. He treated himself to a fresh haircut, eager to present himself with some semblance of dignity and control. Along with a new book and dictionary, he carefully packed his beloved manuscript: "The Crossroads to Your Inner Spirit," a labor of love that had consumed years of his life. Gathering all these items into a simple shoulder bag, David resigned himself to his fate and turned himself in.

As the gates closed behind him and he was led down the winding corridors of the prison, David couldn't help but reflect on the irony of it all – on this day of endings and loss, he carried with him the tools for creating something new and meaningful

Any place that provides an atmosphere where serious introspection can be achieved, is a place worth valuing for its intrinsic purpose. Granted, prison should be the last place a man finds conducive to this need, and David now see that there were far more beautiful places of serenity he could have used for this purpose, but he went there, and his goal was to look within myself and make the necessary corrections.

His cell was small, yet civil in terms of the prison cells he had seen in America. It had windows that could be opened and screens to keep out the flies, his sink and toilet were not the usual stainless steel, instead they white porcelain. There are three buildings that represent various levels of trust; E-1 for problem people, E-2 for a mixture of those attempting change, and E-3, where he was housed was a unit which had forty-eight cells housing a majority of lifers and has the good fortune to be allowed televisions in your cell and music and computers.

This prison has acquainted him with many relatives that he had never known. He found out that Parker was a famous name throughout the island, an old, respected name of English origin.

Despite growing up with the knowledge of his family's complicated lineage, David never took the time to truly understand it. On one hand, he knew that his ancestors included wealthy white families and poor Black individuals who may have been linked through the dark times of slavery. His mother was a Parker, just like her mother before her, passing on the name to any illegitimate child she had. Yet, if circumstances had been different and his grandparents had married or his parents had wed, he would have been known by a completely different surname. It was a common practice in Bermuda for children to take their mother's name in situations like this, a way of either punishing the father or hiding their identity. But for David, it only sparked more curiosity and questions about his own heritage and where he truly belonged.

Despite spending years in Bermuda, David never fully understood the true reasoning behind the discordant genealogy. He couldn't help but wonder if it was simply a way of life on the island, deeply ingrained in its culture. Perhaps there was some endemic sociological aspect that explained the prevalence of sexual promiscuity, even within such a tiny country. It seemed to be an accepted norm, resulting in countless fatherless children and mothers bearing cliché names. David couldn't help but feel a sense of unease as he contemplated the societal implications of this seemingly common practice.

Being forcefully deported to the tropical paradise of Bermuda left David feeling disillusioned and lost. He couldn't shake off the overwhelming sense that his life was over, as if he had already been sentenced to death. And in response, he began to slowly erode himself from within. It wasn't a conscious decision to end his own life, but a gradual destruction of his character and integrity.

Why had he chosen this form of death? The answer eluded him, but his actions spoke louder than any words could. However, being caught and sent to prison for his wrongdoing gave him a chance to reflect on his choices. And in the company of those whose behavior he once despised, he started to see things more clearly. In this environment, he realized that he couldn't continue pitying himself and playing the victim. He needed to grow up and accept that life was not all about him; that he was just one small part in a much bigger universe. It was a tough truth to swallow, but it was necessary for his growth and survival. As Sharon Swan made her way through the prison, she exuded a warm and welcoming energy. The inmates treated her like a mother figure, seeking solace in her presence. Despite the bleakness of their situation, Sharon's visits brought a glimmer of hope to these lost souls.

David couldn't help but notice her infectious smile every time she passed by him. It seemed as though it was meant for him alone. Curiosity getting the better of him, he asked Officer Shannon about Sharon.

"Officer Shannon, who is that lady that roams around here with such purpose and joy?" David inquired.

"That's Sharon Swan. She runs the TLC," Officer Shannon replied. "TLC? What's that?" David questioned further.

"Oh, it stands for Transitional Living Center. It's a program just outside of the prison walls. The guys live there, eat there, attend classes, and eventually they're given the chance to find jobs," Officer Shannon explained.

This program sounded like exactly what David needed to turn his life around. He knew it would be a perfect fit for his plans to better himself and move forward from his past mistakes.

For the past eight months, David had been confined within the walls of the prison, counting down the days until he could apply for the TLC – a program that offered hope and a second chance to those who were willing to work for it. Despite not having enough time served to be eligible, David believed himself to be an exception and began writing daily letters to Mrs. Swan, the head of the program. He poured his heart and soul into each letter, determined to make a lasting impression. And after a month of diligent writing, his efforts paid off when Mrs. Swan put him up for consideration by the parole board. With bated breath, David waited for the final decision and was overjoyed when he received the word that he had been accepted into the program. It was a glimmer of light In an otherwise dark and desolate world behind bars.

David had almost given up hope on Bermuda as a support system. The people here seemed to lack understanding of what drives a man to act against his beliefs. But then, he was offered a chance at true rehabilitation by Sharon Swan. It was a glimmer of light in the darkness that had consumed him.

As he stood in this familiar yet unfamiliar place, his country of origin, he couldn't help but direct his anger towards the way things had unfolded. This was the last place on earth he wanted to be, even though it was where he had grown up. Had he changed since his time away? He couldn't say for sure.

All he knew was that this was not the life he wanted for himself. David longed to be the man he had dreamed of becoming during his childhood. A time when his dreams and aspirations were still alive and full of meaning.

But as he reflected on his past, he began to realize the role *rejection* had played in shaping his life. The scars of growing up without a father ran deep within him, leading him down a path of self-destruction until there was nothing left for him to compete with. In an attempt to cover up his failures, he became someone he wasn't, constantly trying to please those who had brought him into this world and feeling like a fake in the process.

David spent his life living a carefully crafted I, weaving a web of lies and stories to make himself appear greater than he truly was. He hid behind expensive designer suits, Gucci loafers, and a prestigious briefcase, all in an attempt to mask his true identity. He despised being a product of a mixed-race family, ashamed of his impoverished upbringing. Every aspect of himself and his life filled him with disgust and shame, as he struggled to understand his own identity. His self-hatred consumed him until nothing, but an empty shell remained, devoid of any sense of self or purpose.

A gnawing sense of regret consumes David as he reflects on his past choices. He had forsaken education, believing it would take too much time and effort to achieve. Instead, he took jobs that he was not qualified for, lying about his skills just to fit in with a world he never truly belonged to. His entire existence was built on deception and falsehoods, leaving him feeling hollow and disconnected from reality.

But now, after months of introspection and soul-searching, David has been released from a four-year prison sentence and has a chance to start over. He acknowledges the emptiness that comes with wasted time and vows to make every moment count moving forward. With a newfound clarity, he can finally see the path before him and is determined to leave behind his former life of lies and mediocrity. As he begins to rebuild himself from the ground up, a sense of peace washes over him, giving him the strength to face whatever challenges lie ahead.

The final piece of David's broken heart shattered when a good friend, Gayle Stowe, delivered the crushing news to the prison that she wished to sever all ties with him. The mere thought of someone cutting off any emotional connection to him left him feeling dirty and infected with ugliness. He wasn't angry or seeking forgiveness, but he couldn't deny the pain of losing a friendship.

Alone in his cell, David sat with his thoughts, reflecting on the loss of his bond with Gayle. He understood her reasons, but it still stung. He longed for a way to turn back time and undo the actions that landed him in this lonely isolation. But regrets only went so far. What he needed was a path forward, a way to find redemption and use his mistakes for good.

As he pondered these thoughts, a cranky guard suddenly appeared at his cell door. "You've got mail," he grumbled, thrusting a small envelope into David's hands. Confused, David turned it over and saw that it was addressed to him. Who could be writing to him now? With trembling fingers, he opened the envelope and unfolded a single sheet of paper inside. It was a short note from the prison chaplain, inviting David to attend a meeting for inmates interested in restorative justice – a chance for healing and making amends.

David read the note again and felt a glimmer of hope ignite within him. Maybe this was the opportunity he had been waiting for – a chance to be part of something positive and meaningful, to connect with others who shared similar struggles. With renewed determination, he made up his mind to attend the meeting and work towards rebuilding himself from within.

Amidst the chaos of his thoughts, he struggled to pinpoint exactly what role Bermuda played in his actions. It was easy to fall back on the excuses of external circumstances, a convenient way to absolve oneself of responsibility. But being deported to Bermuda forced him to confront his own self and examine his choices with unflinching honesty. It wasn't a punishment, as he initially saw it, but rather an opportunity for growth and redemption. David came from a family that instilled strong values and principles, ones that guide and shape a person's moral compass. Even in this unfamiliar place, he couldn't deny the lessons they had taught him.

Life was never as difficult as he made it out to be. The constant cycle of getting high, cheating in relationships, and the web of lies and hypocrisy were all just a I to appear alive. David felt reborn; liberated from his past mistakes and wrongdoings. But amidst this newfound freedom, there was a subtle feeling of emptiness and lack of direction. For so long, he had dedicated his life to chasing one thrill after another, until the chase became his purpose. Now that he had nothing left to chase, he found meaning in this void, for it brought an end to the pain and turmoil that consumed him. It was a strange and unsettling realization – finding purpose in nothingness – but it was also a relief, a reprieve from the constant chaos of his previous existence.

David's heart ached to see his grandsons, the sons of his son. They were born while he was away in Bermuda, and though he shared a good relationship with his son, David longed for more. He wanted to feel his son's embrace and answer any questions he may now have.

As he continued on this journey, David couldn't help but feel that his son's love was more out of obligation than true connection. He yearned for a deeper bond, one that was not bound by duty.

Each step in time had left him with more confusion than clarity. He couldn't make sense of how his life had unfolded, and he found himself moving forward without truly comprehending the path he was on.

It dawned on him that it was all too easy to take life for granted and let things become imbalanced. But he knew that in order to prevent further damage, he needed to take ownership of his actions as they arose.

David thought he had made the right decision when he brought a motherless child to a childless mother, Susan. But now, he realized he needed to let go of the past and focus on building a new and more meaningful future. He must forgive himself for any choices that may have led him astray and find a new purpose before it was too late.

David's father was a distant figure in his life, only seen on rare occasions during visits to Bermuda as a child. Each time, David was met with the same cold and dismissive reception.

"Stay away from me, stop bothering me or I'll call the police." Frank's words stung David, but he didn't know how to process his emotions in that moment. Was he supposed to feel hurt or angry? He couldn't tell. Instead, he remained calm and neutral, masking the turmoil inside. All he wanted was to be accepted and loved by his father. But did this longing for love stem from his own father's absence? David wasn't sure, but he knew it had affected him deeply. As a result, he struggled to be a good father To his own son, mirroring the patterns set by his own imperfect father.

Chapter 26

Move to England

After being deported to Bermuda following forty-eight years of living in America, David was filled with a deep well of hate, self-pity, shame, and rejection. These emotions fueled his own personal destruction, as if there were two people living inside him - one driven by ambition and a desire for a better life, and the other consumed by darkness.

David spent a year at the TLC program outside of prison, completing every course offered in preparation for life on the outside. Finally, he was ready for a job again. His first opportunity came through a company called Gorham's, where someone saw past his past mistakes and prison sentence and gave him a chance.

For a brief period, everything was falling into place. The company even offered David a managerial position for their night shift with a generous salary.

It was an opportunity for a better life than he could have ever dreamed of. But it all fell apart when David picked up a bottle again.

His time at Gorham's lasted only two years before he relapsed once more. However, this time it was short-lived, and he completed parole. He then took a job as a maintenance man at Beau Rivage Restaurant in Paget. With 12-hour workdays and renting a room in St. David's, he barely had time to think about abusing his life again. Slowly but surely, he rose from the rubble of the war he had been fighting all his life one more time.

Surviving the harsh reality of homelessness in America ignited a fiery drive within him for all things metal. He dove headfirst into studying scrap metal and recycling, pouring over every detail until his mind was saturated with knowledge. And when he landed in Bermuda on his final attempt to make something of himself, he spent every night meticulously crafting a business plan for a revolutionary scrap metal and waste management program. His goal was to sell it to the government of Bermuda, but instead, an affluent air-conditioning company swooped in, offering to buy his plan and hire him as their general manager with a hefty salary attached. But just like that, everything fell apart when the Bermuda government dragged their feet on leasing him a one-acre site on the landfill.

It was then that a friend with connections suggested England as his next move, and this man generously paid for David's trip. On December 13, 2013, he arrived in London with nothing but hope and determination. After catching a train from Gatwick to Victoria Station, he found temporary shelter at the Grange on Rochester Row for an eye-watering £100 per night. Naive and desperate for stability, David had no idea he was spending far more than necessary.

But time was what he needed most - time to find his footing, to carve out a new path for himself in a foreign land. Unfortunately, England was cold and unwelcoming to those without means. Despite having a roof over his head at night, David could feel his funds dwindling each day. So, he resorted to surviving on cheap meals at McDonald's and spending hours riding buses and trains just to pass the time and save money. There were even nights when he would ride buses all through the night just to avoid the cost of yet another expensive hotel room. But despite the hardships and struggles, David refused to give up or let go of his dream of creating a better life for himself in England. He was determined to make it work, no matter what the cost.

David's days in London were a blur of library cards and job applications. He scrounged for computer time, spending one hour at a time in various libraries scattered throughout the city. But despite his efforts, he couldn't secure employment without a National Insurance number.

Determined to obtain this crucial piece of documentation, David made his way to the Job Center, where he was informed that he would need to physically apply for the number at the center in Camden. So, he hopped on the underground and journeyed to Camden Town, where he filled out paperwork.

By now David had found a cheaper hotel where he would alternate the days of sleeping there and days of catching a bus or train to make the time pass more quickly. His friend in England still helped with funds, but it was becoming increasingly difficult to make ends meet. Finally, after weeks of searching, David found a run-down hotel that was slightly cheaper than the others. At this point, he couldn't bear the bone-chilling cold of England any longer and just wanted to find stability.

Realizing that his previous strategies weren't working, David decided to think like a homeless person and turned to a library computer for help. He stumbled upon Betel of Britain, a Christian organization in Birmingham that offered housing and support for those in need. Excited by this potential opportunity, David called the organization and was met with warm reassurance from the woman on the other end of the line.

"We'd love to have you join us," she said kindly. "Just take a coach to Birmingham and someone will be waiting for you at the station. Just give us a call when you arrive."

David carefully packed a bag, making sure to include all of his belongings. At the coach depot at London Victoria, he counted out £15 and handed it over for a bus ticket, hoping that it would be enough to take him to where he needed to be. As the coach rumbled along, David allowed himself to drift off into a peaceful sleep, feeling safe and sound for the first time in what seemed like ages.

When he finally arrived at his destination, David quickly dialed the number he had been given. In just a few short minutes, a man with a weathered face and an old pickup truck pulled up to the Birmingham coach station. David got in and they began driving down a series of winding roads, the trees thickening as they went. After what felt like thirty minutes, they reached their final destination - a grand, sprawling home that exuded both history and mystery.

As David stepped out of the truck and took in his surroundings, he soon learned that this was once a residence for nurses who worked for the NHS. However, it was now owned by an organization called Betel of Britain. He had heard that he could exchange his services for a place to get back on his feet, but little did he know that this was not an ordinary charity organization. This was a cult, filled with people who didn't fit into society any longer - parolees, homeless individuals, addicts looking for help.

The cult was under the control of an American husband and wife team, and they made it clear that in order to stay, you must devote yourself to Christian teachings. This included tasks like furniture restoration for their charity shops or tree surgery or delivering flyers in freezing temperatures. Nothing came for free in this place - even a warm bed meant endless labor and strict rules. It was not simply a place to seek refuge; it was an all-encompassing lifestyle where every move was monitored and controlled.

Despite the initial allure of finding shelter here, David soon realized that this was not the escape he had hoped for. The constant presence of others and strict adherence to rules left him feeling suffocated, longing for the freedom he once took for granted. Even lying in bed and reading a book was unheard of in this place - every moment must be dedicated to serving God, but in this place God was the cult's leaders. This was not the refuge David had been searching for; it was a trap disguised as salvation.

Twice a week, the entire community was required to gather for bible studies. On one particular night, a band was playing, and their voices filled the hall with harmonious melodies. Everyone sang along, fully immersed in the music. However, David sat stoically, seething with anger at how controlled and constrained his life had become within this organization.

The man sitting next to him seemed friendly enough, so David leaned over and whispered, "Is this some kind of cult?"

The man's face turned serious as he placed a finger over his lips and warned, "Never say that. It's forbidden to even suggest such a thing."

David didn't need any further explanation; he sat quietly until suddenly he found himself on his feet, caught up in the music's energy and singing along with the group. For a moment, it felt magical, and he could feel himself breaking free from the hold this place had on him.

The next day, while everyone else prepared for another day of work and study, David decided. He couldn't stay here any longer; he needed to move on with his life. So, he went to the office and asked the man in charge to release him.

"Give me my things," he demanded. "I'm leaving today."

Without question or hesitation, the man retrieved David's valuables from the safe and ordered one of his followers to drive David to the airport. They did so without saying a word and dropped him off at Birmingham airport without so much as a goodbye.

David stood there alone, with no money and no plan. In desperation, he called a relative in Bermuda and begged for help. After successfully getting $100 from his Bermuda account in pound sterling, David boarded a bus bound for London. It was time for him to start again, but this time on his own terms.

When he was back in London, David paid a visit to the agency responsible for his National Insurance application. David waited in line while the support worker argued with a woman who had an African accent. When it was David's turn spoke with the man, the man said,

"Mr Parker, I am so sorry you have waited so long; I see from your passport you are a British citizen and shouldn't have had to wait this long for your National Insurance Number. I will get this sorted right away and you should hear from someone within the week."

He shuffled some papers, made a phone call, and then.

"All sorted, Mr Parker, again my apology for the long wait."

Filled with renewed determination after speaking with the man from the NI office, David left the building and made his way towards the day center where the homeless gathered. The thought of a warm meal and potential help made him eager to arrive. As he walked, he could feel the cold English air biting at his skin, making him shiver. He was missing the warm climate of Bermuda where he had previously lived.

Finally reaching the day center, he entered to find a bustling atmosphere. People were huddled together in small groups, some talking quietly while others ate their meals in silence. David approached the priest who was overseeing everything and introduced himself.

"Morning, Father Pritchard," he said, trying to sound as confident as possible. "My name is David, and I've been coming here for a few days now.

I'm not actually eligible for any services, but they have kindly allowed me to stay for 30 days."

The priest listened attentively as David explained his situation. When he finished, he asked, "Are you Catholic?"

David shook his head. "No Father, just Christian. Although I suppose I'm more spiritual than religious."

The priest smiled kindly and replied, "Well then, of course I will pray for you. Please have a seat." He gestured towards a chair in his makeshift office.

As they sat together in prayer, David felt a sense of peace wash over him. It had been a long time since someone had offered to pray for him.

Before they parted ways, the priest asked about David's living situation. When he learned David was planning on sleeping on the streets, he immediately jumped into action.

"Sleeping rough? That won't do at all," he said with concern. He quickly left the room and returned with a brand-new sleeping bag in hand. "Someone donated this yesterday, and it's yours now."

Overwhelmed by the kindness shown to him, David accepted the sleeping bag gratefully. As he left the center that day, he found a spot to stash the sleeping bag near Victoria Train Station. That night, when he returned, it was still there waiting for him, a small beacon of hope amid his uncertain circumstances.

That night, as David trudged down the dimly lit streets, he clutched the thin sleeping bag tightly to his chest. It had been years since he had last found himself homeless and forced to sleep on the unforgiving pavement. The bustling city of London was a new environment for him, filled with an overwhelming sense of hostility and danger, especially at night when the cold seemed to seep into his bones. He couldn't help but notice the scattered bodies of other homeless individuals strewn about their doorsteps like human doormats, their breathing was barely audible in the night's stillness. Despite his exhaustion, David couldn't shake off the heavy weight of shame and indignity that engulfed him. But his new-found sense of morality wouldn't allow him to give in to the temptation to just find a spot to rest and steal a few moments of sleep. So instead, he continued walking through countless city blocks until his weary body could take no more. Finally, he plopped himself down on the steps of what appeared to be a grand and influential home, seeking solace in its imposing presence.

Homes in London differed from those in the states. In Westminster, the homes appeared out of an old movie. They were ornate and sculptured and had a grand feeling of luxury; he thought to himself. David didn't want to violate these properties with his homeless presence, so he just continued to walk and walk, circumnavigating the entire City of Westminster until his shame of trespassing pushed him closer to the precipice of exhaustion.

He closed in on one particular property that appeared dark and empty. It had a large bank of steps that flowed from the front door out to the pavement, just feet short of the street. It was difficult for him to just spread out the sleeping bag he had lovingly tucked under his arms so instead he took a seat on one of the cold concrete steps, instantly he could feel the dampness breaking through the fabric of his pants and then onto his skin. At the very bottom of the steps, he watched everyone walking by until, around two in the morning, the foot traffic died down, and he braved spreading out the bag, but even then he didn't just crawl into the bag, no, instead he eased in bit-by-bit using his shoes and backpack as a pillow and then the sleeping bag became his cocoon.

Mingled with the night's cold air was a unique moisture more akin to a freezing ocean. It covered him until he fell asleep, and in his sleep he couldn't differentiate between being asleep or awake. The bitter cold held his mind trapped in a mysterious hallucination, making a peaceful sleep impossible. He was sleepwalking in his sleep and going nowhere, only his mind was moving, and sounds became clearer as he heard the footsteps of an intruder, but he couldn't rise from his frozen coma, and so he passed the sounds off as part of his dream. Meanwhile, A man was standing over him watching intently, standing without moving to check if David would notice his presence. When the man was satisfied that David was beyond just sleeping he picked David's head up gently and removed the backpack and shoes that David was using as a pillow, and then the man gently laid David's head down on the concrete and rushed away.

Sometime later that morning, David was aroused out of his sleep by a strong suspicion that something was wrong. He was certain he had heard footsteps, but when he looked around, he saw no one there and lay back down. But as his head hit the cold hard ground he realized his bookbag was gone along with his shoes and socks. *The footsteps I heard in my sleep were real. Someone came into my space, lifted my head, and took my bag and shoes and then lowered my head back down. Only a deadly thief could have been that courteous.* David thought to himself.

Barefoot and freezing, he made his way to the homeless day center where he had received the sleeping bag from Father Pritchard, and there he bought a pair of shoes and some socks and then walked to the passport office to report his stolen passport, which was in the backpack, and from there he walked across the street to the Metropolitan Police and filed a report of the events.

The police was in doubt about anything coming of this or. David went about his usual staggering around the city that day and then tried again to get some sleep that night only this time he put his shoes and socks in the sleeping bag with him. After troubled night's sleep, David was awaken by his phone ringing, he answers,

"Hello, who is this?" asked David barely awake. "Metropolitan police, can I speak with David Parker?"

"This is David."

"Mr. Parker, something strange has happened we recovered your backpack with everything in it, you can come by and pick it up." David thanked the officer and quickly jumped from his sleeping bag. The police had recovered everything, including his passport, the only things missing were his toothbrush and deodorant. David quickly rushed to the passport office to see if he could stop the order on his passport, and luckily it was just being prepared for processing and so the matter was closed.

That day after the ordeal, and another night attempting to sleep, out in the raw cold, David broke down and called a shelter: it was named: No Second Night Out.

"No second night out. How can we help you?" Said a lady on the phone.

"Yes, hi, my name is David. I got the name of this shelter from the Passage, Father Pritchard. I need help to find a place to stay."

"David, are you a resident here in the UK? Are you sleeping rough?"

"Yes, I have a UK passport, I am a British citizen from Bermuda, but I am trying to live here now, but not that easy plus I am waiting on my national insurance number so I can apply for jobs, I just need somewhere to stay for a short time and then I can make it on my own, please."

"Then David, how this works is we come and find you where you are sleeping rough and we take you from there, so David, where are you sleeping rough at night?"

"I'm not sure the name of this place, but It's across the street from a wall with barbed wire at the top, I think it's the back of Buckingham Palace Garden or something like that near a little park by the Victoria train station I am sleeping on the steps of one of the buildings that faces the street."

"Okay, well, we will try to find you. Good luck." And the lady from No Second Night Out hung up.

As the day changed to night, David grew excited about getting out of the cold and into a warm bed. This would be his first in a shelter and he didn't know what to expect apart from what he had seen on TV about the homeless fighting for a bed in a shelter with limited space on cold nights in New York, but this wasn't New York this was London an inhospitable land mine made so by not being familiar with the turf.

David's usual London day continued: long uneventful bus rides, several trips to a few libraries scattered around town, a dozen walks in and out of Victoria station all to fill the passing minutes till night fall. At eleven that evening, he made his way out of the Victoria train station and into the streets where he walked until he came to a clump of shrubbery near the passport office, which was where he had hidden his sleeping bag. He could feel the cold creeping in. His feet were numb from endless uncharted walks, and his clothing seemed to stick to his body and though he had been in England for a little over two months, he felt the stench of street life crawling up his leg, drowning him in the ugliness of a darkened world he was all too familiar.

As he tired from a long monotonous day, his sense of reasoning told him to sit down, or lie down on anything other than continue this useless journey of trying to find solace in an unsearchable life of uncertainty. He felt a bit of fear about returning to the same place where all misfortune occurred, but since he had informed the shelter of his whereabouts, he had little say so in where he slept if he wanted to be found and rescued by the shelter team. So, he went back to his same spot and laid out his sleeping bag again. This time he was more careful. He tucked everything into the sleeping bag with him. After a few minutes of just decompressing, he found himself drifting off to sleep, but he wasn't sure, as it was so cold. Somehow, David felt, sleeping out in the cold produced a different layer of consciousness in his dreams. It was hard to differentiate between dreaming and sleeping. They both seemed to overlap.

Once he had found himself asleep, according to what he thought was sleep, an interruption happened.

"Hello, sorry to wake you, are you David? We are from No Second Night Out," a lady pointed to herself and her male colleague.

"Yes, that's me. I didn't expect you guys so soon. It's so cold out here." David replied.

"It is cold out here, David. That is why we are here to take you back to the shelter where you can get a nice warm sleep and something to eat. How does that sound?"

"I know this is going to sound crazy to you guys, but I am so cold, and I can't get up from this sleeping bag, so can I come tomorrow?" The two social workers laughed.

"Sure, you can come tomorrow. Just inform the day center 'The Passage', and they can call us. They'll probably give you a voucher for a taxi to the shelter, now get some sleep and we'll see you tomorrow."

As the sun began to set, he finally reached the shelter. It was a humble building, no bigger than an average small commercial office. The exterior walls were coated with dirt and grime, giving it a worn and neglected appearance. Inside, there were only two showers, both clogged with debris and filth. The standing water in the trays had turned a murky grey, adding to the overall state of decay.

There were a few offices for staff use, but they too showed signs of neglect with papers strewn everywhere and furniture in disarray. In the rear of the building, there was a small garden area that served as a designated smoking spot. Cigarette butts littered the ground, evidence of its constant use. Near the entrance, there was an open space with a few chairs and a large sofa. It was standing room only, and those who wanted a place to sleep had to squeeze in between other bodies scattered about on the floor.

Despite the less-than-ideal conditions, each night brought a glimmer of hope in the form of a food delivery from 'Pret a Manger'. The popular restaurant chain donated all their leftover food from the day, creating a feeding frenzy among the residents of the shelter. In this world, life was supposed to be fair for everyone, but circumstances differed for each person. As much as we may want it to be so, true fairness is impossible to achieve. Those in power understood this reality all too well, while those without clung to the belief that it was their right to take from those who had more.

The staff at the shelter were overwhelmed by the overcrowding and added stress of welcoming David into their community. He seemed like an anomaly compared to the other homeless individuals they had encountered. Most were struggling with addiction or trying to navigate a new life as Eastern European immigrants in England. But David, having just left paradise in Bermuda, appeared to be escaping from something else entirely. Though his years in Bermuda between ages of forty-eight and fifty-six were better than his time in California, he still carried remnants of his old life with him, especially his battles with drug and alcohol addiction. These demons were ever-present, following him even as he tried to start over in a new country.

It wasn't his intention to change when he arrived in England. He simply went with the flow and embraced being a stranger in a foreign land. The shelter staff couldn't ignore that David seemed to have different needs than the other residents, but they also couldn't turn him away. After exhausting all attempts to convince him to return to Bermuda, with all expenses paid, they reluctantly gave him a chance.

Despite their initial reservations, the staff couldn't deny that there was something intriguing about David and his mysterious past. They were determined to help him and believed that perhaps he could find a new beginning in this unfamiliar place.

So, he stayed, and he waited until one day, after having been at the shelter for three weeks, he received a call from the National Insurance office informing him he now had an NI number. They also asked for his bank details, which he couldn't understand why until he was told.

"Mr. Parker, when you applied for your National Insurance number, we enrolled you in the Job Seekers help program, which is retroactive, and we need to deposit the funds into your account." That very day, they deposited eight- hundred pounds into his account. *What a country*, he thought. At the shelter, he made sure to keep his little secret about the money. The next day the staff informed David he had a meeting with the housing people about getting a place, but David told them he wasn't looking for housing in the capacity it was being offered.

"I don't want to live on benefits. I want a job and a real life of my own. Can't you people understand my goal?" and he walked out and went to a library in Marlybone in London armed with his new National Insurance number, he began vigorously sending out his resume. Strange, though. The next day, he got a call from an organization called Emmaus and David spoke with a lady named Rose.

"Hello, David speaking, may I help you?"

"Hi David, this is Rose Myers from Emmaus in Colchester. Have you ever heard of Emmaus?"

"I haven't, but can you tell me what this is about?" and Rose went into her sales pitch for this organization that takes in homeless people and in return they work for the community, and this community was a group of people unlike the Betel of Britain he had experienced a few months earlier.

"Why don't you come up and spend the night in one of our guest rooms and see how the operation is? Have the people at No Second Night Out call me and we can arrange your train ticket for you." And like that, David was on his way to Colchester the very next morning.

David arrived in Colchester walked the short distance from the train station to the center. Rose and Emmaus Colchester were great. They had a vast building with thirty rooms all ensuites. They had an industrial kitchen where they prepared everyone's meals three times a day. Then, for work, you either went out on the trucks collecting donations or worked in the charity shops. There were other jobs as well, but those were the two bread winners for the organization. David stayed with Emmaus for a little over a year and in that time he helped boost the income in the charity stores, became a rep for the homeless men there, a sort of go-between with the trustees. He helped to bring in a life coach who helped the guys with CV's. and on top of the £32 per week he was paid, Emmaus Colchester had saved over a thousand pounds for David to help him get on his feet when he finally got a real job and moved out.

Emmaus had separate properties for men who were transitioning back into the mainstream of things and so David moved into one of their flats where he shared with two other men who were working. His first job was with RDC, a company in Braintree where he worked on an international sales team selling refurbished laptops and computers in bulk. after getting that job, David met a lady online named Lee Wed. They instantly fell in love, and she asked David one weekend to move in. Throughout the week they both worked, only David had to catch the train to work. It was rough at first, but he was so in love with Lee and thought she felt the same until one day a couple months into their relationships she got a call from her ex-boyfriend's sister who informed her he had died. That night when they were both having dinner, Lee told him the news:

"David, I have some bad news. You remember me telling you about my ex?" "The guy you dated fourteen years ago?"

"Yes, Alfredo, well, I got a call from his sister, and she said he had a heart attack and died. I can't believe he's dead." That night when we were getting into bed, "David, I'm sorry, but this is hard for me. Do you mind sleeping in the downstairs bedroom tonight, just till I get my head around this whole death thing?"

"Sleep in the downstairs bedroom, but why? He has been out of your life for over fourteen years. This makes little sense unless, of course, you are still in love with the guy." And, David marched himself into the other room. It was her house, and he told himself before moving in that he would never put himself in a position like this where the woman had the upper hand on him.

The next day and the day after that, they spoke. David felt humiliated, cheated on with a ghost. His stomach was in knots, he couldn't eat or sleep and so the next day he said to her,

"Lee, I'm leaving."

"Please, David, don't leave. Stay and help me work this out."

"There isn't anything I can do to help you. This is all on you, and I feel like shit. You won't sleep with me. I can't touch you or make love to you, so what is the sense of carrying on like this? I'm leaving next week and going back to Bermuda."

Their life up until this guy, Alfredo, had died was good. David thought he was in a relationship he could relate to and be in, but as the past had always been, relationships comprised two different personalities and not always do those two personalities go further than lust or a momentary purpose, David was just a momentary purpose serving the needs of someone else; he was done. The following week, while she was at work, he packed his bags. He also took all the gifts she had given him over the months and stacked them into a neat little pile and left them on the last bed he occupied, and then he left for the airport.

Chapter 27

Alex and Towards Peace in His Sixties

With a heavy heart, David boarded the plane back to Bermuda, knowing that it would only be for two short weeks before he returned to England. He had learned his lesson and was determined not to fall into old habits again. The thought of seeing his old friends filled him with both nostalgia and fear - fearing that he would slip back into his old ways once more. England seemed like the safest choice for him at this point in his life.

Bermuda welcomed David with open arms, its turquoise waters and sandy beaches providing a temporary escape from the weight of his past relationship. He knew that he still loved Lee, but he couldn't continue being with someone who was stuck in their past. David needed closure, needed to understand why their love couldn't withstand the test of time. As he scrolled through countless articles online searching for answers, he discovered their situation was not unique - many others had also struggled with letting go of old flames from years ago.

David was back in England with no job and no place to live and so he returned to Colchester, to Emmaus, and told them of his situation.

"Keith, I just need a place to stay until I get on my feet. I didn't know that I would go down this road, but I'm there now; please Keith, just a for a week or two?" And the best Keith could do for him was two days.

That same day he was out for a walk on the High Street when suddenly he heard his name being called:

"David!" He looked around and saw Alex, the lady he had recommended to Emmaus Colchester as a Life Coach.

"Alex, how nice to see you! What are you up to today?"

"Nothing, just coming from a session at the Treehouse. You know, the venue I rent when I need to teach a class." Said Alex.

Alex was a beautiful woman in her fifties, from Cyprus who David met when he was working for Emmaus in Colchester. Her father had died a few years earlier and left her with a sizeable inheritance, which was what she mostly lived on because her coaching business was not doing that well. Alex had been in several short-lived relationships, and though she had chosen a profession that helped others in their personal life, she herself was the one in need of help, and the coaching business was how she received it.

"Would you like to get a coffee or a drink?" David asked, and they walked to the Amour Cafe at the top of the High Street.

Alex and David were not that close and have never taken time out for coffee or anything close to that. It was because of their connection with Emmaus, her a life coach and David a regular member. Anyway, they chatted the day away, including lunch and several drinks. The moment was filled with laughter, and David told her about his situation.

"Hey, look David, I have two bedrooms. You could stay in one of my rooms until you get on your feet." And without even discussing the finer points of such an arrangement.

"Are you sure, Alex? Because I can't pay you right now."

"Don't worry, just get yourself sorted and we'll figure something out later."

Never had David entertained a date for the time he and Alex were spending. David could finally see Alex as an attractive woman, and he found himself attracted to her, but he knew from experience this would be short-lived. And besides, a woman wouldn't just invite you to stay at her house without knowing you unless, of course, she herself was getting caught up in some sex driven moment of passion. They left the café around eight that night and headed back to her house, which wasn't far from where they were. Alex showed David to his room, which she used as an office, and then she left him alone to sleep. A short time later in the evening, David woke up to find Alex sitting at the foot of the bed. Alex was dressed in a silk kimono, with her bare legs crossed at the knee. And she looked him in the eye and said,

"David I'm a woman."

"I know you're a woman, Alex, so why are you saying that?"

"Because I want you to know I have feelings for you, had since we first met through Emmaus, but you never noticed."

"Alex, when we first met, it was... I didn't know that today was going to happen. This wasn't planned, it just happened." David could feel the tension building inside him, an uncomfortable feeling that she was letting him know this arrangement was more than just friendly. David found himself backed into a corner and didn't know anyway out other than to comply with what she was implying, a sexual relationship. The single bed in her office was small, but David moved back towards the wall, lifting the covers just enough to motion her in, and she slid next to him without a word. They made love.

David's movements against Alex were fueled by desperation and primal urges, lacking any genuine emotion or connection. He was merely going through the motions, giving little thought to the possibility of building a real relationship with her. As time passed, the initial excitement for Alex dissipated quicker than expected, leaving only the remnants of a fading sexual affair. They now shared a bed, but their routines were separate; she buried herself in books while he escaped downstairs to his computer, avoiding any interaction with her at all costs. He knew it was only a matter of time before she would voice her dissatisfaction with their lackluster intimacy, and the only way he could maintain the facade was by taking on more household tasks that she had neglected. But there were only so many chores to keep him occupied before nightfall arrived, and they were left alone together once again. Alex reached out one night while in bed.

"David, we need to talk. Can we go downstairs and have a drink, and I need a spliff? There is something bothering me about this relationship."

"Sure babe, let's go to the kitchen and chat." David said to her, but deep down inside of him, he was dreading it. He could feel that uncomfortable feeling that comes when he knew he was wrong about something he was doing.

"David, you brainwashed me." She spoke. "Brainwashed, what in the hell are you talking about?"

"When we first made love you were so passionate, even the second and third time there was passion and spontaneity, you whispered in my ear as you made love to me, 'Alex I will never stop making love to you,' and then out of nowhere you avoid me at bedtime, you have quit three different jobs and it seems I am the one who is taking care of all the expenses." She rolled a spliff and lit it. "I can't go on this way, David. I need a man who is going to be part of this relationship, and it doesn't seem like your heart is there." And all he could do was lean against the kitchen counter in silence. He hadn't a thing to come back with. She was right.

"Alex, you are right, and I am sorry, but I don't feel the same way I did when we first got together. I think it's best if I moved out. I am going back to Bermuda."

"Bermuda, what about the money you owe me? What are you going to do about that?" She retorted.

"I'll pay you back. I promise I just need to get myself together and I can't do it here under the pressure."

"Pressure, what fucking pressure? I have given you every opportunity to sort yourself out. David."

Alex's words about David rang true, and he couldn't shake the feeling that his supposed belief in helping others was actually just a way for him to help himself. He had always found himself in relationships with women who fell for him, but never felt the same in return. This pattern seemed to follow him wherever he went, and he didn't know how to break free from it. A day later, while Alex was at work, David made his way to the airport for yet another flight back to Bermuda. It was all too familiar, reminiscent of what had happened between him and Lee just months before.

After a short stay in Bermuda, David boarded another flight back to England. With limited funds, he settled for a cheap room near Victoria train station in London. Feeling lost and unsure of what to do next, he took a chance and emailed his CV and a letter to every Emmaus community in England - around fifty in total. To his surprise, he received a response from Emmaus Gloucester in Gloucestershire, welcoming him to join their community.

As he reflected on his situation, David couldn't help but feel like he was taking a step backwards by joining Emmaus again, but also a step forward towards finding stability and purpose in his life. He knew what not to do this time around and could see a flicker of hope at the end of the dark tunnel he had been wandering through.

David had spent almost two years at Emmaus Gloucester. They helped him get his UK driver's license and then he moved into a house, as a lodger, in Stonehouse. He secured a job as the manager of a charity store for the RSPCA in Stroud, and after a year with that job, he took a position with an American firm called Topcon as a Store Person. While entering his third year in Stonehouse, he received news from a friend back in Bermuda informing David that she had a daughter living in Havant, Hampshire. David had mentioned to Kathey that he was trying to move as close to London as he could, because in London jobs paid better. While still living and working in Gloucestershire, David bought the first car in his life. He was now sixty-two.

David risked it all and moved to Havant. He stayed with Kathey's daughter. Kathey's daughter Tiff was also from Bermuda, and somehow Bermudians just love helping each other whenever they can. David offered to pay the rent while he was staying with her, and he also bought food and other things. Being grateful for the opportunity was not enough, but he made the best of it and shared his friendship with her and her little daughter.

David got an interview with a company called GTR. They did carbon fibre laminating with parts for Formula one race cars. He felt confident that things would go well, and they did. He was given the job as an Inventory Controller. The money was good. And it allowed him a chance to pay back by helping those who helped him. The hours were the shits; twelve-hour nights four days a week, but he had Friday, Saturday, and Sunday to recuperate. He had been at GTR for less than a year when the pandemic hit. They put him on Furlough, which lasted about six months. He thought this was great, like having a holiday with pay, but he had to admit it was a bit confining in that he had to spend more time at the flat with Tiff and her daughter whom themselves had problems and issues that made the space they all lived in more crowded. David tried to find a flat of his own but because of the pandemic he was having little luck. He needed to complete his plan; he wanted his own space. Then one day he got a call from a letting agent:

"Mr Parker, you are in luck. There is a flat in Emsworth available and the current tenant doesn't mind you viewing in person." So, he visited the flat, and in minutes he accepted. He told himself *that anywhere, anything will do as long as I could be on my own* and so he moved in.

Within a matter of months, work resumed. Only now he was working days instead of nights and that meant a reduction in pay, but what could he do? Life moved on and things soon went back to normal, and the night shift was once again opened, and he could take his post as Inventory Controller. David went out and bought a new car, a 2017 Mini Clubman, blue, and he was so proud. He was now sixty-four and into his seventh year in England, and life had never been better. For once in his life, he could understand how it feels to love oneself. In America, he lived in a dream of what he wanted to be and do, but those were just notions. There was no substance, no direction, no truth to his existence.

David is now sixty-eight and retired. His health is good except for a little cholesterol. It has been twenty years since he had left California and his family. He misses them terribly, but has accepted the reality he may never see them again. Life had a strange way of working itself out for David. All the difficulties that would have destroyed another person, but had only forced him to keep pushing forward, trying as best he could to find the better version of himself. This was a wonderful experience for David and sometimes he didn't realize it until he became more tuned into life and the true bliss of growing old. He still can't believe through all the things he encountered in life he is still here and in a better way.

Although he is retired, there was a minor mistake in his life that he didn't see coming. Preparation for retirement in terms of money. He didn't have an adequate pension plan. David never imagined that he would ever reach this point, but he had, and he will figure the rest out as he goes along. What has happened to him could happen to anyone. The key is how you deal with it. You can scream and shout and complain about how unfair life is, but that will make nothing change. All change is within, it is a state of mind, and acceptance and a belief in oneself that anything is possible, and you can do anything you desire, there is no time limit to this thing so get up and pick yourself up and just live.

www.ingramcontent.com/pod-product-compliance
Lightning Source LLC
Chambersburg PA
CBHW030151310726
48970CB00005B/1694